Cover Design and Interior Format

Reforming the Duke

KEIRA MONTCLAIR

TO THE READER:

A previous version of this book was released as *THE DUKE AND THE DRESSMAKER* in 2013.

I have rewritten enough of it that I decided to change the title and the cover.

I hope you enjoy Philip and Sara's story!

CHAPTER ONE

London, Spring 1812

ANGRY SCREECHES PENETRATED THE WINDOWS of the carriage, impossibly high in pitch.

"Someone needs to remind that woman of her place in the *ton*. Why, she acts as if she is the patroness of Almack's." Mary St. James, Dowager Duchess of Brentwood, stared wide-eyed at her son seated across from her in the carriage. "Really, Philip, it would please me if you would do something about the woman. Must she always be the center of attention? Even at someone else's wedding? She's carrying on like a harridan." The duchess crossed her arms.

Unfortunately, Philip St. James, the Sixth Duke of Brentwood, could hardly ignore the situation. If he didn't put a stop to Miranda's undignified behavior, his mother would start needling him about the affair he was carrying on with the bawdy widow.

"Philip?" his mother said sharply.

"Of course, Mother," he hastened to say. "As soon as the carriage stops rolling, I will speak with Lady Montrose."

"Why is she out there yelling at that young woman? She is a pretty little thing. Poor dear. Lady Montrose would frighten the daylights out of anyone." His mother shook her head in pity.

Their carriage sat in a long line of them in front of St. George's Church in Hanover Square. The sound of Miranda's yelling and the sour look on his mother's face both told Philip he would know no rest if he did not intervene in a timely manner. Rather than continue in the procession, he rapped his cane against the roof of his carriage a few times to get his footman's attention.

When the man opened the door, Philip glanced back at his mother. "I will await you at the front of the church, Mother."

He sighed as he headed down the line of carriages toward the screeching woman in front of the church.

Miranda had always savored attention. Why did he persist in carrying on with a woman he couldn't respect? A courtesan would be easier and probably less expensive than Lady Montrose, with all the jewels he lavished on her at her insistence.

And yet, the lady made an enticing picture as he approached her from behind. Her nicely rounded bottom matched her voluptuous bosom. She was beautiful, and he had needs. In truth, it was easier to carry on with someone who hadn't the slightest grip on his heart. His wife— now his ex-wife—had run off with another man, and he couldn't abide the thought of courting another woman.

"You have no right to be here, missy," Miranda shrieked, "so take yourself away. You may have been a member of the *ton* at one time, but no more. I will have you removed if you step inside that church, Sara."

Philip finally took his eyes off Miranda's derriere as he stepped up next to her. "Is there a problem, Lady Montrose?" He intentionally used his deepest voice to make the displeasure known.

Miranda jumped and stared up at him. "Your Grace, I beg your pardon. How may I help you?" She blushed a deep shade of red.

"Why, thank you kindly for offering, Lady Montrose. You may remove yourself. If there is, indeed, a problem, I will take care of it." He accompanied the words with a cold glare.

"But, Your Grace, you do not understand. This chit…" She gestured to the young woman who stood opposite her. His mother had been correct, the lady was indeed beautiful, but he fixed his attention on Miranda, making his glare icy. He needed to stop her verbal assault of the poor thing before his mother drew close enough to descend from her carriage. If the dowager duchess became personally involved in the incident, it would make it into every newspaper in London by morning.

Miranda cut off whatever she'd planned on saying, dropped into a deep curtsy, and then promptly turned and fled.

Thank the saints above, Philip thought to himself as his gaze returned to the young woman whom Miranda had insulted. He guessed her to be in her early twenties. She was tall and willowy, quite the opposite of Miranda's buxom figure, yet full of curves in the right places. He was embarrassed to admit he couldn't stop himself from taking a full-length perusal of her.

Before he could open his mouth to speak, his friend Edward Davis, the Fourth Earl of Ardleigh, appeared at his side. His presence was not unexpected. They had both gone to boarding school with the groom, and the wedding was considered something of an event for the *ton*. What was unexpected was that Ardleigh's first words were for the beautiful lady.

"It *is* you! Lady Downey, it has been much too long. My wife is most eager to see you."

Philip froze. Downey? Lady Downey? Could this be the wife of the man who'd run off with his ex-wife, Caroline? Blood pulsed through his brain, the pressure building until it started to affect his ability to think. His jaw clenched, and his fists tightened so his nails dug into the flesh of his palms. Ardleigh turned to him with a grin. "I say, Brentwood, I see you have finally met Lady Downey. Such a lovely young woman despite, well, you surely know of what I speak. I couldn't help but hear Lady Montrose yelling just now. I can't imagine why she'd speak to Lady Downey in such a rude manner."

"We have not met, Ardleigh," Philip said, his lips like ice. "I just came upon her as she was being treated rudely by Lady Montrose."

"Oh, I beg your pardon, Your Grace." Ardleigh took a step back. "Let me introduce you to Lady Sara Downey." He gave a lazy smile. "Lady Downey, this is the Honorable Philip St. James, the Duke of Brentwood."

Philip's hand brushed her gloved fingertips. He bowed briefly to her as she curtsied, their eyes steady on each other. No doubt she knew about him just as he knew about her. As Sara stood, she pulled her hand back and nodded. "Your Grace."

Philip tried to force his mind back into action. This little thing had been married to the man his ex-wife claimed to love. He assessed her carefully. Her hair was a rich chestnut sable with little curls framing her face. She was dressed in a soft green gown that fit snugly in just the right places and made her emerald eyes glow. Her nose was pert, her lips full and pink. He imagined her long legs wrapped around him and had to mentally shake himself.

It had been a long time since a woman had affected him so. He forced himself to think of the conniving, deceitful ways of the fairer sex…except surely this woman had been wronged just as he had?

"Lady Downey, may I assist you in some way?" he asked. He thought for a moment, then added, "I would be happy to allow you the use of my carriage if it would help. My footman will see you to your destination while we're in the church." There, surely she'd seize upon his suggestion. She could not possibly wish to attend the wedding after receiving such ill treatment from Miranda. Instant quiet descended on the group as the crowd awaited her answer.

Lady Downey lifted her chin a notch. "Thank you, Your Grace, but I am perfectly capable of finding my own way." It only occurred to him then that his words might have offended her. She might assume, wrongly, that he agreed with Miranda, that he thought she ought to leave. And yet, he found he rather liked the way she stared at him, her gaze uncompromising, her posture ramrod straight. Although words did not usually fail him, he struggled for them now.

Ardleigh remained silent, too, watching their exchange with silent interest. He hadn't said a word since making the introductions. But not everyone remained silent.

A rude comment came from the crowd. "She's not your kind, Your Grace. Do not waste your time."

A fire lit in Lady Downey's eyes, turning her into an avenging goddess. An image flickered to life in his head. This beautiful woman, nude, with a large ruby necklace wrapped around her throat, her luscious mouth smiling at him as she writhed in ecstasy beneath him.

Bloody hell! Stop thinking with your favorite organ, Brentwood!

Another snide utterance reached his ears. This time Philip reached out in a flash, grabbing the guilty party and tugging him forward. Tightening his hand around the man's neck cloth, he spoke loud enough for the crowd to hear. "Apologize to the lady, young man." He glared at the guilty party until the offender sputtered, "Your pardon, madam."

He released him, and the man stumbled before running away.

Philip's eyes returned to hers. He couldn't look away; he was mesmerized.

"Thank you, Your Grace," she said after a pause, her eyes holding his, "but that was not necessary. I am quite able to take care of myself."

He didn't wish to break his gaze away, but a persistent tugging on his arm forced him to do so. His mother. Her carriage must have finally reached the front of the line.

"Why, Philip, introduce me to your new friend." The duchess smiled at Sara.

The duke reached for his mother's hand. "Of course. May I introduce you to Lady Sara Downey? Lady Downey, my mother, Her Grace, the Dowager Duchess of Brentwood."

Sara again curtsied and said, "I am pleased to make your acquaintance, Your Grace."

"Oh, child, don't be silly. You do not need to curtsy to me. Why does your name sound so familiar? Sara Downey, hmmm. Do I know your mother, Lady Downey?"

Philip sighed with exasperation. "No, Mother, you recognize her name because it was Lady Downey's husband who seduced my ex-wife."

Sara's eyes went huge at that comment, although he strongly suspected she'd already made the connection. His name would be as familiar to her as hers was to him. His mother grabbed Sara's hands and searched her eyes with sympathy. "Pardon me, Lady Downey, I did not mean to bring up such a painful subject. Why, you have been through quite a time of it, have you not? What a terrible thing to happen to one so young."

Sara glanced at the duchess. "If you will excuse me, please, I really must be going." She curtsied and turned to flee. The crowd of people who had amassed to watch Miranda's verbal attack on Lady Downey slowly began to disperse.

"What a lovely girl, Philip, don't you think?" His mother beamed a smile at him.

"No, I don't, Mother," he lied. "Her husband ran away

with Caroline, and a great deal of our money. I don't think there is anything lovely about her, with all due respect." Philip leaned down and kissed her cheek.

"Oh, Philip, you really must get over it, dear. You are a grown man. Find someone else. Just about anyone would be better for you than the one you married." Having thoroughly chastised him, his mother patted his hand as if he were ten years old again and walked away.

His mother had never set much stock on titles and the like. She persisted in calling him just "Philip" instead of "Your Grace" or "Duke." She did the same with all his siblings, claiming she had the right to call them whatever she pleased because she'd given birth to them. Most of the time, she used his given name, although she had been known in the past to call him some pet names that were best forgotten.

"That was kind of you, Ardleigh, making sure the *ton* has something to talk about tomorrow," the duke said quietly. "Did you really need to introduce us?"

"Actually, Brentwood, I thought it might help you to see you're not the only one your wife and Lord Downey hurt. Of course, the fact Lady Downey is one fine specimen of a woman. But you probably didn't notice, did you? Caroline has ruined you in more ways than one." Ardleigh's gaze pierced his.

Oh, he had noticed what a fine specimen of a woman she was. Zounds, he could not get her out of his mind, and that was what really worried him.

CHAPTER TWO

SARA DOWNEY TUGGED ON HER bonnet in an attempt to hide her face as much as possible as she headed down the street. How embarrassing to be accosted by Miranda Montrose in front of the church before her client's wedding. Perhaps she should not have come, but she did so wish to see her creation on the bride. It was her first bridal dress, and she was proud of the fine muslin gown.

But then Miranda had seen her. Why Lady Montrose hated her so, she didn't know. She had always treated Sara as if she were the lowest of the gentry. True, Miranda had married a wealthy, titled man, but he had been uncommonly old. His death had left her a young widow in the upper-crust Berkeley Square neighborhood.

Sara sighed, remembering how it had felt to be a bride. While she had believed she was in love with her husband, Duncan Stanhope, Baron Downey, on their wedding day, their relationship had quickly soured. In fact, she often felt as though she'd married a different man from the one who had pursued her. She had hoped that other version of the baron, the kind, solicitous one, might one day make a reappearance, but instead her husband had disappeared altogether. Six months after their wedding day, he'd run off with a married woman—the Duke of Brentwood's wife, no less—taking all the money Sara's father had bequeathed them upon his death. What her husband likely didn't realize was that she was glad to be free of him. Even though he'd left her destitute.

Or so he had believed.

She'd been shocked to learn Duncan had sold their shared property and taken the proceeds for himself, but she'd been even more surprised by the revelation that her father had hidden away a small fortune for her, large enough for her to buy a building and open her own dress shop.

That was nearly a year ago.

Anger built inside her again. Why had she not guessed her husband had only pursued her for her fortune? No wonder their marriage bed had been such a bore. She'd thought losing her virginity would be an exciting event. Well, it had not been exciting. Nor had it ever been special.

Thank goodness her father had possessed the foresight to put something aside for her that her husband could not touch. Sewing was her passion, so it had seemed the obvious choice. Establishing the shop had been difficult, but she was proud of what she'd built with her father's money. If Duncan attempted to come back now, she'd send him away.

As Sara reached her shop and stepped inside, removing her bonnet, her mind strayed back to the duke. She had to admit, he was as handsome as any man she had ever met. But the coldness in his blue eyes had cooled her attraction to him. Of course, his wife's desertion must have been hard for him, but at least he had other family and friends he could rely on for support. Sara's parents were both dead, her mother having died when she was young, and they had lived alone in the country with very few acquaintances. The only thing she had left of her mother was a beaded bag, and she treasured it. She had hoped to carry it the day of her wedding, but Duncan had refused, saying it lacked sophistication.

She had lost her father, then her husband, and now all

of her friends—within the same year. Setting her bonnet down on the table inside, she wondered again if she'd be able to make it as a dressmaker, something she'd always dreamed of since she'd lost her dear mother.

To her surprise, the door opened after a hard knock, and the Duke of Brentwood stood inside her door, something she'd never expected to see. Why was he here? Was he bent on harassing her for the spectacle she'd been a part of in front of St. George's?

"Lady Downey, may I have a moment of your time?"

She nodded briefly. "Of course, Your Grace."

"My apologies. I fear I've done the inexcusable, treated you as though you were the one who ran away with my wife. My guess is it had nothing to do with you." The duke was a little breathless, a clear indication of the effort he'd expended to follow her. Which also meant he'd be late for the ceremony.

Even flushed and ruffled, his dark good looks were still part of a commanding presence that she wasn't accustomed to in her past. "Your Grace, if I had anything to do with my husband leaving with your wife, I am unaware of it. His sudden change of heart was a total surprise to me, as it probably was for you."

"Indeed. I apologize for my boorish behavior. I'll leave you to your tasks, my lady, but please be careful walking alone. It's…simply not done and could prove dangerous." His gaze settled on her and stirred something deep in her belly, but she ignored it. His eyes were anything but cold at the moment.

"Thank you for your concern. Enjoy the wedding," she said, standing up as he took his leave. She watched him as he left, and she had to peek to make certain his carriage wasn't down the street, but it was not.

He had followed her. She decided not to ponder his motives for long.

After all, she was a dressmaker now, well below his station. Everything for her had changed.

The glorious *ton* wanted nothing to do with her now that her husband had abandoned her and taken her father's fortune with him. Although few people were as outright rude as Miranda, there was no denying the invitations had stopped coming after his departure. It made it worse, she knew, that she lived in the small room above her shop. Originally, she'd moved into a boardinghouse down the street, an acceptable choice for a woman in her position, but she could no longer afford it.

As far as the aristocracy was concerned, she was just a common laborer now.

Alone.

She suspected she'd stay that way, and yet, as she moved to the back room in her shop, her thoughts strayed once again to the duke with the ice blue eyes.

CHAPTER THREE

PHILIP STROLLED INTO HIS BREAKFAST room the next morning and stared out the window. He loved Hearthstone Manor, his main estate, at this time of year. The spring flowers blossomed in beds accented by beautifully maintained grass. The sight was almost enough to make him hope again. He chided himself for being foolish and sentimental, but from the gardens to the lake to the estate itself, Hearthstone Manor was truly the most glorious place he'd ever seen. It had been his privilege and joy to grow up there—fishing, racing horses, and having shooting contests with his brothers and his father. He had hoped to do the same with his own sons someday, but it seemed life was not going to accommodate him.

He sighed and grabbed a plate. Ambling to the sideboard, he helped himself to coddled eggs, ham, and toast, and nodded briefly at the servants. The sight of the newspaper in front of his usual seat caused him to sigh again. Picking it up after he sat, he promised himself he would ignore the gossip page. He expected to find his name linked with Sara Downey's, and he did not need to be reminded about how he'd defended her. His mother flurried in, swishing her skirts as she traversed the breakfast room.

"Good morning, Philip. Are you having a better day today?"

"Better than what, Mother?"

"Why, better than your usual days, of course. You should be having a better day today," she replied.

"And why is that, Mother?" He set the paper down. He was not anxious to hear her answer, but he knew his mother would have her say eventually, so he might as well get it over with as quickly as possible.

"Well, I believe you should be happy after meeting that beautiful young lady yesterday, Sara Downey." She took a seat as the servants bustled around, bringing both of them tea and seeing to the duchess's needs.

"And please tell me why meeting Lady Downey should make me happy?" he ground out.

"Why, chemistry, of course! Anyone within fifty feet of the two of you could feel the chemistry between you." She smiled over the rim of her teacup.

"Chemistry! Are you out of your mind?" His hands curled into fists on the tablecloth, but then he forced himself to pick up the paper again.

"Why, Philip, I do disagree with you. We all witnessed the sparks flying between the two of you. They were as strong from her as they were from you." She gave one vehement nod of her head to emphasize her point.

"Mother, I am beginning to really worry about you. How could you mistake my reaction to her for anything other than rage?" He dropped the newspaper in frustration. "That woman you are so taken with is Baron Downey's wife."

His mother just smirked. "There is a fine line between love and hate. Are you just learning that?"

"I think I know all I care to know about love. I have my lovely ex-wife to thank for that instruction. I will never fool myself into thinking I'm in love again, Mother. I told you, give up on me."

She clucked her tongue. "Caroline did do a nice job of wrapping you around her finger. You were young and clearly in lust when you married her, but you weren't in love. There is a difference."

Philip spewed his tea halfway across the table. "Mother! Could you speak a bit more appropriately? What if Emma were to walk in and hear you?" The servants rushed over to clean up after him.

"Oh, pah. And your sister would agree with me. It is time someone spoke the truth to you to get you out of your snip. It happened a long time ago, young man. You've had plenty of time to heal. Get over it and start living your life again."

Philip stared at his mother, speechless. Heal? How was he supposed to heal from the humiliation of his wife leaving him for another man? Thanks to Caroline, half of England knew of his embarrassment. He could see the spiteful glances from his peers, even in the House of Lords. Why, even the gentry eyed him with pity.

The most embarrassing part of all was that he'd loved Caroline. Desperately.

Hadn't he? Or was it possible his mother was correct in her assessment? Had it been lust and not love?

"Oh, Philip, speaking of your sister, I plan on taking her to the new dressmaker this week, and I would like you to go with us. What day is good for you?" She donned her sweetest smile.

His mother's request startled him back to the present. "To the dressmaker? Since when do you need me to go shopping with you? I have to meet with my steward this week. I am scheduled to visit many of my tenants as well."

Philip shook his head in exasperation. What had gotten into his mother?

"Emma is fourteen years old. In case you have not noticed, she is blossoming into a beautiful young lady. And I do not like the leering glances she is getting from the men in town. I think it would be beneficial if you would go with us. Your presence would remind those men that she is off limits. Your brothers run like wildfire wherever they wish, but you have a duty to your sister as the head of the family. Are you too busy to be a good brother?"

She gave him that stare she was so good at, the "dare to disagree with me" look. He'd learned long ago not to challenge her at such times.

"Of course not, Mother," he said, sufficiently chastened. "I will be glad to accompany you and Emma this week. Monday would be fine."

Why had his life taken such an unusual turn this week?

CHAPTER FOUR

SARA STRAIGHTENED UP HER LIVING area. It was small, but it was hers in a way her husband's townhouse never had been. She had designed the curtains and upholstered a small couch to match. A table and chairs sat alongside her bed. It had been her idea to fashion the attic of the dress shop into a living space. Society frowned on matrons living alone, but her father had raised her to be her own person and to make her own decisions. If her shop continued to be successful, she would be able to afford a safer place soon enough. In deference to public opinion, she stepped out of the shop's front door every night, locked it, and turned the corner before slipping inside her back door, attempting to create the illusion of going to the boardinghouse.

She shuffled down the stairs carefully since it was such a steep staircase. The base of the staircase opened into the back room of the shop, where she kept bolts of beautiful fabrics. She'd purchased only the best—an expensive investment, to be sure—but skimping on fabric was not the way to run a business that served the ladies of the *ton*. As she passed through her back room, she ran her hand across the large flat table she used for cutting and developing her patterns. Every item in her shop had been purchased with love.

The next room was her favorite. She stole a moment to stand on the viewing platform that sat in the middle for her customers. The looking glasses were arranged just so to allow her clients to see both the front and back of their gowns. The walls were lined with a few readymade gowns for those who could not wait for custom-made creations. The dresses hung on T-shaped wood brackets her father had designed for her. She had labored furiously to build her inventory of dresses, but she was only one person, and sewing one gown took so much time and effort, especially the beadwork. The room was completed by her desk, tucked in one corner, and a changing screen in another.

She straightened everything and dusted as she moved through the space, humming as she thought of the week ahead. Her bridal gown design had been well-received, which should garner her some new clients. As she neared the front room, the bell above the door tinkled. Her heart leapt into her throat when she entered the space and saw the disheveled, dirty man who'd just stepped inside. He closed the door behind him and locked it.

Trying not to show her fear, she said, "I am sorry, sir, but I am not open for business yet. If you return in an hour, I would be happy…" The menacing look in his eyes cut her offer short.

She stepped back, planning to run for the back staircase, but he grabbed her arm and twisted it viciously.

Tugging her closer, he sneered, "No, I will not be returning. We will finish our business now."

Attempting to push away from him, she groaned as his powerful grip detained her. The man reeked of unwashed sweat and whisky, his teeth were black stubs, and his gaze was flat and cruel. Her stomach churned with anxiety, but what was she to do? He was more powerful, and she could not escape him. She hated how easy it was for a man to control a woman.

Hoping to reason with the brute, she stated, "I'm sorry, sir, but I don't know you. Please release me this instant." She did her best to hide the fear that gripped her body.

He leaned in, twisting her arm painfully. "My boss has a message for you. He needs the money by next week, or else."

Sara started. "Money? What are you talking about?" She twisted again, trying to break free of his grasp, but the man only squeezed tighter.

"Maybe you don't, but your husband did."

Her fear increased exponentially. "My husband left me. I have not seen him in almost eleven months, and I don't ever wish to see him again. Why would he owe you money?"

"Your husband liked to gamble money he didn't have. He owes my boss a fortune." He looked around and whistled through his damaged teeth. "I see a lot of money hanging on the wall here, and you have some pretty fancy clients. I suggest you sew until your fingers bleed. You have one week from today."

"But how much does he owe?"

"I'll tell you next week," he said with a chuckle.

He pushed her away, but before she could feel a moment's relief, he grabbed her left wrist in one hand and her pinky finger with the other, thrusting her finger backward. She screamed from the pain before falling to the floor as he released her.

"If I don't get my money next week, I will break it." The foul man leaned over her as he spoke. "I'll start with the little one, but I'll break another finger every time you are late with a payment. From there, I'll go to your arms and proceed to your legs until you are unable to work or even move anymore. I may break every bone in your body before I am done. Do you understand?"

Sara whimpered, gasping in pain as she cradled her finger. Peering up at him, she nodded.

"And do not think of going to the authorities, or I will have my way with you until you won't be able to walk." He said this with a foul grin, as if he wished her to test him. "I don't care where you hide. I *will* find you. Am I making myself clear, Lady Downey?"

Sara nodded again, tears streaming down her face. He unlocked the door before turning back to her. "You have one week." He turned and left, as casual as if he had not attacked her in broad daylight in her own shop.

Sara stood carefully and tried to slow her breathing. She moved her finger, saying a quick prayer of thanks when it bent freely, although the pain in both her arm and her finger was nearly more than she could bear. Now that he was gone, she wished she'd done something—anything—although she doubted anything would have stopped the foul man.

What was she going to do? He'd hurt her so badly it would be a struggle to work today, but she couldn't afford to send for a physician. The man had never told her how much Duncan owed.

Panic claimed her mind and her body as the stark reality of the situation set in. She had no one to go to. No one to help her. And the shop that had seemed like her salvation was no longer a safe place.

How could her new life have been turned upside down so quickly?

Philip held out his hand to help his sister down from the carriage. His mother already stood beside him.

"Oh, Philip, I do hope you will help me pick out some of my gowns," Emma prattled on excitedly. "You know everything about the *ton*. You will know exactly what sorts of styles I should be wearing. Someday, I hope you'll help me find a handsome husband, too. He'll be part of our family, after all, so I should think you'd like to help me pick him. You'll get along with him well, will you not?"

He merely smiled in response.

When Philip glanced at his sister, he still saw the dear little girl who used to hold his hand. Sit on his lap. Where had the years gone? And now she was talking of marriage? True, it was still years off, but he could not imagine her as a woman grown. She was only fourteen, twelve years his junior, and sometimes she still babbled like a young girl. Emma was such an innocent.

He had hoped to drop his mother and sister at the modiste and run, but his sister had made it clear she expected him to join them inside. His mother gave him a beseeching look, but she needn't have—he couldn't deny Emma. Not when he'd neglected her so during his short marriage to Caroline. With the benefit of hindsight, he realized he'd allowed her to take him away from his family, from Emma. He had much to atone for.

Philip smiled as he pushed open the door to the shop, holding it for his mother and sister.

A little bell tinkled as they stepped inside. He glanced at the items in the glass case in front, thinking he should probably purchase a small bauble for Miranda. The little incident in front of the church had likely upset her, but her affection was easily won with gifts, the more expensive the better. He heard a familiar voice—"welcome"—and turned around slowly.

Lady Sara Downey stood before him.

Ah, now he understood his mother's motivation. She had a reason for everything she did, and the reason for today's visit was now smiling at his sister. He nodded to his mother, accepting she had out-maneuvered him this time.

But his attention was quickly diverted back to Lady Downey. His mind stopped functioning when she curtsied to him. Her lips were lush, her teeth perfect—she had a beautiful smile, although something told him it was forced. Her hair was pulled back simply, but a few strands had escaped and caressed her cheeks, highlighting how pink and flushed they were. Why?

He assessed her again, head to toe, and liked everything he saw, other than the fact that something had clearly upset her. She met his gaze briefly, long enough for him to notice the gold flecks in her green eyes and her gloriously long lashes, then looked away.

His mother gave him an innocent smile. "Wait here just a minute for us, would you, Philip? We would like your opinion on some of Lady Downey's colors and creations." Philip felt himself nod to his mother, still unable to speak. He caught himself staring at Sara again. Even though she'd been relegated to the working class, she possessed an air of nobility. He wondered if that was the real reason why Miranda had accosted her in front of the church the other day—Sara Downey had class in her bones, the kind Miranda coveted. When she turned to exit the room, Philip caught a quick look at the roundness of her bottom. He was instantly hard.

Bloody hell! No woman had been able to affect him so since Caroline's departure. He turned back to the window in the hopes that Lady Downey hadn't noticed his reaction. What was happening to him? He was usually so good at controlling his emotions and desires, but something about this woman affected him on a deep level. That made her dangerous. And yet, he found himself contemplating Sara's forced smile, her flushed cheeks. Whereas she'd radiated self-confidence the other day, she seemed nervous today. Insecure. Something was wrong.

Despite himself, he wanted to know what had happened.

He watched as Sara led Emma about the shop. His sister had a bright, natural smile on her face as she piled gowns over her arms—one that brought Sara's forced smile into harsh relief. Once Emma had a few gowns to try on, she disappeared into the back with the dressmaker.

In a few minutes, Emma called out to him excitedly—"Philip, come look!"—only for their mother to remind her she was to address him properly in public.

"Come quickly, Your Grace," Emma said. "Tell me what you think." His sister stood on a platform in front of two mirrors, swishing the skirts of the pale pink gown she wore, radiating pure joy. "Isn't it beautiful? I love this! It is the prettiest shade of pink. I wonder if I can find slippers to match. And I need a bonnet, too. What do you think?" Emma turned to him.

"It is beautiful on you, princess. We will find whatever you need to go with it," he said softly.

"Indeed. Quite becoming," his mother agreed.

Philip darted a glance at Lady Downey. His earlier assessment had been correct—something was indeed wrong. Visible pain radiated from her eyes. Why? Did he remind her of her husband? What was wrong with her?

Then he noticed the way she guarded her arm. Unable to stop himself, he strode over to her and carefully grasped her wrist. She winced in pain just as he spotted the swelling of her smallest finger.

"Philip!" his mother exclaimed. "What has come over you? You are being improper. You have no right to grab Lady Downey's hand."

He knew she was right, and yet he couldn't step away. Barely aware of what he was doing, he turned her arm over, gently tugging the sleeve of her gown up. A set of fresh bruises assailed his vision.

His mother gasped, but she recovered quickly, stepping onto the platform and ushering Emma back into the changing area.

Lady Downey glared at him, yanked her arm back, and pulled her sleeve down.

Blood pulsed through Philip's body at an alarming rate. Someone had assaulted this beautiful, strong-willed woman. He fisted his hands by his side, filled with hot rage and the need to kill whoever had hurt her.

He stared into her eyes but couldn't control the gruffness in his voice. "Who?"

Sara lowered her lashes. "I am sorry, Your Grace. What exactly is your question?"

"Who assaulted you? Who twisted your arm?" He waited a moment, glaring at her. "I demand an answer," he whispered.

"I don't know what you are talking about. I fell. I fell down the stairs this morning and my finger caught on the railing." Her chin came up as she returned his glare.

His mother led Emma, who was once again in her own gown, toward the back room. "Lady Downey, perhaps we will take a look at those bolts of cloth now."

Philip stepped closer to Sara. She did not back down. Neither did he. He couldn't—not when he was certain someone had deliberately harmed her. He ran his finger softly along her cheek. "Someone did this to you. I would know who, please."

He caressed the pulse in her neck, unable to stop himself, and breathed in her sweet scent. Tears formed on her lashes.

"You are wrong, Your Grace," she whispered. "It was just an accident." She lowered her eyes and turned away from him. She let her breath out. "It is not your concern."

"I just made it my concern. I will find out, Lady Downey," he promised. "And whoever hurt you will pay."

CHAPTER FIVE

SARA TURNED THE SIGN AROUND immediately after the St. James family's departure. She could not bear to see any more customers. Her hand shook as pain jolted up her arm from the small movement. Truth was, the Duke of Brentwood totally unnerved her. She'd expected him to be as distant and cold as he'd been in their first encounter, but he'd surprised her. He was so sweet with his sister, and his blue eyes glowed with warmth whenever he spoke to her. And the way he'd touched Sara's arm. Her neck. The gentleness of it had shocked her. Although he was stronger than the man who'd assaulted her earlier, and so tall he could look down on Sara—who'd always been quite tall for a woman—he didn't frighten her. Quite the opposite. Her stomach churned with butterflies in his presence. No one had ever affected her so, including her husband, but she told herself it was merely the man's rank that impressed her. Surely it was.

She had so wanted to confide in him. How wonderful it would have been if she could have leaned into him and allowed him to hold her. If she could have poured out her heart in the warm safety of his embrace. Fear had held her back—the dirty man had been very clear in his threats. Besides, the Duke of Brentwood would hardly have taken an interest in the woman whose husband had broken up his marriage.

To think otherwise was to dream, and Sara was quite sure she'd done enough dreaming for two lifetimes.

Philip had tried to forget Lady Downey, both the way she affected him and those bruises he'd seen on her arms, but he'd spent a sleepless night thinking of nothing but her. He'd awakened twice last night—once from a very pleasant dream that had aroused him to the point of pain, and another time from a nightmare of a man beating Sara. Both circumstances had left him so frustrated he was forced to take action.

In fact, he was so taken with her that he'd decided it was time to end things with Miranda, although he hadn't found the time to attend to that yet. He doubted she would care overly much—their interactions had lacked emotion from start to finish, which was precisely why the relationship, such as it was, had worked.

He left early for White's the next morning, intending to speak to his friend Ardleigh. Philip had decided he would find out everything he could about Sara's situation. It was the only way he could help her, and helping her was the only way he could get her out of his head. He hoped.

He strode into the club with a stern look on his face and found Ardleigh in the corner reading the newspaper.

"Brentwood," Ardleigh announced. "What brings you out so early this morning?"

"I am here because I need information. I require someone who will discreetly ascertain some facts for me. But no one can know what I am doing, especially my target."

Ardleigh chuckled lightly. "Sounds like another female has gotten into your head, Brentwood. The only question is, who is she?"

"None of your concern," Philip said, his tone sharp. "And you are a good example of why I need someone who can be discreet."

"Ah, but you know I cannot wait to see you settled with

another woman, my friend. But this time, I encourage you to choose someone of better character," Ardleigh said with a smile.

"Worry about your own woman, not mine. Lady Montrose meets my needs perfectly." Philip strode to the window and stared through it, deliberately turning away from his friend. Ardleigh had always possessed an enviable ability to detect lies, and Philip wasn't ready to tell him about his decision to break ties with Miranda. Not yet. Something told him Ardleigh would find the timing suspect, and he was not inclined to explain himself.

"Oh, I do worry about my woman. But then you know how much I adore my wife. It is because of Phoebe that I am always after you. I would be lost without her. You deserve to have a wonderful woman at your side, too. A real wife." Ardleigh stared at Brentwood with a serious expression. "I am not jesting; I mean what I say."

"It isn't that easy," Philip said as he shook his head. "Back to my original purpose, can you help me? Is there someone trustworthy and discreet you can recommend?"

"Yes, as a matter of fact, yes. Just tell me why you need him, and I will gladly give you the name." Ardleigh peered over the edge of his newspaper.

Brentwood's fist came down hard on the small table in front of his friend. "Give it up, Ardleigh! It is none of your concern."

"Bloody hell, Brentwood. Calm down," the other man said, raising his hands as if to say he conceded. "What has you in such a state? All right, I will give you his name." Ardleigh wrote the name on a piece of paper and handed it to Brentwood. "But you are to inform me if there is trouble."

Brentwood grabbed the paper from Ardleigh's hand and studied it carefully, then he stormed out the door without another word.

CHAPTER SIX

SARA SAT AT HER TABLE counting her coins. Almost a week had passed since the attack. She didn't have as much money as she'd hoped, but then again, she didn't really know how much she needed. Why hadn't Stinky told her? She smiled at her name for him, wrinkling her nose at the memory.

It felt good to smile at his expense, especially since the memory of his invasion had kept her from sleeping soundly for the past several days. When she was awake, she jolted at every sound; when she was asleep, she suffered from nightmares. The fear she had that he would return before the end of the promised week churned in her belly. Sara placed her money back into the box and hid it.

Fortunately, her business had been successful. With the St. James order, she almost had more work than she could handle. She stayed up late many nights working on Emma's gowns, even though the duchess had given her a very reasonable amount of time to complete them. Of course, she would not get paid until the order was delivered. If the dowager duchess was satisfied with her work, it would go a long way toward helping establish her business. Many of the *ton* followed the duchess's lead.

She had one other affliction she couldn't control. Every time she worked on the St. James order, her mind drifted to Philip St. James, the handsome duke. Could she believe what he'd said the other day? Would he try to find out who had hurt her?

At night, when she could not sleep, she let herself pretend. In those precious moments, she imagined what life would be like if the duke were her husband. They would adore each other, and he would ensure her attacker was arrested for his crimes. And since it was a dream, she also entertained the notion that he'd encourage her to continue working as a dressmaker even as he asked her to be his duchess.

A ridiculous thought, of course. No duke would allow his wife to work in a dress shop. Nor would anyone in the *ton* wish to marry an abandoned woman, even if such a thing were possible.

There was no harm in dreaming, fortunately.

Sara checked her image in the looking glass across from her. Her eyes remained red and droopy from exhaustion. She yawned. There was nothing for it—she wouldn't be able to sleep soundly until after Stinky was paid off and promised to leave her alone.

He *would* leave her alone, wouldn't he? She cringed at the thought, but fortunately, her mind was distracted by the ringing of her front bell. She pinched color into her cheeks and forced a smile as she walked into the front room.

"Oh," she said softly when she saw her visitor. Miranda Montrose stood in the middle of the front room with her hands on her curvy hips. The lady was a notorious beauty, from her voluptuous curves to her dark hair, blue eyes, and lovely olive-toned skin. However, no one admired her beauty more than Miranda did. In Sara's opinion, Miranda's vanity only fed her tendency to be difficult.

"Well, if it isn't the mousy girl that spends all her time trying to be part of the *ton*. You can no longer act that way, Sara." Miranda eyed her viciously, as if daring her to retaliate.

"Act what way, Lady Montrose?" Sara asked, all innocence.

"Stop playing the martyr. I know your kind. You are trying to find some rich nobleman. Who could possibly be interested in a homely girl who spends most of her time on her knees, pinning hems?" Miranda's chin tilted in the air as she glared at Sara.

Sara's blood boiled. She counted to ten, reminding herself it wouldn't help her get business from the *ton* if she told Miranda exactly what she thought of her.

"How can I help you today, Lady Montrose?" Sara asked, her head held high.

"Stop acting like you are something special, Miss Sara. After all, whose husband took off after only six months? You must have been wonderful in the bedroom. Six months. You couldn't even keep a man happy for *six* months." Miranda sneered at Sara, perusing her up and down.

Sara blushed but refused to back down.

"You better keep your eyes off my man, Miss Sara. If I ever see you talking to him again, you will regret it. Of course, I am not worried, he knows a real woman when he sees one." Miranda continued to stand there with her hands on her hips, tapping her foot rudely as she studied Sara. If she expected some sort of reaction, she was bound to be disappointed.

"Lady Montrose, I do not know who your man is. But do not worry, the last thing I am interested in is another husband."

"Who said anything about a husband? You will never get another husband." Miranda leaned over and peered into Sara's face with an expression of sheer hatred. "But you better stay away from the duke. Do not even look at him. He is mine."

At that moment, the door opened, and the bell tinkled.

"Why, whoever are you talking about, Lady Montrose?

Who is yours?"

Miranda spun around and found herself staring into the expectant gaze of the dowager duchess.

"Good morning to you, Lady Downey." Mary St. James peered around Lady Montrose and smiled at Sara.

"Oh! Your Grace," Miranda sputtered. "I didn't realize you were there."

"Well, of course not. I just walked in. But it seems that you were taking issue with Lady Downey over something. Can I be of any assistance, Lady Montrose?" The duchess stood squarely in front of Miranda, staring at her with open amusement. Her small frame did not detract from her presence. Mary St. James could cast an intimidating air with just a glance. Presently, that look was directed at Miranda Montrose. Sara felt quite lucky that it was not directed at her instead.

Miranda squirmed. "No, everything is fine, Your Grace. Actually, I believe it is time for me to depart." She hurried to the door, pausing to glare at Sara one last time before slamming it shut behind her.

The duchess smiled at Sara. "Why a woman of such beauty would be so unpleasant is beyond me. Do not allow Lady Montrose's threats to frighten you, my dear. She enjoys hearing her own voice."

Sara's relief was immediate. "How can I help you today, Your Grace? I am sorry, but I don't have any of Emma's gowns ready yet, but I will have the first two as promised next week."

"Oh, that is not why I am here, Lady Downey. I so enjoyed examining all of your new bolts of fabric that I have decided to order a few new gowns for myself. Would you have time to take my measurements?" she asked with a smile.

"Oh, of course," Sara said, already calculating the coin this would bring in. And if the duchess praised her work...

The word of mouth alone would be an invaluable boon. "Please come right this way." Sara ushered her into the measuring room.

"Please, Lady Downey, call me Mary. We need not be so formal. May I call you Sara?"

"Of course, Your Grace, I mean, Mary. Of course you may call me Sara. May I ask what types of gowns you are interested in?" Sara smiled at the lovely woman. Emma was lucky to have such a thoughtful and caring mother. Although how the duke fit in with the other two, she wasn't quite sure. He was capable of kindness, but there was a fearsome intensity to the man.

"Well, take my measurements first, then we will look at the cloth again. Does that sound acceptable to you?" Mary asked.

"Certainly. Step right up here, and we will get started." Sara led her to the platform in the center of the room.

"Sara, do I know your mother?" Mary asked. "You look so familiar to me, my dear."

"No, I don't believe so. My mother died when I was young. I was raised by my father, and he died about a year ago." Sara bustled about, picking up her tape and paper to write on.

"Oh, child, I am so sorry! Do you have other family in London?"

"No, I don't have any other family I am aware of. My father never spoke about family much. I'm not sure where he made his money, but he took good care of me. We were alone, but happy. I miss him very much," Sara said quietly. She set to work taking the duchess's measurements.

"You have had a tough life for someone so young." Mary shook her head. "By the way, how is your arm faring? You say you fell down the stairs?"

"Yes, I fell." She peered at her finger anxiously. "But my finger is fine. No reason to concern yourself, Mary. It is easily kept out of the way."

"Oh, you poor thing. It troubles me that you're here all on your own. I understand your husband has left you in a terrible situation, but your father would surely not approve. How are you managing?"

Sara's eyes misted slightly, but she refused to give in to tears. How she craved the opportunity to share her fears with someone, but Mary was a duchess. She had many more important things to do than to listen to Sara's troubles. No doubt she was just being polite.

"I am getting along fine. I enjoy sewing, and business has picked up. I am too busy to feel sorry for myself." Oh, how she wished that were true. Well, it *used* to be true. Or at least mostly true. But ever since Stinky had barged into her shop, she'd started to wonder if fate was tilted against her.

"Now, you listen to me, young lady. I know it is none of my business, but I am going to make it my business. I see a very proud young woman in front of me trying to put up a good front while her world tumbles down around her. You probably feel very alone but will not ask anyone for help. You mind my words, Lady Downey. When your troubles become too much for you to handle, you must share them. No one should be alone in this world. In fact," Mary St. James implored, "I want you to promise me that you will come to me when you need help."

"Your Grace, that is very kind of you, but I am fine," Sara insisted.

"Mary…" The dowager tipped her head at Sara.

"Your pardon. Mary." She blushed again, feeling like a child in the presence of this kind yet powerful lady. Being reprimanded, no matter how sweetly, never pleased her.

"I can see it in your eyes. You're in trouble. You may not be ready to ask for help yet, but when you are, will you promise to come to me?" Mary's eyes never faltered.

"Really, there is no need." Sara blushed as she stared at

the paper in front of her.

"That is not what I asked. Will you promise?" The duchess reached down and tugged her chin up until she met her gaze.

Sara didn't think she had much choice in the matter, so she promised. "All right, if you insist, Your Grace."

"Thank you. Now, do you know how to get in touch with me?" Mary asked.

"Yes, I know where you live, thank you." She barely managed to stutter the words out through her shock. Could she actually do it? Could she call upon Mary St. James and ask her for help?

"Well, then, now that you have finished with my measurements, I will let you choose the materials for three walking dresses for me. I am in no hurry. And here is partial payment for all the work you have to do for me." She picked up her reticule, paid Sara, and strode toward the door. Her footman had already opened it for her from his position outside of the shop.

"Oh, and I will expect you for dinner at four o'clock on Sunday." Mary walked out with a smile on her face before Sara could accept or refuse the offer.

Of course, it wasn't really an offer, but a command.

CHAPTER SEVEN

A LONE IN HER BACK ROOM, Sara paced from one side of the small space to the other. Stinky would return to her shop soon. He hadn't said it would be exactly one week, but if so, that would be tomorrow.

Maybe she could hit him with something, a piece of wood, or a poker. Maybe she could get a gun. But where could she get one? They probably didn't give guns to women. Maybe the duke would help her. No, she doubted that. Although he'd seemed intent on protecting her the other day, he hadn't been back since. She was but a common laborer. Why should he help her? Especially considering what her husband had done to him.

She wished she could ask the duchess. Mary had been quite adamant that she wished to help her, however, the duchess could hardly have suspected she would need assistance with a situation like *this*. It wouldn't be appropriate to go to her, and she didn't want to take advantage of the older woman's kindness.

Suddenly desperate to leave the shop, Sara made her way into the front room, gathered her reticule, and opened the front door with no destination in mind. She had to get out. Scurrying along, she searched the street for the mad man to make sure he wasn't stalking her. Nothing. After a time, her eye caught the sign for Gunter's. True, she shouldn't be outside alone, but she was a married lady, which made it less improper…even if her husband had abandoned her. She'd barely eaten all day, and it was quite warm outside.

On a whim, she decided to buy an ice.

She procured a lemon ice in the small store, then stepped outside and found an empty bench. Heaving a sigh, she sat down. Maybe this was what she needed. She loved ices, after all. Perhaps the cold delicacy would calm her. Every crisp, citrus-laden bite melted slowly against her tongue, relieving her anxiety. She savored each taste, remembering all the occasions her father had brought her here for a treat when she was a little girl. Smiling, she closed her eyes and savored the memories of kinder days.

Feeling a sudden change around her, she opened her eyes and jumped in surprise. Towering over her, blocking the sun, stood the Duke of Brentwood. She gazed up at his imposing presence, from the top of his tall, dark head down to his impeccably dressed body. Then, realizing what she was doing, she blushed at her boldness and dropped her eyes.

"Lady Downey, may I join you?" he inquired with a rather husky voice.

"Of course, Your Grace." She smiled politely at him, secretly wondering what interest he could possibly have in her. She was beneath his station, every person in the *ton* would say so. Besides, it was her husband who'd run off with his wife, so she wouldn't be surprised if he remained cold and aloof.

Perhaps he wished to ask her questions about her husband.

He sat down, searching the area with his eyes before directing his attention at her. "Are things slow for you, Lady Downey? My sister did not give you enough business?"

"Oh no, Your Grace. Business is very good. I just stepped out for a short break. I have many things to do. You are correct, I should go back and work on your sister's and your mother's gowns." She gathered her reticule and stood.

The duke bounded from the bench. "Please stay." He reached for her, but pulled his hand back at the last minute. "My mother's? You have gowns to make for my mother?" he asked with raised eyebrows.

"Why, yes. Your mother stopped in yesterday and ordered some day dresses. Is that a problem?"

Philip smirked. Wasn't that typical of his mother? If she had wanted a gown, she certainly could have ordered it earlier in the week when they had been there with Emma. He wondered what her ulterior motive had been. How he wished he could have been privy to their conversation. His mother had apparently decided to take a personal interest in Lady Downey. She'd never been fond of his wife, but for some reason this woman in front of him, whom the *ton* was casting aside, had become her newest venture.

Were Lady Downey not still legally married to her cad of a husband, he would have suspected his mother of matchmaking. But even his mother heeded to the most basic tenets of propriety, although the moments she took leave of it gave him great delight.

"Is something amusing, Your Grace?" Sara's chin jutted out another inch.

She's a feisty one. He controlled his grin. "No, forgive me. I was thinking about how lovely you are today. Is your gown your own design?" His gaze perused her from head to toe.

Sara blushed, but her eyes blazed. She'd set her things down, but she stood before him undaunted. "There is no need to flatter me. No one can hear you, and I am certainly not in the market to be anyone's mistress, so there is no reason for false compliments."

"False compliments?" He stared at her in disbelief. "I assure you, I am not known for dispensing empty flattery. And I am not in the market for a mistress, as you so crudely stated."

"Well, my husband reminded me every day how homely I am and how lucky I was to have his attention, so I am not a young one of the *ton* to be easily taken in by your sweet words. I know full well what my attributes are…and what they are not." He noticed her hands trembled as she spoke. Philip had no notion of what to say. How could he respond to such a remark?

Homely?

What the devil was her husband's game? The woman was a sheer beauty, gorgeous to his eyes.

"Good day, Your Grace." She whirled around and headed back toward her shop.

He watched the sway of her hips, the arch of her back as she left. Her chin was held high. Society was not going to ruin Sara Downey. She obviously had much more character than the *ton* could stomp out of her.

He knew one thing for certain: her sexuality would flourish with the right man. Apparently, her husband had not been the right man. Philip's loins told him he was.

CHAPTER EIGHT

SUNDAYS IN SPRING WERE GLORIOUS. Daffodils and tulips blossomed, adding splashes of bright color to the greenery, and it was an ideal time to fish.

Philip had only one purpose in mind when he returned home from church. He took the stairs two at a time, changed his clothes, and returned to the morning room in record time with a smile on his face. He was on a mission.

His mother looked at him with sparkling eyes.

"Where are you going in such a rush, Philip?"

"Ah, Mother, 'tis a fine spring day and I think it is time to find my pole again. I am headed to the lake, unless you need something from me." He actually smiled at the thought of fishing again. "In fact, if Graham is bored, send him along to join me." Graham was only a year younger than Philip, and the two had gone on many jaunts together as boys, often with their father. Their other brothers, Adam, four years younger than Philip, and Ben, six years younger, had spent more time together in their childhood. The two were nearly inseparable.

"Why, what a splendid idea! You will, of course, be around to dine with us later this afternoon?" She gave him a smile in return. "I have informed your brothers they all need to be here as well."

"Of course, I would not dream of missing our family meal. I will return with plenty of time to dress for dinner, Mother."

The duchess tipped her head as she eyed her eldest. "Well,

then, enjoy your time. But please remember to wash those fishy-smelling hands when you return. Fiddlesticks, your father's reeked to the heavens after a long day fishing."

Philip chuckled and turned to leave the house. "I think I am old enough to remember to do that." The door banged shut behind him.

Whistling as he walked, he thought of the wonders of spring, how a mere change in the air could motivate people to put down the work and take to nature. He stopped at the stables to pick up his fishing gear in the storage room. While he was there, he reached up to his hidden cupboard and opened it.

He stared at the carved toy sailboat inside for a second, grateful it was still there, then tossed it into his pocket and walked toward the lake. As he walked, he glanced up to check for rain clouds. The sky was clear, a perfect accompaniment to the brilliant thatches of flowers covering the meadow.

When he reached the tranquil setting, he paused to take it all in. He hadn't been here in a long time. His last visit was probably right after he had married Caroline. She hadn't liked swimming or boating, so the visits to the lake had ended.

The dock was in sad need of repair; parts of it creaked under his weight. He stepped carefully and set down his gear. He stared at the lake, visions of his childhood reflecting in the glassy pool. This lake had been one of his favorite spots. He'd come here often with his father and Graham. As his younger brothers grew, the four of them had tried to fish together, but the fish had always seemed to know when they were coming. Adam was quiet, but baby Benjamin had been a chatterbox, as his father had oft called him.

The brothers had enjoyed swimming together, too, and they'd compete to see who could make the biggest splash jumping off the dock.

Sighing, Philip threw his line out and waited. It struck him as sad that there were no children out here to enjoy the lake anymore. He should be reclining on a towel in the grass next to his wife, watching their little ones splash in the shallow water. That wouldn't be happening anytime soon, would it?

Well, he could still enjoy his heritage. He made a mental note to encourage his brothers to join him in a fishing competition soon, something they hadn't done in years.

He fingered the wooden sailboat in his pocket. Pulling it out, he rubbed his thumb across the well-used toy. His father had given each of his children their own boat to play with in the water—his attempt to cease the squabbling between the boisterous brothers. But it hadn't worked out as planned. For some reason, the younger St. James brothers had all thought Philip's boat was best, so they'd often try to steal it. It had become a joke amongst the four boys. But Philip knew the truth—it wasn't better than the others, he was just more careful with it. Even now, it was in pristine condition. Time had dulled but not broken it.

Philip tucked the worn toy into his pocket. He was glad he had saved this piece of his father. It was a treasure to him, one he had saved to give to his own son.

If he had a son.

Philip could no longer imagine having a wife, a family. He was the duke. It was his responsibility to fill the nursery, but he doubted he could ever trust another woman after the way Caroline had betrayed him. In dark moments, he wondered if he was even capable of siring a child. Caroline had never carried, a peculiarity given the number of times they'd tried over their two-year marriage.

And yet, as he stood before the lake, staring out at the vivid blue water, a pair of gold-flecked emerald eyes forced their way into his mind. He thought of Sara's soft, swaying hips, her strength of resolve. Of her fierce self-possession.

How unusual that she ran a business alone and was doing a fine job of it, apparently. Why couldn't he have met someone like Sara Downey long ago?

Could he love a woman like that?

No, lust was all he was capable of anymore.

Reaching into his pocket, he stroked his fingers across the tiny wooden boat one more time for luck as he used to do. He set it down in the water, his hands steadying the wooden toy, and a part of him hoped it would still float. He grinned as soon as it did, but then it tipped over, and he grabbed it to keep it from going under.

Sara rubbed the sleep from her eyes as she noticed the brightness of the day. Unable to fall asleep, she had climbed down the stairs in the middle of the night to work on her sketches. Drawing used to calm her, especially when she created wedding gowns. But it had not worked last night. Visions of Stinky had hidden in every shadow, haunting her.

How she wished she did not live alone.

When she headed down to the shop on Sunday morning, she spent over an hour straightening her work area. The occasional glimpses of her reflection in the mirrors made her cringe—her eyes were red, underscored by circles. Once she finished, she partook in a simple breakfast of dry toast and tea. The day still loomed before her, so she decided to work on Emma's gowns. With the shop closed, she had little else to occupy her time, and she didn't wish to sit around waiting for Stinky to assault her.

You could take the duchess up on her invitation, a little voice reminded her. Although the thought was threaded with longing, she steeled herself against it. Encroaching on their family dinner would be inappropriate. Her mind returned to her visit with the duke at Gunter's shop. Did he think her lovely? In truth, she had no idea what people thought of her appearance. She did the best with what she had, though her hips were too narrow and her lips too plump in her mind. Other men in the *ton* had given her compliments, but she assumed that was customary. She hadn't been courted by anyone other than Duncan, and after their wedding, he'd made it quite clear how he felt about her appearance.

But if the Duke of Brentwood thought her lovely, she'd savor the thought, especially because he was probably one of the handsomest men she'd ever met. If only his personality were a little less abrasive.

She might as well continue to cherish her daydreams, she supposed. They would never amount to anything.

Her eyes became heavy as she worked. Although she fought sleep, she didn't fight it too hard—all the doors were locked. She had been especially careful about checking the shop's security since Stinky's interruption last week. Her last thought was that perhaps he wouldn't come after all.

Suddenly, a grimy hand grabbed her from behind and yanked her out of her chair, slamming her against his body. She gasped for air, gagging at the odors that immediately attacked her senses.

"Where's the money, Lady Downey? I'm here for my payment." He rubbed his arousal against her backside. "Of course, I am hoping you don't have it and I can take payment in other ways."

Retching from his stench, Sara vomited. She tried to stop it from happening, but she couldn't help it.

"You filthy bitch!" He shoved her away from him. Her arms swung wildly in an attempt to keep her balance, but she lost the battle and sprawled onto the floor. Wiping her face with a nearby cloth, Sara tried to catch her breath, pinching her nose closed to keep the fetid air from assaulting her senses. Stinky was upon her in a moment, towering over her and kicking at her bottom. She tried to curl into a ball, but he kicked her again.

This is it, he is going to kill me. Her breath came in pants as her eyes darted across her workroom, searching for a weapon, anything within her reach, but there was nothing. All of her scissors were stored elsewhere. She darted a quick glance at him, long enough for her to see the madness in his eyes. What could she do to stop him?

"Please," she cried. "The coins, I have enough, I think."

He grabbed her by the hair and jerked her back up so she stood in front of him.

"You better have the bits, Lady Downey, or you will regret it."

The foul air surrounding him reached her nostrils again. She shut her eyes because she couldn't bear to look at him and hugged her belly for protection. Fighting another wave of nausea, she thought of her father, anything but her attacker. On impulse, she hid her fingers.

He took a handful of her hair and wrenched it until she screamed.

"Get it!" He shoved her. "Show me the tanners."

Sara wiped her mouth as she stumbled to the front room, tears blurring her vision. Finding the small bag of coins she'd hidden in her front cupboard, she handed it to him, not wanting to count the pennies and thruppences. It would be too painful to watch the shillings and half crowns go to this fool.

He snatched the bag out of her hand and emptied it over a nearby table. He spread the coins out as he counted.

"This is it?" he snarled. "Where is the rest?"

"That is all I have. I am not wealthy. You never told me how much."

He threw his head back and laughed, showing his black teeth. Rough stubble covered his face, bits of dried food caught in the whiskers. Sara shuddered.

"Your husband owed us three times this sum. And now that he is dead, you have to pay his debts." Spittle flew as he barked.

Shock dizzied her. Duncan was dead? She was a widow? She reached for the side of the table. "Dead? He's dead? How?" she asked through numb lips. "Do you know what happened to him?"

"He is dead because my boss wanted him dead. He was still gambling, ignoring his payments. So he is dead. Did I neglect to tell you that I killed him? He died a slow, painful death. Is that what you want?" He grinned at her. "I can arrange it if you would like."

Her knees buckled and she gripped the table, leaning over it because she feared she would faint, the reality of the situation coming at her from so many directions she was quite ill. Her husband was dead. They—Stinky's group—had killed him because he couldn't pay his gambling debt.

Her eyes came back up to her attacker, the true understanding of her predicament finally dawning on her.

If she didn't pay, this awful man would kill her, just like he'd killed her husband.

And no one would know...

Her attacker grabbed her hair again and tugged her forward. Sara's vision blurred. Her will faltered. She knew she would never, ever be able to earn that kind of coin.

No, Sara, no! Fight, daughter. You have much to live for. Fight! For your children, fight!

Sara's eyes snapped open. Where had her father's voice come from? Her eyes searched the room, but they only found Stinky.

"Two weeks, do you hear me?" He kicked her side. "What is wrong with you, girl? Listen to me! You have two weeks to get me the money. Three times that amount. And if you tell anyone, remember, I will find you in your bed and enjoy you all night long."

Stinky collected the coins and dropped them into his pocket. He walked toward the back door then stopped and turned, an evil smile on his face.

"Oh, how could I forget?" he said as he strolled back to Sara, his gaze on her fingers.

CHAPTER NINE

PHILIP WHISTLED AS HE MADE his way back to the house. He'd already left his fishing pole and toy sailboat back in the cupboards. All he had to do was dress for dinner and wash his fish hands, as his mother had called them. He thrust his hands in his pockets and walked back toward the side entrance to his estate, but something caught his eye.

A woman stumbled up the front walk, headed for the main entrance. Stopping at the end of the staircase, she glanced up but didn't move. She was so clumsy that he doubted her ability to walk up the stairs.

She looked familiar.

Sara? Was that Lady Downey trying to make her way up his front steps?

"Sara!" he bellowed, running toward her. He had no idea what had happened to her, but if he didn't reach her in time, she'd collapse and probably knock herself unconscious.

When he was nearly upon her, he caught the confusion in her gaze, and something else.

Fear and pain.

"Sara?"

Sara collapsed into the arms of Philip St. James. He tore up the steps, bellowing for his butler. The door swung open and he barked orders at the help as he continued down the hallway.

Philip raced through the door and into the sitting room.

He placed Lady Downey on the divan and turned to the butler.

"Summon the physician, Stevens, and tell him to hurry."

Stevens left and Philip turned to Sara. He froze at her beauty, the striking contrast of her rosy lips against her creamy skin, framed by her lovely chestnut hair. The days since he'd last seen her had done nothing to weaken her effect on him. He reined in his thoughts and reminded himself of her present condition.

"Sara?" He jostled her shoulder, but no response. Why had she passed out? His eyes ran down the length of her right hand to her delicate fingers and then switched to her left hand.

"What the devil?" Hot rage coursed through Philip when he saw the damage that had been wrought on her left hand. He roared again for Stevens. His mother rushed in.

"Philip, what is the problem? Why are you yelling?" Mary St. James stopped in her tracks, her mouth forming an 'o' as she took in the sight in front of her. Philip's three brothers ran in behind her.

"Dash it, Philip, what happened?" Adam asked. "She's quite a beauty."

"Touch her and you are a dead man!" Philip snarled, although he wasn't quite sure why he was so angry.

"No need to get nasty. He meant it as a compliment," Graham offered.

"Just make sure none of you get any ideas," he said, wondering why he'd become so possessive about Sara.

Mary immediately took charge. "Philip, stop shouting at your brothers and help the girl. Carry her up to one of the guest rooms. Has Stevens sent for the doctor?"

"Yes, I already spoke with him." Philip carefully gathered Sara in his arms and headed up the stairs.

"Do you want help?" Adam called after him.

"I will take care of her," Philip said. Although he didn't wish to interpret his feelings, he couldn't bear for another man to touch her just now, even if it was his brother. His mother gave him a look of interest as she followed him up the stairs.

Philip carried Sara into the first guest room and lowered her onto a chaise while his mother bustled in behind him.

"What happened, Philip?" She reached for Sara's left arm to remove her cloak. "Careful, Mother, be wary of her hand. I don't know what happened. I was just returning from the lake when I noticed her walking toward the front door. I knew something was wrong right away. Her steps were uncoordinated. I suspect she fainted."

When his mother had removed the cloak, he took Sara into his arms to move her to the bed. Her eyes fluttered open. She glanced up and started when she saw Philip. "What happened? Why am I here?"

He carefully lowered her onto the bed. "You've had a bit of a shock," he said.

Sara's brow furrowed. "I am sorry to bother you. I will go home now. I…I didn't mean to come here."

He sat on the side of the bed and rubbed her arm as he spoke. "Lady Downey, you are not well enough to go anywhere. You fainted on your way to our front door. I must ask you what happened to your hand." He said the words softly, tenderly. Obviously, the poor woman had suffered some sort of ordeal, and he certainly didn't wish to make matters worse for her.

Sara glanced down at her hand with a perplexed look. "My hand, why I don't…" She closed her eyes and lay back, sinking into the pillow, as she groaned. "No!"

Philip held her right hand in his and brushed his thumb across the back of her fingers. "Lady Downey, you can trust me. I will help you. Please tell me what happened."

Sara shook her head as she gazed up into his blue eyes.

The hopelessness in her gaze moved him. He knew what it was to feel that way.

The duchess waved a hand in front of her face. "Philip, please go wash. You reek of fish. You must be making the poor girl sick."

Sara gave Philip a small smile and closed her eyes again. "It's all right. The smell of fish doesn't bother me. It reminds me of my father. He always loved to fish."

Stevens appeared at the door. "The physician, Your Grace."

Philip stood immediately. "Of course, Dr. Newberry. Come right in. Let me introduce you to Lady Downey. She must have taken a fall or something." He hovered as the doctor approached the bed.

"Lady Downey, it's my pleasure to meet you," the doctor said, nodding politely. "That's quite a bruise on your hand, young lady."

"I'm pleased to meet you, too, Dr. Newberry," she said, her voice soft.

The doctor turned to Philip. "With all due respect, Your Grace, I would like to examine the lady in private. Of course, Duchess, you may stay if you like and if Lady Downey is agreeable." He bowed to the dowager.

"Of course, she may stay." Sara offered a weak smile.

Mary ushered Philip out the door and whispered, "Go wash up, please. You are rank, my dear."

Philip left, although nervous energy coursed through his body, and he found himself pacing the hall beneath the stairs as he awaited the doctor.

A short time later, Dr. Newberry descended the stairs.

Philip rushed to his side. "Dr. Newberry, what happened? Is she all right?"

"Oh, I expect she'll be fine. The lady doesn't want to talk about what happened. But she has a broken finger. I suspect it was done intentionally by someone. It has an odd angle to it."

"What did she tell you?" Philip asked.

"Something about falling down a stairway, catching her fingers on a railing. I don't believe it myself." He shook his head, crossing his arms.

"Why did she collapse?" Philip led the doctor into his library, then motioned for Dr. Newberry to take a chair and asked the butler for tea. His mother came down the stairs and took a seat on one of the other chaises. Philip still couldn't bring himself to sit.

"Probably shock," Dr. Newberry answered. "Breaking a finger causes considerable pain, and she did walk all the way from her shop. Frankly, I don't know how she made it this far. She also bears several bruises on her body. Someone knocked her about pretty well."

Philip's blood boiled at the thought of someone beating Sara. He stared at the physician. "Any idea who?"

"No, and she is not saying. Where is her husband? She is married." His gaze went from Philip, who'd started pacing again, to the duchess.

Stevens arrived with the tea on a tray with some biscuits, which he left on the table in between the duchess and the doctor.

"He ran away with their money," Philip said once Stevens had left. "I believe he was with my ex-wife." He stopped and stared out the window for a moment.

"Then who would you suspect? Do you know of anyone else she might have angered?" Dr. Newberry asked as he sipped his tea.

"I am afraid I don't know much about Lady Downey's life. I only recently met her. She has been making gowns for my sister and my mother." And he had not yet heard anything from the investigator he'd paid to look into her problem.

"Well, try to find out. Someone could cause serious

injury to this young lady, and she refuses to get the authorities involved." Dr. Newberry pointed a finger at him. "She needs some protection in my opinion."

"Thank you, Doctor, I will keep that in mind," Philip said, shifting his hands into his pockets.

Mary shook her head. "Poor girl."

"Duchess, I gave her some laudanum. She should sleep for a while. I would advise bed rest for a couple of days." He pushed away from the table. "Thank you for the tea, Your Grace."

"Thank you for your prompt attention to this matter, Dr. Newberry," Mary said. Stevens escorted the doctor to the door.

When they were alone, his mother looked at him with a thoughtful expression.

"Tell me your thoughts, Mother. I know you want to." Philip smiled cautiously, but he didn't feel much humor about the situation.

"Dr. Newberry is correct, in my opinion," she said, rising to her feet. "Someone has to protect that girl. She looks like she could break easily, but you should see the bruises on her body. Philip, it is awful. You need to do something about this."

The more she talked, the closer she came to her son.

"Mother, what would you have me do? I'll admit that I've taken an interest in her situation, but she is not forthcoming about her business and we have no idea what's going on. I'm attempting to get information in other ways, but to no avail yet." Philip's eyebrows rose as he stared at his mother.

"Well, you better make it our business, young man. How are you going to feel if she turns up dead one day? Do you know how much guilt I will bear if that happens, Philip? You better act while you still can. She has no one. We must help her."

Philip turned and stared out the window. "I intend to, Mother. Believe me, I will find out who is hurting Lady Downey, and I will stop him."

CHAPTER TEN

WHEN SARA AWOKE, IT WAS morning. For a moment, she couldn't place her surroundings—she only knew the beautiful, refined room was not her own. Pain drew her attention to her left hand, and when she saw the splint on her finger, the memories came flooding back. She was at the St. James home. Although she recalled starting out to see the duchess, she could remember nothing else.

She was attempting to get out of bed, poorly, when a maid appeared in front of her. "My lady, you should not be getting out of bed. Her Grace will be very upset."

"Well, I need to wash up and take care of certain needs."

"I will help you, my lady."

Sara did not want to give in, since she'd never had a maid around to help her before, even during her short-lived marriage to the baron. But if ever she'd needed one, it was now. Every bone in her body ached. Sighing, she allowed the maid to help her get clean with the water on the side table. There was a fresh night rail on the chair for her to wear, but she could not get back into bed. There was simply too much to be done. She only had two weeks to raise the money.

The maid, however, tried her best to coax her back into bed after seeing to her needs.

"I am sorry," she said, tugging on her shoes, "but I must go home. I have many things to do." Sara tugged at her shoes.

The duchess strode in quietly. "Are you feeling better, Sara?"

"Why, yes, Your Grace, I am." Sara stood quickly and brushed the wrinkles from her gown. "I appreciate your help, but I really must be going. I have much sewing to do."

"Remember, you agreed to call me Mary. Would you please do me the honor of coming downstairs and having breakfast with me? I am sure you must be hungry by now."

Mary's voice soothed her immediately. Sara realized the duchess was right; she was starving. What could it hurt to have breakfast before she left? She realized it would be rude to walk away without properly thanking the woman for her help. Breakfast would be a great way to accomplish that, and besides, she had very little food at home and no coin.

"Of course, Mary, I would be delighted to have breakfast with you." She followed Mary out the door and down the stairs, her cloak over her arm.

The two sat in the breakfast room. The maids served plates of coddled eggs and ham, toast, and pastries with icing. Sara's mouth watered. She had not eaten well ever since Stinky had first arrived. Nerves had held her back—and so had the money. Any money she spent on food would not be going toward her husband's debts.

The duchess filled Sara's plate. "Here you are, my dear. I gave you a bit of everything. We have a wonderful cook here. You must try her pastries." Mary smiled as she set Sara's plate in front of her and poured her a cup of tea.

"Thank you, Mary." Smoothing a napkin on her lap, she settled her left hand on the table and took a sip of tea. As soon as she picked up her fork, the duke entered the room. She couldn't help but stare at him. The man truly was magnificent to look at. His hair was dark, his eyes a light blue. Everything about him was perfection, even his cravat. When his gaze met hers, she almost choked on her food.

Mary had the grace not to comment on her blush.

"Good morning, Your Grace," Sara said, setting her utensils down to regain her composure. "I thank you for your hospitality last night. I remember little, but I owe you both for your fine care."

The duke sat across from Sara. "You are welcome, Lady Downey. But you certainly do not owe us anything. Well, other than an explanation for what happened to you. How did you end up in such a predicament?"

Sara swallowed hard and cast her eyes down. "I don't understand, Your Grace. What predicament?"

"How did you come to collapse on our doorstep? And who broke your finger? Perhaps you were not comfortable talking about it with Dr. Newberry, but I think you should be truthful with us."

The duchess brought her hand down abruptly next to her plate. "Philip, where are your manners? You will not bother the lady while she is eating. Your rude interrogation can wait." The dowager glared at her son.

Philip nodded slowly. "Of course, Mother, you are correct. I apologize, Lady Downey." He accepted his mother's chastisement without another word.

Sara took a timid bite of egg as the duke continued to stare at her. Finally, he heaved a sigh and stood up to fill his plate.

"Sara, tell me, is there a friend you can stay with while you are recovering? Is there perhaps someone at the boardinghouse who could assist you?" asked Mary.

Sara played with the napkin in her lap, her eyes darting to Philip as he returned to his seat across from her. "I am afraid I do not have many friends. Ever since my husband left, people have avoided me. You know how demanding the *ton* can be. I am now a working woman, and there is little appreciation for my place in society." She then lifted her chin. "I will be fine, Your Grace. I appreciate your concern, but I assure you that I am capable of taking care of myself. I have much work to do."

She looked into Philip's eye as she said that last bit.

He'd allowed his mother's chastisement quite simply because she was correct. He hadn't noticed how thin Sara had become.

What was going on with her? Thin, nervous, using poor judgment, frequent injuries. It all reeked of something he didn't like to think about. Someone was either threatening her or abusing her, but who? Was her husband returning to frighten her for some reason?

He could not fathom what was going on in her life, but he vowed to find out.

Philip curbed his tongue at her declaration that she would return to work. A broken finger and a bruised body and she planned on continuing to sew? The woman had an iron will. Perhaps she had succumbed to exhaustion yesterday. Was she that desperate for money? He reflected on his visit with the private investigator earlier in the week. The man better be a fast worker. He didn't care how much it cost. He wanted to know who was beating his woman.

His woman? Where had that thought come from? Philip stared at Sara, shock running through his mind. The woman did have a way of making certain parts of his body stand at attention every time she was in the room. He wanted more food right now but didn't dare get up to go to the sideboard. He sat directly across from the siren, and she would surely notice if he stood. Instead, he motioned to one of the servants to fill his plate.

He would have understood it better if it had been a mere physical attraction, but his feelings were much more complicated than that. He longed to hold her. To soothe her and protect her. To make her smile.

Philip didn't remember having the same feelings for Caroline. What was happening to him?

They ate in silence until Emma strolled into the breakfast room.

"Oh, Lady Downey, I am so excited to see you!" Emma ran over to the table, her face flushed with excitement. "Do you know when my gowns will be ready? I was really hoping that my pink one might be ready this week. It would be perfect for the Earl of Ardleigh's ball next week. Philip is allowing me to attend, since he is friends with the earl, isn't that so, Philip? He is going to escort me. I am so thrilled to be going. I cannot wait to see what everyone else is wearing. How many gowns are you making for the ball?" Emma finally ran out of words when she noticed the splint on Sara's finger. "Oh my goodness, what happened to your finger?"

"Emma, cease your chattering tongue, child," the duchess said. "You are exhausting Lady Downey with your prattle. Stop, please. You will not be in attendance if you cannot demonstrate better manners." She pulled on her daughter's arm and gave her a harsh look.

"I am sorry, Mother. I am just a bit excited. Pray forgive me, Lady Downey." Emma blushed.

"Emma, you have no reason to apologize," Sara said. "I am working on your pink gown now. I plan to have it finished for you midweek. Hopefully, if you could, we might schedule a fitting for Wednesday. That's why I need to get back home. There is much work to be done."

Sara made a motion to get up from her chair and a servant appeared at her side to assist her.

The duchess stood quickly and grabbed her daughter's hand. "Come, Emma, I need your help in the kitchen for a moment. Please excuse us, Lady Downey."

Philip thought to applaud his mother's timing. She truly did have a quick mind. It would be impossible for Lady

Downey to depart without taking proper leave of her hostess.

"Now, Lady Downey, you were going to tell me what happened to you yesterday, were you not?" Philip studied his companion. "That is if you have finished eating." He did not intend to let her leave without some kind of explanation. He hoped she understood that by his look.

She took a sip of tea and set her cup back down. A moment of silence passed between them, and then she met and held his gaze. "All right, Your Grace. I will tell you what happened. But you won't be happy. I cannot tell you much."

"Please, let me decide that."

"It is very simple. I am being blackmailed. I do not know who he is, just that he has threatened to break every bone in my body if I don't pay him what he wants. As you can see, he has made a great start." Sara didn't pull her gaze from his as she held up her left hand.

Philip fought to keep his rage under control. He would kill the man.

"This man broke your finger?" He could hear his own pulse in his eardrums.

"Yes. He threatened me for the first time a week ago. Yesterday, he returned and broke my finger."

"Why is he blackmailing you?"

Tears welled in Sara's eyes, although she kept them contained by what could only be sheer force of will. She turned her head and stared at the sideboard. "I think that is my business and not yours, Your Grace."

Philip reached across the table and, with one finger on her jaw, turned her face to him. Those tears she'd contained finally spilled down her cheeks. He fought the need to pull her onto his lap and wrap his arms around her.

Her strength humbled him.

"I cannot help you if I don't know everything," he whispered.

Sara sighed and twisted her napkin again. She pulled
her face away from his touch and glanced at her lap. "My
husband was a gambler, apparently. He gambled when we
were married and did not repay his debts. My attacker tells
me…he tells me he's killed him. They now expect me to
pay what he owed."

"Are you certain your husband is dead?" Philip's mind
flew. His first emotion was relief—if the baron was dead,
Sara was a free woman. His next thought was that Caroline
had likely been with the baron at the time of his death.
Would she return to London? Would she attempt to return
to Hearthstone Manor?

Sara nodded. "The man told me so."

"Fine, then I will pay him whatever he wants. He will
have no choice but to leave you alone."

Sara jumped from her chair. "No! You mustn't! He said
if I told anyone, he would make me pay." The fear in her
eyes broke his heart.

"What could be worse than allowing him to break every
bone in your body, Sara?"

Sara's face turned red as she closed her eyes and turned
her head away. "Please," she whispered. "I could not bear
what he threatened. Promise me you won't do anything."

Oh. The rage that had lit him up from within roared
with renewed vigor. Death would not be punishment
enough for such a man. But it wouldn't do to react with
rage just now—he knew what his mother would say; she
needed sympathy. A soft hand.

"Ah, yes, I forget there are worse things for a woman.
Pardon my insensitivity, but I will not promise you any
such thing. The man will never touch you again."

Philip observed the woman in front of him. His heart
broke at the fear in her eyes. He wasn't quite sure how he
would accomplish it, but he would do everything in his

power to protect her.

Philip stood and held his hand out to her. "Come, I will escort you home, Lady Downey."

"Oh, but I must thank your mother for her assistance."

He remained standing with his hand outstretched. "I will convey your appreciation. You probably would not want Emma to see you right now. I'll take care of everything."

CHAPTER ELEVEN

I'LL TAKE CARE OF EVERYTHING. Sara wanted to believe him. She'd never wanted anything more, but her hands trembled as she climbed into the carriage with the duke's help. Stinky could be out there watching right now. What if he came back tonight?

A low, velvety voice cut into her thoughts. "I will not let him hurt you again." The duke had taken the seat across from her, the better to hold her gaze.

"How can you say such a thing? I do not even know who he is. Why, he could be out there right now watching me." Sara searched his blue eyes. The ice was gone, replaced by a tenderness she had never seen before.

Her heart skipped a beat.

"I will find out who he is. I have my ways. I will protect you." He spoke with certainty.

When he looked at her like that, his blue eyes filled with intensity, she could almost believe him. She certainly *wanted* to believe him. Butterflies fluttered in her stomach, warmth pooled between her thighs. She wondered what it would be like to kiss him.

Kissing had never been an especially pleasant event with her husband. His mouth had always covered hers roughly, leaving saliva over half her face. Somehow, she didn't think it would feel the same with this man. He probably would not shove his tongue into her mouth far enough to gag her.

Of course, such a fine man would never, ever want to

kiss her. Would he?

Philip reached over and held her gloved hand. "You don't believe me," he said, stroking her wrist at her pulse point.

Sara allowed the simple caress, but she kept her head bowed, her gaze averted to hide what her eyes might reveal. She let herself be entranced by his touch, permitting herself a moment's pleasure before saying, "I don't know what to believe anymore, but I cannot expect you to pay my husband's debts. He has done enough to you…and I could never hope to repay you."

The carriage arrived at her shop. The duke helped her down and unlocked the front door for her.

"Your Grace, I cannot thank you enough for your assistance."

Sara turned to enter her shop, expecting him to just leave, but he gently pushed his way past her through the open door.

"If you don't mind, I would like to look around first."

Sara stood frozen in her front room, thankful that he was willing to do this for her, and listened as he opened doors. She heard his boots on the stairs up to her rooms. His footsteps descended the stairway a few moments later, followed by the sound of water being thrown out the back door. Oh, her tub. She had forgotten it.

He strode back into the front room.

"The lock on your back door was picked. That is how he got in. I will send a locksmith over to change your locks. You need something stronger. I don't think anyone has been here in your absence. Nothing else seems to have been disturbed."

She peered up at him nervously. "Thank you, but I cannot take up any more of your time."

Philip stepped closer to her, pinning her with his gaze. "You live here instead of in a boardinghouse? May I ask why? Could this not be part of your problem?"

Sara dropped her gaze. "I have my reasons, Your Grace. I would appreciate it if you could recommend a good locksmith. I certainly can handle it myself. I would be happy to pay him a fair price for his work." Her lower lip trembled slightly.

Philip grazed her cheek with the back of his hand. "He struck you here, didn't he?"

Sara shivered at his warm touch. "No."

"Your skin is red and raw."

He was so gentle. Duncan had never touched her this tenderly, even when courting her. Philip stood close enough for her to catch his scent. She inhaled deeply before speaking again, as if she could draw some of his strength from his essence.

Turning her face away in embarrassment, she whispered. "He licked my cheek. I had to scrub it to feel clean again. Perhaps I was a bit excessive."

"I am so sorry I could not protect you from him." He ran his thumb across her lip and leaned down to brush his lips across hers. It lasted only seconds.

Shock and pleasure blasted through her, but she forced herself to take a small step back. "Please, Your Grace, I don't need your pity." Sara didn't know what else to say. She certainly was not pretty, so he must feel sorry for her.

"Is that what you think this is? I assure you it is not." He cupped her face and kissed her more deeply. His tongue mated with hers briefly, the effect so powerful Sara's knees buckled. He caught her and pulled her in closer yet. His hard member pressed against her belly, and her eyes flew open as she pulled back.

He smiled a mischievous grin. "As I said, this is not about pity. I will return to check on you, Lady Downey. And now that I have tasted you, I hope I may call you Sara and you will call me Philip. Promise that you will contact me if you have any more problems?" He waited for her answer.

Sara didn't know what else to do, so she nodded her head, swallowing hard.

The duke turned and left.

Sara went to work immediately on Emma's pink gown. The locksmith came in the afternoon and changed both locks. She had to admit, she felt safer. Although the locks would not keep a truly persistent intruder out, they were certainly better than what she'd had. She attempted to pay the man, but he declined adamantly.

There were no visitors that day. She finished Emma's gown and started on one of the custom-made gowns Mary had commissioned. She chose a rich cinnamon color for her. The shade would complement her complexion quite nicely.

After hours of fitful sleep, she finally got up to work on some sketches. Stinky had left her paralyzed with fear, but she refused to give in. If she did, he would win. While she could not sleep as she liked, at least she was able to continue her work.

Mid-morning, while Sara sewed at her desk, she smiled as she thought of Mary, Philip's dear mother, wearing this gown. She wondered if her own mother had been anything like the duchess. Setting aside her work for a moment, she opened her drawer and retrieved her mother's beaded reticule. Running her fingers over the beads, several of which were missing, she thought of the wedding gown she'd designed to match the bag. A quick perusal of her sketchbook unearthed the design.

She'd never had a chance to make the gown of her dreams. Although she'd looked for the ivory beads she would need to fix the reticule and make the dress prior to her wedding to Duncan, they'd eluded her. After a month of searching, she'd declared it a lost cause. Without them, she could not make the perfect dress. Besides which Duncan, her husband-to-be, had refused to spend any money on a wedding, declaring such events to be wasteful and boring. He had convinced Sara and her father they needed to save the money in order to secure their financial success. Now Sara realized he was only interested in his own coffers. He must have gambled that money away. No matter. She was glad her design had not been wasted on such a despicable man. A knock on the door interrupted her thoughts. She crossed into her front room, looking outside to see who had knocked. A familiar face smiled back at her. Phoebe Davis, wife of the Earl of Ardleigh.

"Sara? Sara, is it really you?" Phoebe said. "I have been looking for you for months! When last I saw you, Duncan had just disappeared. The next time I came calling, you had left, and no one had any idea where you had gone."

Sara opened the door and ran to her friend.

"Oh, it is so good to see you, Phoebe," she said, hugging her without any thought to propriety. It was so wonderful to see a friendly face. She'd thought about going to Phoebe, sharing the full extent of her troubles, but the last thing she'd wanted was to seem desperate. It had struck her that the countess, or perhaps her husband, might think she was looking for charity. Besides which, her friend had been expecting at the time of Duncan's disappearance. She hadn't wanted to stress or worry her. Now, she wondered if she'd made a mistake. Her friend's husband had been so kind to her at the wedding, and Phoebe seemed overjoyed to see her.

"Why didn't you visit me?" her friend asked, pulling back to look at her. "I have been worried sick over you. I asked everyone about you. It wasn't until my husband came home last week that I discovered where you were. He told me you had started your own business. Of course, my dearest Ardleigh then reminded me I'd been busy with our baby, so I was a little distracted. And I didn't leave the house much while I was carrying either."

Sara peered at her friend sheepishly. "Duncan sold the townhouse, just as he'd sold all of my father's properties, but I discovered my father had hidden away some money for me. Although it would have allowed me to pay for lodgings for some time, I used it to open my dress shop. I did not think you would be interested in continuing our friendship."

"Oh, poppycock, Sara Downey. You know I don't care what the *ton* says. I have my own mind. All that matters to me is what my dear Ardleigh thinks, and he encouraged me to visit you today. Now, I've heard talk that the baron is dead. Is it true? Has the cad left you a widow?"

Sara nodded, a slight bowing of her head. In her mind, she heard Stinky say, *"He died a slow painful death."*

Phoebe pulled her into another hug. "I *am* sorry. Not for him, mind you, the man treated you abominably. But you've dealt with quite enough trouble." Pulling back, she smiled. "I must admit, I would love to see your shop, and for slightly selfish reasons. I remember admiring your sketches. What do you think would look nice on me?"

Phoebe had always known when to change the subject, and Sara was only too happy to oblige. She escorted her friend to the measuring station, and they chattered on in the same fashion as schoolgirls. Once they were finished, Sara showed her around the rest of the meager space. Her friend immediately noticed the sketchbook that lay open on the desk.

"Oh, Sara, this gown is divine. Have you made it for anyone yet?" Phoebe asked as she ran her finger down the page.

Sara shook her head. "If you like, I can make it for you. We can choose the fabric today."

"I would love to see what you have. But wait. Isn't that

your mother's reticule? You have kept it all this time?" Phoebe picked up the bag and ran her fingers carefully across the satin. "It is still beautiful after all these years, isn't it? The missing beads don't change that."

Sara nodded. "Yes, it is. But I would still like to find beads that would match."

"The other day, Ardleigh brought me to an accessories shop on the other side of town. It is a ways off, but the shopkeeper had some lovely beads. Would you care to go with me some time? We could certainly use my carriage. Perhaps on Thursday."

"Oh, I would love that, Phoebe." Sara clutched her hands to her chest.

"Gadzooks, Sara! What happened to your hand?" Phoebe exclaimed.

"Oh, 'tis a long story, one better suited for another day." Sara turned to search for fabric in the hopes of distracting her friend.

"Well, you better be careful. You need a good man to look after you, not a halfwit like your late husband. I am sorry, but I never liked that man. Hmm…I have something new to think about. I love playing matchmaker." She bounced her index finger on her lips as she gave the matter thought.

"Phoebe, I don't need anyone. I am fine alone, please."

"Forgive me for saying so, but it doesn't look to me like you are fine alone. Do you feel all right? You are quite pale, Sara…and thin. Have you lost weight?" She paused for a while, then her mood brightened. "Why don't you come and stay with me for a while? Business will wait for you. You just opened. You can't have that many people waiting for you."

Although the offer was tempting, the last thing she wanted to do was bring trouble to Phoebe's doorstep. "On the contrary," she said, "I have too much work to do. I am tired, but once I get adjusted to my new life, I will be fine. I would be happy to go shopping with you one morning, Phoebe, but that is the only free time I have. I have gowns I must prepare for your ball next weekend."

"Oh, of course. You will come, Sara?" Phoebe grabbed Sara's uninjured hand. "Please say you will come. Had I known you were here, you know I would have sent an invitation."

"I don't think so. I have too much work to do. Thank you for the invitation, but I must decline. Besides, I have nothing to wear. I am too busy sewing for others." Sara glanced down at her own gown self-consciously. She hadn't made herself a new gown in a very long time. Though her things had all been nice at one time, many of them were fading. At this point, everything was about putting money aside for Stinky. She must not forget about him.

"All right, if you insist. But I will be back to pick you up Thursday morning. I won't take no for an answer, Lady Downey!" Phoebe gave Sara another quick hug and left with a swish of her skirts.

Sara sighed. How lucky Phoebe was. Her husband was the sweetest man. They were always touching and talking sweetly to each other, their love for each other clear in everything they did. Was it possible to enjoy the physical part of marriage? She had to admit, kissing Philip St. James had been a singular experience.

Once again, her imagination conjured up a different sort of marriage—one forged between two people who enjoyed each other's company. If she were married to the duke, he'd touch her softly, like he'd done at breakfast. He'd ravage her mouth. He'd touch her even if they weren't in the marriage bed.

Sara's head drifted slowly to the table as she thought of that other life, that fantasy life, and she fell asleep dreaming about a duke reformed.

CHAPTER TWELVE

PHILIP MADE A TRIP TO town later that afternoon. He let himself into the private investigator's place of business and barged straight into the office.

"What have you found out, Ridley?"

"Hell's bells, Brentwood. Thanks for knocking." Ridley sat up straight in his chair and stared at the duke.

"I need information. And for the money I am paying you, you'd better have some for me. Who is bothering Lady Downey?" He stood over the investigator's desk, leaning toward him.

"Unfortunately, I haven't been able to figure that out yet." Ridley rested his arms on the desk. "But I will tell you what I do know."

"Go ahead," Philip said, exasperated. He'd have to get after Ardleigh to find him a better investigator. Unfortunately, Ridley was all he had at the moment.

"Lord Downey left to escape the loan sharks, true enough. He was in way over his head but couldn't stop. He decided to skip town instead. Some think he went as far as France, but he was followed, and it's said that he lost his life when he fell off his horse, breaking his neck, though I suspect that could be a tale created to hide the truth of his death."

"Good enough. I care only that he's dead, not how it happened. Tell me who he owes and I will pay him off." Philip was satisfied. This situation would be easily resolved.

"Not so simple. There are several loan sharks in London,

and no one wants to name his debtor. Some say he paid much of his debt down with the jewels he got from your wife. One red necklace in particular was worth a fortune. It's a wonder they're still after the dressmaker given all the jewelry your wife gave the man." Ridley looked at him with a small smile on his face. "I do hope they weren't heirlooms. They are mostly sitting in pawnshops from here to the coast. You were a generous man to your wife."

"I don't care about the jewels. I want nothing that reminds me of my former wife. Find out who is bothering Lady Downey. And put a man outside her shop to keep an eye on who enters. I don't care what it costs, just do it." Philip left and slammed the door.

He didn't want to care, truly, but it was a bitter pill. He'd given Caroline that ruby necklace for her birthday, and she'd thanked him quite well for it. But obviously the necklace meant nothing to her. She'd given it away to some swindler.

What the hell had Caroline seen in Lord Downey anyway? Philip gave her gifts; Downey took her pretty things and gambled them away. Philip had loved her, but Downey was clearly only capable of loving himself. Well, no more. The man was dead.

After the pulsating of his blood through his veins slowed, Philip found himself standing in front of the jewelers. He walked in the front door and over to the counter. Red stones had always drawn his eye, so he took special notice of the ruby necklaces in the case. He'd intended only to buy one, a parting gift for Miranda, but he recalled his vision of Lady Downey in rubies. Perhaps he'd procure one for her, too. He'd already asked the clerk to show him the necklaces when a third piece caught his eye: an exquisite emerald pendant. It would suit Sara's soft green eyes. He envisioned her standing in his bedroom, adorned only in the emerald necklace and her sable curls.

He purchased all three necklaces and left.

Philip strode up the steps and knocked on the door. He should have done this long ago, but he'd put it off, knowing the theatrics it would bring. With any luck, the gift he'd brought her would help him avoid a scene.

The door opened quietly and he entered.

Which was when the screaming started.

"How dare you treat me so!" Miranda railed at him, hands on her hips. "You told me you would be here last night. How dare you ignore me! When I said you could come to me, I expected you to be here. I will be treated with respect. Do you hear me, Brentwood? When I want you, you are to come!" Miranda paced as she yelled.

Her thin night robe fell open, allowing Philip a clear look at her bared breasts, which bounced becomingly with her furious tirade. She was beautiful, but she was also controlling, manipulative, nasty, and vindictive.

Had he purposefully chosen to involve himself with a woman he could never love?

"Aren't you going to say anything? No apology? Nothing?" She glared at him with her hands still on her hips, making no attempt to cover her nudity. She knew how to flaunt her best assets.

Philip reached into his pocket and pulled out the package. He held it out to her. "Miranda, our time together has been wonderful, but it's over. Accept this gift as a token of my appreciation for everything we've shared."

Miranda reached out to grab the package. She quickly tore the wrapping off, her mouth forming a perfect circle.

"Oh, Philip! It is beautiful. You know how I love rubies."

She put the necklace on quickly and fell to her knees in front of him, but he caught her before she could touch him. "I'm not here for that. Our time is done."

"Allow me to convince you otherwise," she said, reaching for his pants.

"No. It's over. Good-bye." He intended to leave, but she grabbed his neckcloth. He turned back to face her, surprised to see her expression.

Miranda's face had turned a deep shade of red, something he'd not seen often. Then she surprised him even more.

She slapped him.

"You bastard! Who is she? How *dare* you." Her arms rotated like windmills, her nails trying to rake every part of him within reach.

"Miranda, stop." Philip grabbed both of her wrists to put an end to her flailing.

"No, I won't! You son of a bitch. Nobody leaves me. I leave them. Get out! Get out and never come back. But you *will* be back. Two days from now, you will be groveling at my doorstep. I am the most desired woman in London. You will want me, Brentwood, and I won't give you the time of day."

Philip let go of her hands. There was only one thing he could say: the truth, though he guessed it would be a while before she believed it. "It's over, Miranda."

Miranda slapped him again, hard across the cheek.

Philip opened the door and left.

CHAPTER THIRTEEN

THREE DAYS LATER, SARA PEEKED out the window and saw Phoebe's carriage pull up in front of her store. She set her sign to "Closed" and locked up with her new set of keys.

The door of the carriage opened, and Phoebe beckoned to her from inside. "Come on, Sara. We have important work to do...shop!"

She giggled as her friend tugged her inside. The cushion was made of fine velvet, a fabric that would have made a lovely winter gown, and she ran her fingers across it as Phoebe leaned forward to give the driver instructions. "You recall that wonderful shop with all the buttons? That's where we're headed today."

"Aye, my lady." The man climbed up to his seat and flicked the reins. The horses began moving forward at a steady clip, the carriage rolling smoothly over the road.

"Phoebe, I have been anticipating this outing all week." It felt as if her smile warmed her entire face.

"Sara, I have forgotten how stunning you are." She shook her head with her pronouncement. "You, my dear, need a man."

Sara blushed. "Don't be ridiculous. Duncan told me every day of our marriage how homely I am. Please stop flattering me."

Phoebe's voice softened. "Ah, you are modest and innocent still, I think. Trust me when I tell you that many men would wish to take you to wife."

"Enough about me. I want to hear about your family. Were you not expecting a short while ago?"

"Oh, yes! Ardleigh and I have a precious little girl, Abigail. Why, she lights up my day. You should see Edward with her. I swear she already has him wrapped right around her little finger. He just cannot stay away from her, he adores her so." Phoebe's face radiated excitement as she spoke. It was obvious Abigail had her mother wrapped around her finger as well.

"Goodness. Who is she with while you shop?" Sara asked.

"Oh, Ardleigh is home along with her nanny. He has been pushing me to go out more lately. I don't want to leave her, but I think he is right. I am so glad you came today, Sara." Phoebe reached over and gave her a quick hug.

They discussed all the current fashions and accessories. Time passed quickly, and they soon found themselves in front of the shop Phoebe had told her about.

When they stepped inside, Sara released a slow sigh, turning in a circle to admire the containers of beads lining the walls. She'd always loved shops like this. Although she had few memories of her mother, her father had told her plenty of stories. Her mother had loved sewing just as much as she did, and the treasured reticule was of her own creation.

There were two rooms for them to go through. They selected beads for Phoebe's ball gown. Then Sara found beads the perfect shade for the dowager duchess's gown. By the time she was done, she had chosen several varieties to use in her shop.

"We did not find what we came for, though. I am sorry, Sara. I really believed there was a large enough selection to find every kind of bead. I had hoped you'd find the ones you're seeking."

Sara placed a hand on her friend's arm. "It is all right that

I didn't find the exact kind to complement my mother's bag. When I need to, I will find them. I am happy I found the ones that I need right now. If the Dowager Duchess of Brentwood is happy with my designs, I'll get more business than I can handle. Thank you, Phoebe."

They waited while their purchases were wrapped, and then they climbed back into the carriage.

"Now I must insist that you come to my house to see my lovely daughter. We can have tea and sandwiches while you are there."

Sara turned her head so Phoebe would not see the tears in her eyes. "I would love nothing more."

Philip sat in Ardleigh's library.

The Earl of Ardleigh shook his head and said to his friend, "Tell me again what you know so far, Brentwood."

"Lady Downey is being blackmailed for her husband's gambling debts. They killed him first, presumably to put an end to his gambling, but now they expect her to pay. That's what your man told me, though he could work a bit faster. He is awfully slow, Ardleigh."

"You wanted someone discreet," his friend said with a shrug. "He's discreet, though he may not be the best. Never mind that. Lord Downey is really dead? I've heard the rumors, but is there any proof?"

"No, but I'm having your man look into it." Philip couldn't stop himself from pacing the room.

"I knew he was a gambler, but I didn't realize his problem was so serious. He must owe a bundle to have lost his life over it. And if it's true, where do you suppose Caroline is now?" Ardleigh steepled his fingers. "How were you able to get a divorce from her? Must have cost you a great deal of money, since I have only heard of one other divorce granted this year." Ardleigh waited for an answer but didn't get one. "I suspect it was a wise move as you may see her again soon. Do you think she will attempt to come back to you if the baron's dead?"

"I don't know and I don't care. Tell me what you know about Downey."

"You aren't going to like what I tell you. I can see you have some special interest in Lady Downey, and I know how protective you can be." Ardleigh raised his eyebrows at Brentwood to gauge his reaction.

"Never mind about my interests. Tell me about their marriage." Philip continued to pace around the room as they talked.

Ardleigh leaned back in his chair and stared out the window. "Well, I am not sure how they met, but Duncan was as happy as any man when he married her, although I suspect it was more over her dowry than any special feelings for her. She is not from London. It was an arranged marriage. Her father's health was not good, and he wanted to make sure she was taken care of before he died. He was of new money, apparently. Wanted to get his daughter a title to go with her fortune. He just wasn't thorough enough about looking into the baron's background."

Philip stopped to ask, "When did her father die?"

"Shortly after their wedding. Phoebe met Sara at a dress shop in town. They became fast friends, but Phoebe didn't like the things she heard from Sara about her husband. She always wanted me to intervene. I felt uncomfortable with the situation, but she had no family to support her after her father died."

Brentwood flexed his fists as he paced. He stopped occasionally to focus on his friend. "Why did Phoebe want you to intervene? What did the bastard do to her?"

Ardleigh frowned and sat up in his chair. "He beat her once. Phoebe was upset because she hadn't seen Sara at any of the recent *ton* events. She called on her and was shocked to see her condition. Her face was black and blue. Phoebe actually thought she saw fingerprints on Sara's neck. I did threaten the bastard over that one. Phoebe was beside herself. I think he got my message. As far as I know, he never beat her again."

"Anything else?"

"My only other recollection is that he always belittled Sara. I don't know how anyone could look at Sara and call her homely, but he did. I remember one particular night at the opera he ridiculed her dress. He wanted to know why she didn't know enough to dress like the other women. I think he called her a cow. He was trying to whisper in her ear, but I caught bits and pieces. I asked Phoebe about it later. How could anyone look at Sara and call her a cow? The woman is exquisite. I guess he was one of those sick bastards who control women through intimidation. They did not go out much after they married. He probably did not want to spend the money."

Philip finally sat in a chair and leaned forward on his elbows. "Rotten bastard. I wish he were alive so I could kill him again."

Ardleigh spoke quietly to his friend. "What I can't figure out is why Caroline would go with him. No offense, Brentwood, but your wife was not the type to be easily intimidated."

On their trip back to Phoebe's home, Sara finally confided a bit of her troubles to her friend. Phoebe promised to speak to Ardleigh about Stinky's visits. Although nothing had been resolved, Sara allowed herself to hope. It had felt good to unburden herself—she already felt so much less alone.

They walked up the steps to the estate, overloaded with packages, laughing over a story Phoebe had just finished.

"Come, Sara, I cannot wait to show you my Abigail." The butler helped them move their parcels into the day room. A maid took their coats, and Sara dropped onto the settee, a joyous feeling permeating her body, something she had not experienced for a long time.

Phoebe stood at the door. "Pardon me just a moment. I will run up to the nursery."

She returned shortly with her beautiful, plump daughter in her arms.

"Sara, I want you to meet our daughter, Abigail." Phoebe's face beamed with pride as she turned her baby toward Sara.

Sara froze. She had never seen a baby up close, only from a distance. What a beautiful child. She reached over and ran her finger down Abigail's arm. Her skin was soft and flawless, and she smelled like sunshine. Sara smiled at the cherubic face, surprised to see her smile returned. Abigail kicked her legs and bounced her arms up and down.

"Oh my!" Sara exclaimed as she started. "Why, she is so expressive, Phoebe. What a happy child."

"Have you ever held a baby before?" she asked. "Would you like to hold her?"

"I have never held a baby. You will have to show me how." Sara blushed.

Phoebe motioned her to the wingback chair in the corner. "Sit right here, and I will set her on your lap. Can you manage with your finger?"

Sara hurried over and sat gingerly. "I am sure I can manage. You won't leave me, Phoebe. I wouldn't know what to do if she cried." She held her arms out to her friend.

Phoebe carefully placed Abigail in Sara's arms. "Why, there is nothing to it, Sara. You will be a natural. So long as a child knows they are in loving arms, they will be fine. You just have to support her neck when you move her."

Sara settled the baby into her arms and stared at her,

spellbound by the tiny creature.

"I must let my husband know we've returned. I'll be right back. You'll be fine with her." Phoebe left quickly before Sara realized what she'd said.

Alone in the room, Sara smiled down at Abigail. "Oh, my word. You are a precious thing." She gently kissed her cheek, taking in the child's scent. Abigail smiled up at her.

"Oh, Abigail. I didn't think I would ever want a child. But perhaps I was wrong. What a wonderful gift you are to your parents. Of course, I would need to be married. I certainly couldn't bring someone like you into this world without a wonderful father. And the last man I married would have been a dreadful father. I guess motherhood wasn't meant to be for me. Hopefully, your mother will allow me the pleasure of watching you grow." She sighed when the little girl grabbed her finger into a tight fist.

Sara heard a noise and turned to see Philip St. James standing in the doorway observing her.

Philip had watched from the library window as Phoebe and Sara disembarked from the carriage. It had given him pleasure to see Sara look so lighthearted with her friend, laughing and smiling as if she did not have the weight of the world on her shoulders. She was even more beautiful like this.

"Ah, good," Ardleigh said. "I see Phoebe had a good time with Sara today. I can tell by the number of packages she has in her hands."

Some minutes later, Phoebe strode into the library and gave her husband a kiss.

"Ardleigh, we had such a wonderful time at the shops. Greetings, Your Grace. It is so nice to see you." She offered her hand to Philip and curtsied.

Philip smiled at Phoebe. He couldn't help but smile

whenever he saw his friend with his wife. They truly were in love. Would he ever know that feeling?

"You look lovely today, Lady Ardleigh. Excuse me for a moment, won't you?"

Philip stepped out of the room. He felt like he was intruding and wanted to give them a moment alone. Meandering down the hallway, he heard a soft voice and followed it. Stopping outside a doorway, he peeked in to find Sara with the Ardleigh baby in her lap. He listened to her prattle on to the child for a moment before realizing she wasn't cooing sweet nothings. She was talking to the babe, very seriously, it seemed, about her chances of ever becoming a mother.

Seeing her like this tugged at his heart. Oh, she was lovely. Sweet and kind and beautiful. How was he going to be able to ensure that Sara's troubles were over? He wanted to do that for her. He needed to protect this woman, to stop the pain and tragedy in her life. She did not deserve it. He vowed to help her, whatever the cost.

CHAPTER FOURTEEN

THE DAY OF THE ARDLEIGH ball had finally arrived. Sara had refused Phoebe's repeated invitations. Although it would be viewed as acceptable were she to attend alone—she was a widow, after all, and Phoebe was a close friend—she didn't wish to be maligned by gossips like Miranda Montrose. The world didn't know her husband was dead, though some had surely heard the rumors. Besides which, she knew she didn't have much time to raise money for Stinky.

Sara counted her coins again, sighing as she realized she was one-third short of what she needed. One large order hung in the front room for a very wealthy client to pick up. If she received the money in time, she should be safe from Stinky. Only a week had passed, but Sara could not depend on Stinky's ability to count the days correctly.

She paced through her shop. Both doors were locked and bolted, but she checked them multiple times to be sure. Finally, she forced herself to sit at her table and work on her sketchbook. She loved to design most of all.

After a few hours, she noticed the sun had dropped. She grabbed a piece of stale bread from her cupboard upstairs. One lone apple sat on her kitchen table. She sighed and brought both things back downstairs to eat while she sketched. Her mind needed to stay busy or nerves would overtake her.

The rush of traffic had died down outside. Not many were on the street at this hour, especially since the members of the *ton* would be in line at the Ardleigh estate or at the opera or the theater. Most of the shops on her street closed early. After lighting her oil lamp, Sara stood from her desk, listening to the eerie quiet. Chills ran down her spine at the thought of how alone she was at that moment. No one would hear her scream; no one would be there to help, if needed. Perhaps Philip was right, and she should return to the boardinghouse for safety reasons. Cradling her head in her hands, she thought about the futility of such a move. It would be impossible to earn the money she needed if she were forced to leave the shop at sundown.

Allowing herself a few minutes to daydream, she thought about her friend's ball, and wondered what it would have felt like to stroll into the ballroom on the arm of the Duke of Brentwood. He was by far the most handsome nobleman she had ever seen. Without really thinking, she reached up to touch her cheek where he had caressed her. Would he be that gentle if he made love to her? She envisioned Philip smiling at her with his fine-looking mouth, no coldness in his gaze, maybe his hand at her waist, caressing her.

Then Miranda Montrose popped into her mind, causing a shudder to course through her. Oh, the tongue-lashing she'd give Sara if she ever saw her out in public with the duke.

Unfortunately, it was only a dream.

Philip held out his hand to Emma as she stepped from the carriage.

"Are you ready, pretty one, for your first ball?"

"Oh, Philip, I am so excited! How many people do you think will be here? I hope my gown is appropriate. I do love this gown Lady Downey fitted to me. I've never seen another like it. Did you pay her something special? I am sure no one else will have a gown like this. She is a very special lady, don't you agree?"

Mary St. James, who stood on Philip's other side, peeked around her son to glare at her daughter. "For heaven's sake, Emma. Cease your prattling and do remember your brother's title, please. I know you are nervous, but if you continue babbling to your brother, he will escort you home in a hurry."

"It's all right, Mother. Emma is fine. I am sure she will calm down once we're inside." Philip leaned over and gave his sister a peck on her cheek. "You are truly beautiful, Emma. You'll be the loveliest lady at the ball."

Philip had chastised his brothers for not attending with them, but now was glad they'd begged off. They would have teased Emma too much. She didn't need that on the night of her first ball.

Emma blushed and gazed up at him with a sweet smile. "Thank you, Your Grace."

"Remember you are to be with me or your brother at all times tonight," the duchess warned. "You will not go off by yourself for any reason. Is that clear, Emma?"

"Yes, Mother. I will behave. You have reminded me several times now." Emma's eyes rolled up to look at the sky as she sighed.

"Mother is right this time, Emma," Philip admonished. "You are too young to go off by yourself. There are likely to be many young men searching for innocent females. Of course, with me by your side, they will stay away." Noticing the frustration on Emma's face, he couldn't help but smile. She might think her mother and brother were spoiling her fun, but this night would be memorable for her.

He wondered how long he would have to stay. He'd quickly tired of attending balls after the divorce became public knowledge—aggressive mothers had taken to shoving their awkward young daughters in his face. The fact that he had, indeed, obtained a divorce had caused a bit of a stir, but it meant he was once again marriageable material in the minds of his peers. Then there was Miranda. She had sent several notes to his house, hoping to reconcile. He had only responded to one. "It is over" was all he had written. Apparently, she still did not believe him.

His best strategy was to stick by his sister's side all night. His mother had made it clear she intended to guard Emma closely, and Miranda wouldn't dare cross her. The duchess wielded a colossal amount of power with the *ton*.

The butler announced them as they entered the foyer and made their way down the steps.

Philip strode directly to their hosts, Ardleigh and his wife. "Lady Ardleigh, you are a vision of loveliness tonight," he said as he took her gloved hand.

"Why, thank you, Your Grace," Phoebe said with a curtsy.

Philip noticed most eyes in the ballroom had turned to them, so he introduced his sister. "May I present my sister, Lady Emma, and my mother, Mary, the Dowager Duchess of Brentwood."

Phoebe took Emma's hands in hers. "Lady Emma, you are breathtaking tonight. Pink is a lovely color on you. Your gown is divine. As is yours, Your Grace." Phoebe turned to the duchess.

Emma curtsied as she blushed. "Thank you, Lady Ardleigh. Lady Downey designed my new gown. I hoped it would be appropriate for my first ball."

Phoebe's eyes lit up. "It is more than appropriate. You will steal many hearts tonight, I am afraid. All eyes will be on you."

Emma's face beamed as she turned to her brother. "Thank you, Your Grace, for allowing me to come with you."

"Come, Emma, I will find you some lemonade, and we will allow Lady Ardleigh to greet her other guests." Philip bowed briefly, holding his elbow up to his sister, and led his family into the crowd, peering into many sets of male eyes as he passed to make sure they understood his sister was off limits.

Sara jumped at the distant yowl of a cat down the street. Her nerves had been on edge ever since dusk had settled on the city a couple of hours ago. She brushed a fallen hair out of her eyes as she worked, thinking how much she wished she could afford to return to the boardinghouse. At the time, she'd been happy to leave, but her circumstances had changed. If only she could spare the money.

She paced in her showroom, ears attuned to the sounds outside. Although it wasn't close to the end of the two-week period, something told her she was in imminent danger. But what could she do? She certainly couldn't visit the duchess; she would be at the Ardleigh ball tonight. The duke had said she could get in touch with him, but where would he be tonight? Perhaps she could attend the ball— Phoebe would be delighted—however, she no longer owned appropriate attire. She had some nice gowns, but none were truly lavish. Her husband had always encouraged her to be more understated.

Her gaze shot to the readymade gowns, some decorating a chaise, some on her father's T-bars bracketed to the walls. Two of them, she knew, fit her. One gown was soft lavender with dark purple ribbons. Lavender was a little light for her since she was apparently a widow, but the dark ribbons were beautiful. The other choice was yellow, which would be totally inappropriate for Phoebe's ball. She did not wish to stand out, especially not for ignoring the conventions of widowhood.

Foolish girl! Why would you think about attending a ball? You are no longer part of the ton. She paced again. A handsome duke popped into her mind. She had flushed to her roots when she'd caught him staring at her at Phoebe's estate the other day. He was so gorgeous, so unexpectedly kind, that her heart melted a bit more each time she saw him. But he also tied her tongue into knots, and she'd struggled for words. They'd stayed like that, her cradling the baby, him watching her, for a long moment before Phoebe returned.

Strange noises brought her abruptly back to reality. Freezing in her path, she listened to voices outside the shop.

"What do you think you are doing, man? Can't you see that her shop is closed?"

Her shop? She rushed to her window and peered through the curtain. Two men argued a few feet from her door. One man she had never seen before, but the other looked familiar.

Was that Stinky? She watched as the stranger threw a fist at him. The punch landed square in Stinky's gut. He yelled and swung back but missed his target.

"Get the hell out of here, you dirty scum!" the stranger yelled at Stinky. A few more punches were thrown before Stinky finally escaped down the street.

Sara raced to her door to thank the other man, but he disappeared.

Where had he gone?

She opened her door and shouted down the street. "Come back! Don't leave me here alone. Please, come back!"

Sara searched the street for her savior before slamming the door closed and locking it.

He would probably come back for her. She had to get out, but where could she go? Her only choice was to attend Ardleigh's ball. Maybe Philip was there, someone who wouldn't abandon her if she feared for her life.

She ran to the middle room and pulled out the lavender gown. Removing her clothes, she threw them in the back room and tugged the gown on over her corset. Her trembling fingers had a hard time with the buttons, but she finally did them up. How could she get to Ardleigh's? Phoebe's house was closer than the duke's, but it was still quite a distance. And what if Stinky was watching the shop? Maybe he was out there right now waiting for her to make a move.

Another thought struck her. Had the fight been a ruse? Perhaps he'd set the whole thing up to get her to walk outside? Maybe he couldn't get through her new locks. In that case, he would have to get her to leave her shop to get the money.

Perhaps she should stay. Was it safer here? Or would it be safer at Ardleigh's? Sara cradled her hands in her face, wracked by uncertainty and desperation.

Papa, what should I do?

She made the bold decision to leave, even though she would have to go alone, something that just wasn't done. She didn't have a companion to travel to the Ardleigh's with her, but once inside, she could remain near Phoebe, an acceptable arrangement. Staying in one place was impossible now that she had seen Stinky again. If he followed her and tried to kill her, then she would fight. If she lost, so be it. At least the torture would finally be over.

Sara fixed her hair, found her reticule and bonnet, donned her cape, and locked her shop. Glancing over her shoulder when the cold air hit her face, she was thankful there wasn't a soul in sight. She hurried into the night, aiming blindly toward the Ardleigh estate.

CHAPTER FIFTEEN

PHILIP WANDERED AIMLESSLY AROUND THE edge
of the ballroom. Not really understanding why, he continued as if he had a destination. He had left Emma with
his mother by the punchbowl. A couple of young bucks
had tried to talk to her, but he knew his mother would
have her in hand. He smiled when he thought of Emma's
excitement. There was something so innocent about her
joy.

Of course, Caroline had loved balls too, but she'd savored
them for the attention. With her stunning looks and her
body, Caroline had always drawn plenty of interest from
the men and jealousy and admiration from the ladies. He
hadn't realized it until they had been married for a while,
but life was always about Caroline, no one else. He had
certainly never seen his ex-wife stare at a baby the way
Sara had gazed longingly at the Ardleigh baby yesterday.
But then, Lady Downey wasn't self-centered like Caroline.

He stopped for a moment as he caught quick movement
across the ballroom. Was that Sara? His gaze followed her
around the edge of the room. He couldn't tell where she
was headed, but she was clearly in a hurry. Although she
looked as beautiful as he'd ever seen her in a lovely purple
gown, she seemed panic-stricken. In fact, she stumbled as
if she was on the verge of fainting. He charged across the
ballroom, trying not to draw attention to himself. Edging
through the crowd, he finally stepped in front of her.

"Sara?"

Sara dodged him, startled. "Oh, Your Grace. Pardon me. I didn't..." Her eyes darted at the people around them. She appeared to be looking for someone—or perhaps running from someone.

Acting on impulse, Philip quickly grasped her hand and escorted her toward the dance floor as the band started the next piece.

"Waltz with me, Lady Downey?"

She searched his gaze for a moment, long enough for him to count the golden flecks in her eyes, then hastened onto the dance floor with him. He drew her in closer, savoring the feel of her in his arms.

"Sara, look at me," he whispered. "I have you now. You are safe. What's wrong? Remember, whatever it is, I will protect you."

Her eyes searched his then dropped again. She looked lost and frightened, and he'd never wanted anything more than to bolster her. Protect her. She leaned in closer, and he whispered in her ear, "Sara, relax. I will not let him hurt you. You'll stay with me tonight. He'll not frighten you again." Her body relaxed slightly in his arms, and that small sign of trust moved him more than he could say.

"He came for me again," she whispered.

"What happened?" He forced a smile for the crowd as they continued to dance.

"Nothing. He was at my door, and someone scared him away. But I couldn't stay. What if he returned? What if he came back for me?" She closed her eyes and leaned in closer, her hand stroking the fabric of his dark coat in a way that summoned images from his dreams. They stayed like that for a moment, swaying, but then she smiled and raised her head. That smile was so radiant and glorious, he struggled not to kiss her then and there, in front of every-one. Then the smile wavered.

"Your Grace, help me. What do I do?"

"You needn't worry any longer, Sara. I will take care of everything."

Emma tugged on her mother's arm.

"Mother, look! Over there, see who Philip is dancing with? Isn't that Lady Downey?"

"Oh my word, I think you're right, Emma, but when did she get here? I didn't even see her arrive. I must say she appears to be upset. What do you think, my dear?"

"Oh, I think they make a beautiful couple, Mother. Look at Lady Downey's gown. Is it not gorgeous?"

The duchess's eyes narrowed as a small smile crept across her face. "Why, they really do make a perfect couple. Now, how long do you think it will take before your brother realizes it?"

Philip hastened Sara out through the side terrace doors, then called for his carriage. Keeping a tight hold on her, he called out to Ardleigh on the front steps.

Ardleigh strode over to them, his eyes widening when he caught sight of Sara—and the location of Philip's arm, which cradled her lower back.

"Good evening, Lady Downey. Everything all right, Brentwood?"

"No, everything is not all right, but I'll handle it. Would you please tell my mother that I'll be unable to escort her home? Tell her not to wait up for me. I will explain in the morning."

"Of course," Ardleigh said, his brow furrowed. "Do let me know what's happening when you have the chance. I'm certain Phoebe will be concerned."

He bowed to them and took his leave, and Philip tightened his arm around Sara. He didn't want her to get a chill while they waited.

Their carriage arrived, and the duke helped Sara inside. Before following her in, he noticed Miranda Montrose traipsing around the side of the house with a murderous look on her face. Apparently, she wasn't pleased to see he'd formed a friendship with Sara. Perhaps it would encourage her to finally find a different paramour.

He climbed in and sat across from Sara, gazing into her emerald eyes. He realized how happy he was to be looking at Sara instead of Miranda.

"You're ravishing tonight, Sara, and please do not argue with me. You were the most beautiful woman in the ballroom."

Sara blushed and averted her eyes, although he didn't miss the glimmer of pleasure in her gaze.

Philip reached over and tugged her onto his lap. She came to him willingly, and when he traced his thumb across her lower lip she released a lusty sigh that had him hard in an instant.

"Your husband was totally wrong about you and I suspect a little mad," he said in her ear. "Have I told you that you have the most kissable lips I have ever seen?"

He leaned forward and placed a chaste kiss on her lips. Thoughts of chestnut locks falling over her breasts ran through his mind. How would she feel in his arms? He was surprised by how much he wanted her. His lips descended on hers again and he deepened the kiss, satisfying a hunger inside him that he hadn't even identified until now. Sweeping his tongue inside her mouth, he changed the angle of the kiss, giving him better access. Her arms wrapped around his neck, a small moan erupting from the back of her throat.

His thumb brushed her ankle, caressing her soft skin, and he ran a line of kisses down her jaw, across the pulse in her neck. His tongue found its way down her collarbone. Her fingers tightened their grip on his shoulders with every caress.

He broke away and held her in his arms, his fingers stroked her hair, pulling the pins out. What was this woman doing to him? He'd never wanted any woman the way he wanted her.

Already, he knew she would be a passionate lover. He was never wrong about such things. Loud moans of ecstasy tore through his mind as he thought about bringing her to climax.

The carriage pulled to a stop in front of his townhouse.

The door opened and they stepped inside. Sara was a nervous wreck. Her fingers trembled in the duke's hand.

"Alfred, this is Lady Sara," Philip said to the man who'd opened the door. A matronly woman stood beside him. "We shall remain here tonight. Please ready the bath."

Philip's butler nodded. "Of course, Your Grace." Alfred motioned to the housekeeper and sent her on her way.

Sara had thought Philip would bring her back to Hearthstone Manor, but instead they'd come here. What did it mean? Would they have a chance to be alone together? Still holding her hand, he led her into a large bedroom and helped her with her cape.

"Where are we, Your Grace? Where have you brought me?" Her eyes roamed the beautifully outfitted room, lingering on the bed, the largest she had ever seen, which bore a navy blue coverlet and numerous pillows in different shades of blue. There was also a hearth, a couple of luxuriant rugs, and a table and chairs.

"Philip, please. My name is Philip. No 'Your Grace' allowed here. We are in my townhouse. Do not worry; my staff will not speak a word of your arrival. They are paid handsomely to be discreet."

He motioned her to a chair in front of the hearth and

started a fire. As she sat, she could not help but stare at him. He'd removed his jacket to bank the fire, and his muscles rippled through his white shirt. Philip St. James was a fine-looking man from head to toe, but he was off limits… wasn't he?

"I'll not allow you back in your place with that man watching for you," he said. "It's not safe for you there." As if guessing the direction of her thoughts, he added, "There's another bedroom down the hall. It will suit my needs perfectly well."

Sara continued to watch the man in front of her, blushing a little as he bent over. Her eyes lingered on his bottom. Even that was muscular. His strength vibrated in his legs as he worked.

She came to a surprisingly easy decision: she would sleep with this man. Just once she wanted to feel loved, protected, cared for, and admired. The duke didn't truly love her, of course, but he made her feel special. Couldn't she pretend for one night?

"No," she said softly. "We'll both sleep in the bed, if 'tis acceptable to you."

Her fingers twisted her gown in her lap, bunching folds of the fabric. Doing so brought a painful reminder of her broken finger. But she was safe now, wasn't she? She squeezed her eyes shut to make sure this wasn't a dream. When she opened them, Philip was still there. So was the bed.

She stood and tiptoed over to it, caressing the fine linens with her fingertips, luxuriating in the richness of the fabric. He came up behind her, circling his arms around her waist, and leaned in to kiss her neck. She tensed at first, nervous, but then closed her eyes and allowed herself to relax into his embrace.

Sara didn't understand the feelings she had whenever he was near. Heat pooled in her belly. Her breasts tensed against the constraints of her gown, begging to be set free. She had never experienced such sensations with Duncan. Her senses were inflamed by Philip's touch, his scent, and his soft words. She didn't feel his touch on the buttons or ribbons of her gown, but it was suddenly pooled at her feet.

She turned to stare at him, only to see his blue eyes were already boring into her. How had he done that? He unlaced her corset, reaching around her, his hot breath on her bare shoulder making her tremble. Then he lifted her as if she weighed nothing and settled her on the bed.

She followed his every movement as he removed his shirt. Unable to tear her eyes from his torso, she licked her lips at the muscles in his arms and the flat plane of his belly. Her hand reached up to touch the dark hairs on his chest, but he was still too far away. Her husband had been a handsome man, too, but his cruelty had made him ugly to her.

"Do you like what you see, Sara?"

Nodding, she could feel the blush start at her head and travel to her toes.

"Good. I was getting a little nervous." He removed the rest of his clothes and slid between the sheets. "You are agreeable to this? You do want me?"

Astounded that he awaited her response, she nodded again as she gazed into his eyes. "Yes, Philip. I *do* want you. So much. But I am nervous."

He kissed her cheek and a path down her jaw. "Then I must make you forget your nerves. We'll not do anything you don't wish to do." His hand trailed a slow path from the side of her knee up her thigh, rotating in slow circles by her hip before finally reaching up to cup her breast.

"You are absolutely beautiful, Sara. Every part of you is meant for a man's hands—my hands." Philip leaned down and covered her mouth with his, kissing her with a growing urgency. Moving lower, he suckled her nipple and she cried out, arching her back, pressing into him.

His soft caresses, his warm breath, his hard muscles... she wanted more of him. Touching his coarse chest hairs, she teased her hands down his rippled abdomen until she found what she was searching for. She wanted this man with a frenzy she couldn't comprehend.

Philip pulled her hand away. "Not yet, love. You will make me embarrass myself like a schoolboy." The heat in his eyes warmed her belly, pooled between her thighs. She smiled inwardly, hoping she had made the right decision to share herself with this man.

His lips found hers again, and she opened willingly for his tongue to explore the wet cavern of her mouth. Tangling his hands in her hair, he tugged her closer as if he couldn't get enough of her. A loud moan interrupted her thoughts, and it shocked her to realize had come from *her* lips. She wrapped her hand around his arm, digging her nails into his bicep, relishing the hardness, the power she found there.

What was happening to her?

He rained kisses down her neck and across her collarbone until he found her nipple once more. He teased each velvety tip until they reached hard, taut peaks, as if begging for more.

Pulling his head from her breast, he whispered into her neck, "Sara, you're so beautiful. You have no idea how much I want you." She was shocked to see the raw passion in his eyes, turning the color to a deep, dark blue. A low, husky groan erupted from his throat before he took her mouth again, plundering her lips with sweet torture.

Returning to her nipple, he pulled hard on the tip, then ran his teeth across the tender apex, his breath rasping against her skin until she wanted to scream.

Would Philip hurt her when he entered her? It had

always been painful, or nearly so, with Duncan, but he'd never been gentle with her. He'd never touched her like this, as if he savored her.

Philip ran kisses down her belly as she watched, clinging to him. His tongue ran down the inside of each thigh as his hands reached for her tangle of curls. Her breath grew ragged, and she panted at each further touch of his tongue. When his tongue touched her nub, she screamed.

Her hand clutched his hair as he lowered himself between her legs. "Philip, I don't understand. What are you doing to me?"

She couldn't believe what he was doing, yet she was powerless to ask him to stop. She didn't *want* him to stop. His tongue probed her most tender parts at the juncture of her thighs until she cried out in sweet surrender, pleasure rippling through her.

He rose up to his knees and gazed at her. "You drive me to madness. I cannot wait any longer."

Lowering himself over her, he settled his broad frame between her knees and teased her entrance. Touching her with his hands, he inserted his finger inside her slickness.

"Oh, sweetheart, you do want me. You are hot and wet for me."

He removed his finger and entered her swiftly. She cried out from the sheer pleasure of it, shocked it did not hurt as it always had with her husband.

"Philip, oh my heavens, what are you doing to me?" She gripped his arms as if to keep him exactly where he was at the moment.

"Relax, sweetness. Let it come. It is meant to be," he whispered in her ear.

What? What was meant to be? She lost all coherent thought and strained her hips toward him, trying to take him in deeper, fighting for every part of him. She stared at the glistening sweat covering his perfect body, grasping at his hips to urge him deeper, faster.

"Philip, please." Totally powerless against the demands of her body at that moment, all she knew was that she wanted more. And he gave it to her—again and again and again. Her back arched just as she tumbled over the edge.

"Philip," she screamed. "Oh my God, Philip." Her world turned upside down, inside out. She gasped as wave after wave of pleasure rippled through her.

He groaned as he pumped harder into her, then climaxed with a roar, burying himself into her as far as he could. Once he caught his breath, he lowered himself enough to kiss her brow and smiled at her—a radiant smile she wished to see as much as possible. He rolled onto his back, pulling her with him. He nestled her under his arm, with her head on his chest. Duncan had always pushed her away after sex, but Philip continued to caress her back and her arms. She noticed the sweat beaded on his chest, licked a drop, and smiled at his saltiness.

"I had no idea," she finally whispered when she was able to speak.

"Was that your first orgasm?" Philip tipped her chin up so he could look her in the eyes.

"Yes, and it was wonderful, Philip. I thought only men enjoyed sex." She ran a finger over his flat belly and circled his navel.

"Ah, sweetness. That is your husband's loss. He had no idea what a treasure you are." He kissed the top of her head.

Her head lifted and she searched his eyes. "Treasure? I don't understand you."

"It's up to the man to pull all the passion from his lover. I knew from the beginning you were filled with passion. You have a goldmine of loving inside you, Sara."

Sara peered at him curiously, considering his words.

"I promise to show you, if you'll allow me," he whispered.

She leaned her head back on his chest. *Would* she let him? He certainly would never offer her marriage, would he? She didn't know, although she knew men were less likely to make such a leap if there was no need. She'd given him what he wanted without marriage. What motivation would he have to change things between them?

Life was very cruel.

But she wouldn't think of tomorrow right now. She wished to enjoy herself while she could.

CHAPTER SIXTEEN

PHILIP ROLLED OUT OF BED and held his hand out to her.

"Come, Sara, I need to relax you even more."

Taking his hand, she followed him into the adjoining room.

He didn't have to look at her to know she was blushing as she trailed behind him. Why did women hide their nudity so?

Sara gasped when she entered the next room. He turned to catch her expression when she noted her surroundings. In the middle sat a huge porcelain tub filled with steaming water. Next to the tub sat a small table topped with two glasses of wine and a platter of cheese and fruit, and a rack of thick, lush towels.

"I had this made special. Do you like it? Come. Climb in. You must relax your strained body, my sweet." Philip stood in front of her, holding his hand out to help her into the tub.

"This is wonderful, Philip." She stuck a toe in the water and then moaned becomingly as she climbed into the warmth.

"Move over, sweetness. It is big enough for two. I am joining you."

Sara squealed as he climbed into the tub and sat down. She giggled when water lapped over the sides onto the rack of towels. He situated himself so he was facing her and handed her a glass of wine. After retrieving his own glass of wine, he wrapped his free arm around her long legs.

Sara leaned her head back against the tub. "Oh, Philip, this is heavenly." As she moved, she brushed up against his leg and giggled again. "And you have very hairy legs."

"Oh, do I now? And do you want to see what else I have that is very hairy?" He grabbed her hand, but she pulled back screaming.

"Stop, stop!" Sara's laughter echoed in the room. What a beautiful sound it was to him. He didn't think he had ever heard her laugh before tonight.

"Your word is my command," he said, smiling as he leaned back. They sat in silence for a few minutes, enjoying each other's presence, sipping their wine.

"Sara?"

"Yes?"

"Do you want to talk about it?"

"Talk about what?"

"Your marriage to Duncan. Why you know so little about sex?" His eyes bored into hers. He stroked her leg as he talked, hoping it would ease her mind.

Sara stared at the water for a few moments. When she spoke, her voice was quiet, raspy. He could tell she fought back tears.

"What do you want me to say? That my husband was no lover? Well, clearly he was not, but I had nothing to judge him by. I was a virgin when I married, and my father had always protected me from boys. Duncan was the first man I ever kissed. In fact, I had no idea what took place between husband and wife. My father said it was my husband's job to teach me."

"But he taught you the hard way, didn't he?"

"Before our wedding, I thought he loved me." She paused, took in a deep breath, and forced herself to continue. "I cried when he ripped through my virginity, and he…slapped me. So I never spoke another word to him in the bedroom. I thought it was the way it was supposed to be for a woman. Painful."

Philip continued to massage her legs, sensing it was important not to show her his anger, although he had never wanted to kill a man more. Duncan had gotten off easily.

No man had ever looked at her before as Philip was looking at her now. It was as if she were his only focus. As if she were the most important woman in the world.

"Your husband did not appreciate your beauty, did he, sweetness?" he said at last.

Sara gulped her wine as she shook her head.

"Do you know what I think?" Philip asked as he reached for her, setting their wine glasses down first. "I think he insulted you to tear apart your self-regard." He gently eased her toward him. "He ridiculed you so he would have complete control over you. He wanted to be sure you would never challenge him."

Sara's whole body trembled as Philip reached for the soap and a small cloth. He rubbed them together until the cloth was lathered in suds. Lifting her arm, he gently ran the cloth down it, washing her with such reverence she felt like a queen.

As he washed her arms, he whispered to her, "You have the slender, graceful beauty of a noblewoman. The class many women strive to attain is your natural right. Your body and your blood overflow with elegance. I can't imagine the things he must have told you to try to kill your spirit."

He placed his hand behind her knee and gathered her bent leg to his lips. "Don't let him win. Don't let his attacks on your loveliness, your refinement, stay with you. Fight his wickedness. Get his cruel, ugly words out of your head."

Sara reached out and grabbed his arms as tears flowed down her cheeks. "But I'm not beaut…"

"Yes, you are. You have the most gorgeous set of legs I have ever seen. Your breasts are the kind men dream about at night. Your skin is soft and flawless." He washed her shoulders and her breasts. She leaned toward him and dropped her head to his shoulder as the tears continued to flow.

"Tell me that you realize how stunning your face is." He soaped her back and then held her as quiet sobs racked her body.

"Tell me, sweetness." He grasped her chin and held her head up, gazing at her tear-stained face. "Tell me that you are beautiful. *Please,*" he implored.

Sara's voice broke as she gazed into his blue eyes. "I am…beautiful." She kissed him hard on the mouth, then retreated to stare into his eyes again.

"Yes, you are. Do you believe me?"

"Yes."

"Do you believe yourself?" he asked, his eyes flashing.

"Yes."

"Tell me you won't let him win."

"I won't let him win."

"Louder."

"I won't let him win."

"Louder."

Sara shouted, "I won't let him win!"

"That's better." He drew her close and held her until her tears subsided.

"The water is getting a bit cold." Philip stood and helped her out of the tub, although she noticed he stayed in the water.

"Dry off, and then I have something to ask of you."

She wrapped a thick, luxuriant towel about her body,

and once she was dry, she returned it to the rack. "Yes? What is it?" she asked.

He took hold of her hand and placed a cloth in it. "Now, you may wash me, if you're agreeable." He stared at her to gauge her reaction.

Sara smothered a gasp, but she decided it was a fair request. He'd cleaned her, after all, and while his body frightened her, she was also curious. Her husband had never allowed her to touch him. She glanced down at his maleness, but it didn't look quite as big and intimidating as it had before.

He reached for her chin, pulling it up. "Start with my chest."

Sara ran the soapy cloth over his chest and discovered that she liked his coarse, dark hairs. She ran her fingers through them, gliding the cloth lower.

"Careful, sweetness." He winked at her.

She was surprised to see that his chest hair was thinner near his waist. Mesmerized by his body, and how very different it was from hers, she ran the cloth toward his pubic hair.

"Oh!" she remarked as her eyes shot back to his face.

Philip chuckled. "See what you do to me? I tried to warn you. Look again, I don't mind."

Sara marveled as his member grew. She stared at it, wide-eyed with delight.

"Can I touch you?" she gazed at Philip with a small smile.

"Please do. Believe me, I will enjoy it."

She touched him gingerly, then ran her finger down his length. "Oh, Philip! You are so soft."

A laugh choked out of him. "Promise me never to repeat those words to anyone but me. Men do not like to hear they are soft."

"Well, you are very hard, but the skin is so soft, like velvet." She wrapped her hand around him, wanting to feel his girth under her fingers, but Philip groaned loudly.

Snatching her hand back, she looked up at him in surprise. "Did I hurt you?"

"No, you didn't hurt me. Do it again."

Sara smiled and took him in her hand again, sliding her fist up and down on him.

He groaned again and stilled her hand. "Stop before you unman me, woman." He gave her a playful shove and said, "Into bed with you, you have tormented me enough."

She flew into the room, giddy, and he followed her. When he caught her, he lifted her up into the air from behind and pulled her in close.

Her whole body tensed as horrible memories pummeled her. "No, no, Philip, please don't spank me. Please, no."

Philip released her instantly. "Spank you? Is that what he liked to do?"

Sara flew over to the wall, cringing as she stared at him.

"Sara, look at me." He pointed to his now-flaccid penis. "I do not get pleasure from hurting women. See how fast it went down. I will never hurt you."

Sara studied him for a moment. He was right. His penis had been hard and erect; now it was soft. With Duncan, the more he hit her, the more she screamed, the harder he got. Oh, glory be, they were different. She ran to Philip and threw her arms around him. "I'm sorry. I didn't realize."

"It's all right." He held her tightly, his arms cradling her. "In fact, we are going to do this differently."

She pulled back. "What do you mean?"

"*You* are going to make love to *me*. I want you to see how passionate you are." He kissed her neck. "I want you to understand that I don't have to be in control. You decide what we do."

She'd never heard of such a thing, but when Philip led her to the large chair in front of the hearth, she followed.

"I don't understand, Philip."

"You will. Be patient, and you will."

One towel still lay on the chair, so he spread it out and sat, tugging her closer. "I want you to straddle me, one knee on either side of my legs."

Sara settled herself and looked into Philip's eyes. "Now what do I do?"

"Ah, sweetness, that is the beauty of this position. We will do whatever you want to do. You are in control. I think you'll surprise yourself." He ran his hands over her bottom reverently.

"Oh, Philip," she said softly. He had already done so much for her. If she weren't careful, she would find herself falling in love with him.

She kissed him tentatively on the mouth. Pulling back, she ran her tongue along his bottom lip. He opened his mouth and pulled her in closer, deepening the kiss. Possessing her. Gazing into her eyes again, he let her know how much he wanted her.

"Sorry, you're in charge," he said, sounding chagrined. "I lost myself."

Sara giggled and decided to tease him. She found his nipples with her thumbs and then traced the round peaks with her tongue. He groaned as her teeth scraped his right nipple. Never in her life had she felt so powerful. So beautiful. Only one thing would make this better.

She glanced at him furtively. "I think I would like you to touch me."

"Oh, would you like that? And where would you like me to touch you?"

He ran his hands up the backs of her legs, caressing her buttocks.

"Oh!" she started at the intimate caress. "I like that, but I think I will have you start on my breasts." She reached back and strategically placed his hands on her breasts. "I think you know what to do."

She smiled at him, wiggling her bottom over him, and he ran his tongue over her nipple. A small moan escaped her throat. Letting her feelings guide her, she grasped his head and pulled him in closer.

"Ah, you like this?" He sucked hard, and she threw her head back as she wove her fingers through his hair. Her hand reached around for his nipple and she pinched it as she moved against him. His hardness stroked her cleft. He groaned as he caught her other breast and ravaged her nipple, and she responded by rubbing herself along the length of him between her legs.

She spread her legs wider, giving him access to her entrance.

"Philip, can I touch you? I want you inside me. I need you now." She stared into his eyes, shocked at her wantonness.

His eyes smoldered as he gazed into hers. "Do whatever you like, love. I'll let you know if I don't like it."

Shocked by her own boldness, she reached down between her legs and grabbed him, running the tender end of him against her pleasure spot. She rocked against him, building the pleasure inside her core, then dipped the head of his manhood inside her briefly before running it around the outside of her entrance. Her other hand clenched his shoulder at the unexpected pleasure.

"Sara, you're killing me," Philip ground out through his teeth. "I don't know how much more I can take." His blue eyes reached hers, hazy with passion. She was lost when he gazed at her that way.

"Take me in you," he whispered, running his fingers across her cheek. "Take me."

Sara plunged him inside her womanly sheath, wrapping him in her wetness. They groaned simultaneously. She slowly retreated, then brought herself down on him again. She lost control of her thoughts, driven by sensation alone, her body screaming for release. Drawing him inside her again and again, faster and faster, she clenched her muscles around him.

He groaned and reached for her bottom. Pulling her in close, he caressed her two globes softly as Sara arched her back, trying to get him in deeper. Reaching a frenzied pace, she brought herself up and down his length, moaning with each push. He changed his tactic and reached in front to touch her nub. Within seconds she screamed, exploding with an orgasm that was so intense it sent Philip over the edge with her. He yelled as his seed shot into her.

He gathered her to him as their panting subsided, and ran his hands softly up and down her back.

"Philip?" Sara spoke softly between pants.

"Yes?" His hand was still caressing her.

"Is it always this good?" she whispered with her eyes closed, enjoying the scent of their lovemaking.

"No, sweetness, we're especially good together."

A few minutes later, he put his hands on her waist and kissed her forehead, then lifted her and set her down on the floor.

He led her over to the bed and pulled the coverlet back.

"I think I have kept you up late enough."

They climbed into bed together, and Philip tucked her head onto his shoulder.

She fell asleep instantly.

CHAPTER SEVENTEEN

WHEN PHILIP AWOKE AT DAWN, he gazed at the beautiful woman sound asleep in his arms. He could feel her soft breasts moving as she breathed, teasing his chest hairs. Her eyes still had dark circles under them. He was partly to blame. He had kept her up.

Waking her early probably wasn't the right thing to do, however, his member had its own opinion about that. Philip stared up at the ceiling, trying to calm the lust in his body. If he didn't look at her, it had to get better, right?

It wasn't working. He stared at the tent the sheet made over his engorged penis. How was he going to fix this without disturbing her?

A giggle of laughter erupted next to him.

"Again, Philip? Twice last night, and you already want to do it again?" Mirth bubbled in her voice as she turned to look at his face.

Philip growled and rolled her over onto her back.

"Yes, I want you again, beauty. But this time I'll be on top." He leaned down and pulled her nipple into his mouth. A responsive moan reached his ears. "That is the only answer I needed." He smiled and proceeded to ravage her mouth.

Philip hopped out of bed and covered Sara with the blankets. "Stay in bed, my dear. I will arrange a bath for you and see to it that breakfast will be ready shortly."

Sara sighed as she pulled the covers up to her chin. Her

thoughts ran back over the previous night. Astounded would be the best way to describe how she felt at the moment.

Phoebe had been right. A relationship between a man and woman could definitely be better than her relationship with Duncan had been. Wouldn't it be amazing to wake up in Philip's arms every day? She daydreamed briefly about what her life would be like if they married. Perhaps they could have a child, like Phoebe and Edward's beautiful baby girl. Was that too much to hope for?

Of course it is. He is a duke.

The reminder of his title soured her mood. A wedding between a duke and a dressmaker could never be. She would do best to set that silly notion aside. Sighing, she made her way to the tub. The steaming water awaited her, and she slid into its warmth.

She'd do best to enjoy this while she could.

When Sara was dressed, she headed downstairs and found Philip in a small breakfast room sipping tea. He quickly stood.

"Good morning, sweetness. You are lovely this morning." He leaned in to kiss her cheek. "May I serve you breakfast?"

"Yes, please." Sara blushed with a smile. "I admit I'm a bit hungry this morning."

Philip filled a plate from the sideboard of eggs, sausage, toast, and fruit. He set it in front of her with a smile. "I suspect you do need to replenish your energy."

Sara was thankful they were alone. She would extremely embarrassed if he spoke in such a manner in front of the servants.

"Thank you, Your Grace."

Philip reached for her fingers and brushed his lips across them briefly. "Philip, please. I enjoy hearing my name on your lips."

They ate in silence for a bit. Philip appeared lost in thought. Finally, after she filled her plate a second time, he spoke softly. "Can we talk, Sara?"

"Of course."

"I would like to talk about your situation at the dress shop."

"I told you all I know about last night. I don't know why someone stopped Stinky from breaking in, but I am thankful he did. I didn't recognize the other man."

"Stinky?"

She gave him a sheepish look. "I don't know his name. That's how I think of him."

He arched a brow but said nothing. "I suspect it was a man I hired to watch your place. I have someone there every night to protect you and find out who is blackmailing you."

"What? You hired someone to watch me?"

Philip sighed. "Watch over you, not watch you. I worry about your safety. I'm trying to find out who is bothering you, but so far I have been unsuccessful. It seemed to be the next best way for me to see to your safety, especially since you sleep at your shop. It's not safe for a woman to be alone in the middle of London."

"Philip, I appreciate your concern, but I cannot expect you to continue this." How long could he possibly hire someone to protect her? The threats could go on for months.

"I don't want to continue this. I have a suggestion for you that I would like you to seriously consider." His feet shuffled as he straightened his napkin.

Piercing blue eyes stared into hers. He took hold of her hand and ran his thumb across the back. "Sara, I would like you to stay here. No one else comes to this house. It would be just the two of us. You risk danger every time you step into that shop now."

"You want me to move here?" Her gut clenched at the possibility of what he suggested.

"Yes, I believe it would be a satisfactory solution for both of us. After last night, it's clear we have a mutual affection for each other." He cleared his throat and dropped his eyes. "You risk too much working and sleeping in the heart of London all alone. You stubbornly refuse to listen to me."

"Stubbornly? And what about my business? What about the gowns your mother and sister have ordered from me?" She set her fork down and pushed her chair back from the table.

The duke's brow furrowed as he shook his head. "My mother and sister have plenty of gowns. They would not want them if they knew they were placing you in danger. You cannot be in that shop alone anymore. I forbid it." His chin went up, his look stern.

"You *forbid* it? Since when do you issue me orders? I'm not part of your family." She shot to her feet, the better to glare at him. "And what would you have me do all day, Your Grace? Stare out the window waiting for you?"

"I don't know. What do other women do? What did my mother do?" Philip was clearly irritated with the direction their conversation had taken.

"Your mother took care of her many children. Phoebe takes care of her daughter. But I suspect children are not part of this. Oh, but they could be. Because I suspect that you want me sexually available to you at all times as part of this deal." Her hands went instinctively to her hips.

"There are ways of preventing children. Once you move your things in here, I will have you consult discreetly with a woman who is an expert at preventing children. It's done all the time, Sara. After wives give their husbands an heir and a spare, many of them decide to stop having children."

Rage licked at Sara's insides. The same man who had insisted she recognize her value was now treating her as if she had none. "Forgive me, but please allow me to clarify the situation. You want me to move in here and give up my business so that I can be your mistress. Oh, and consult with a courtesan so everything will be exactly as you wish."

Philip adjusted his cravat. "Certainly you were not expecting me to propose marriage. You know I cannot do that. Although you no longer have any attachments to prevent it, I am still a duke. My wife needs to come from a noble bloodline. *If* I ever marry again. I doubt I will after the fiasco of my first marriage."

"And what will I say when I come upon your mother in the street? Or your sister? Oh, I'm sorry, Emma, but I'm living sinfully in your brother's townhouse. Of course, perhaps you would keep me here and never allow me out. That would prevent that from happening, would it not?"

She threw her napkin onto the table and stalked over to the doorway, turning as she reached it. "Excuse me, Your Grace. I have work to do. I shall be leaving now. Thank you for your offer, but I have no interest in being your whore."

Philip followed her. "What is your hesitancy? I don't understand. You're a widow. This is done frequently in the *ton*. No one will think any less of you." He reached for her.

She pulled her hand out of his reach. "I will. *I* will think less of me. The biggest insult you've leveled at me is the supposition that I would sit here waiting for you all day. Do you think me so ignorant as to be satisfied with such an arrangement? I do have a mind, *Your Grace*. And I prefer to use it. For your information, I love designing clothes. Seeing my creations in weddings and at balls makes my heart sing. Or perhaps you don't understand that kind of devotion to a craft. It isn't always about the money."

Sara turned to leave, but it felt something important had been left unsaid. "This is partially my fault," she said. "I take responsibility for my actions. I did whore for you last night. I wanted to know how it felt to be held in another man's arms. I needed to know what relations would be like with a different man. Well, now I know. So I thank you for that. In a way, I used you."

"Clearly, it was not like this with your husband. So, after the intimate relations we shared—which you cannot deny were extremely satisfying—how can you walk away?" Philip stared into her eyes, gloating over what he no doubt thought was a compelling argument.

"Because now I know what I don't want. *You*."

Sara stormed out of the townhouse.

CHAPTER EIGHTEEN

PHILIP STRODE INTO HIS ESTATE, still fuming over Sara Downey's refusal. How dare she turn him down! The front door slammed behind him as he made his way to his library, ignoring his servants as he passed them. He was in such a state he ran right into his mother.

"Philip, is that you? For heaven's sake, what is making you carry on so? Must you slam doors?" the duchess scolded him. "I think you could behave a bit more civilly, my dear."

"Pardon me, Mother, I did not mean to startle you. I'm having a bad morning." His mother followed him into the breakfast room, sitting beside him as he poured himself a cup of tea. Philip rolled his eyes, all too aware he was about to be interrogated.

"How are things with Lady Downey?" his mother asked, tipping her head to the side as she studied him.

"Lady Downey? Why would you concern yourself with her?" Sweat broke out on his forehead as he searched his mother's face.

"Well, I noticed the two of you dancing last night, and she appeared to be upset. Is everything all right with the poor girl?" Her brow furrowed with concern.

"Lady Downey is fine. I escorted her home safely, that's all. You needn't worry about her." Philip picked up the newspaper on the table in the hopes it would put a stop to the conversation.

"I do worry about that young lady. Although her husband was a despicable person, and I daresay she is better off as a widow, London is not a good place for a beautiful young woman to live alone. She has a wonderful business, but she has no one to look after her."

"Mother, please do not concern yourself. I am sure you have better places to focus your efforts."

Her eyebrows rose as she surveyed him. "You are right, Philip," she said at last. "I am a very busy woman. But I do need to pick up Emma's other gowns later this week. Perhaps you would consider escorting us again?"

"Of course, Mother. Whatever you say." He snapped the paper in front of him, only to put it down a moment later. Something she'd said had stuck out at him, in light of his conversation with Sara. "Ah, just a moment, Mother. Did you say you are busy this week?"

"Why, yes, I'm very busy this week. But I shall attempt to assist you with whatever you need. What is it?"

"No, I was just wondering what kind of things you will be busy doing." He stared up at his mother, attempting to hide his curiosity. He certainly didn't want to explain the reason for it.

"Philip, you have never asked me such a question before. Why the concern?"

"I am just curious. Would you mind answering the question?"

"Of course not. Let's see, I have to go to the orphanage on Monday. We have a meeting about renovations. I also need to find more donations of clothing for the little ones. And Tuesday, I must go to the library. Wednesday, I need to visit with your father's solicitor. He has some questions for me. That may be a good day for our visit to the modiste. Or perhaps we could do it on Thursday after I interview the new dance instructor for your sister. And of course, I have many things to do with the house. There are some changes in our menus I would like to initiate and…"

"Thank you, Mother. I see your schedule is full. Would

you not prefer it if you could sit at home instead? Did you not enjoy taking care of Father?" He was sure he knew what her answer would be, but he asked anyway. Wouldn't everyone prefer to have little to do?

"Oh, pah, you think I stayed at home every day while you were a child? How boring would that be? I loved your father, Philip, but you cannot spend every minute of every day together. Your father and I both agreed that we needed to have some interests that were ours alone. Oh, heavens, we would have made each other miserable otherwise." She shook her head at the thought. "Actually, speaking of menus, perhaps I shall speak to Cook about our dinner tonight. Excuse me, Philip, would you?"

Philip's lips curved at the edges as his mother orchestrated a swift departure for the kitchens. He had to admit, she did appear to be active most of the time. Perhaps Sara had a point. Would she agree to the arrangement if he ensured she could continue making dresses?

Briefly, his mind drew him back to a steaming bathtub. His body responded instantly. He found himself rearranging himself in his chair to make room for his erection. It befuddled him that the mere memory of her should have such an effect on him.

His brother Adam strolled into the breakfast room.

"What brings you home so early, Philip? Must have been a bad evening." Adam smirked at him as he strode to the sideboard. He filled a plate and sat at the table with a smile.

"There was nothing wrong with my evening. In fact, it was one of my more enjoyable evenings of late," Philip answered as he sipped his tea, glancing at the newspaper so he didn't have to look at his brother's smug expression.

"I would expect so. My guess is you had a little taste of the delicacy that was here with the broken finger. Dem, but she was a sweet thing."

Philip bounded out of his chair in a flash, grabbing his

brother by the neck cloth before he slammed him against the wall. His plate went flying, striking a glass off the table, and the sound of glassware breaking brought his mother running into the room.

"Rot it, let me go!" Adam squirmed under his grip.

"Philip, stop acting like a madman this instant!" His mother's voice reached the rafters.

Red-faced and furious, he reacted instantly. "If I ever hear you speak of Lady Downey in a disrespectful manner in the future, I promise you, we will finish this outside," he growled, inches from Adam's face. "Do you understand me?"

"Philip!" his mother shouted. "Enough!"

"All right, I have it. She is yours," Adam choked out, his face turning red. "If you hadn't pledged you'd never fall in love with another woman, I would have kept my mouth shut."

Philip released his brother, who slumped down with his hand on his neck.

"I do not have feelings for her," Philip announced, proud of his calm tone. He certainly didn't feel calm, although he didn't understand why he should be so angry on Sara's behalf. Such loose talk was not uncommon for Adam. He'd chastised his brother for it before, but it hadn't bothered him this much in the past. "But I will not tolerate you talking about her as if she were a trollop."

Adam ran his hand across his throat before returning to the table. "You said she is a widow living alone."

"That does not mean she is a trollop!" Philip yelled.

"Somehow, I don't believe most of the females in the *ton* would agree with you. But I'll cease." His brother aimed a mock bow at him.

The duchess folded her arms across her chest. "Although I dislike the way he chose to express himself, I have to agree with him, Adam. You are speaking inappropriately of Lady Downey. I will not have that type of talk in this house. Keep it at White's. I don't care to hear it."

"Sorry, Mother, you were not in the room at the time. It was not meant for your ears," he offered sheepishly.

"Don't you know yet, young man, that my ears hear everything in this house?" Her finger pointed at him. "You should remember that. And, Philip, look at the mess you've made. Why, it will take the servants an hour to clean up after you."

"Pardon my thoughtlessness, Mother. I'll have better control in the future." He glared at his brother while he returned to his chair.

A few moments later, Emma burst into the room with a smile on her face. "Oh my, wasn't that a wonderful ball last night? Everyone complimented me on my dress. Even Lady Ardleigh thought I was the prettiest girl there. But I couldn't agree with her. I must say that Lady Downey was the most beautiful. Do you remember her gown, Mother? The color was fabulous on her, and when she was dancing with Philip, the lavender was even more stunning. I also thought Lady Ardleigh's gown was lovely. But I'm not surprised as she told me Lady Downey designed it for her." Suddenly Emma stopped and glanced around the room. "Oh, goodness. What happened?"

"Nothing, child. It was just a small accident. We'll clean it up later. Please be careful of the glass in the corner." His mother stepped into the hallway. "Celia? Could you clean up this glass when we are all seated? I don't wish for it to be carried throughout the house."

Emma sat down at the table, eyeing her brothers to gauge their temperaments. "What was that loud noise earlier, Mother?"

"Nothing, my dear. Do not concern yourself," the duchess said.

"Philip, are you and Lady Downey in a relationship? Is

that the correct way to ask, Mother?" She blushed as she glanced at her mother.

"No, we're not, Emma." He hid his face behind the newspaper again, hoping that would put an end to it.

"Well, Philip, you should hear how all the ladies were talking about the two of you last night. They all think you are in a relationship now. And some of the things they were saying were not polite, if I do say so myself."

He couldn't stop himself. He sprang out of his chair, tossing the paper onto the table. "That's enough. I will not sit here and listen to any more gossip about me or Lady Downey." He stalked out the door and down the hallway, heading for the stables. He could hear his mother's chastisement all the way to the end of the hallway.

"That is exactly why you do not belong at balls yet, young lady. You're too young to understand the meaning of the word 'discretion.' You will not be going again for a while."

The last thing he heard was his sister bursting into tears.

Philip propelled himself from the house as quickly as his feet would take him. He needed to get away. In a matter of days, his whole life had become focused on a young woman with chestnut locks—a turn of events he frankly didn't understand given that he'd promised himself he'd never let another woman into his heart. The only way he could make sense of things would be if he removed himself to a peaceful environment.

His lake soothed him like nothing else could. He took off his shirt and settled himself on the dock, his feet hanging off the end. His toy sailboat sat next to him, as it always did on such outings. Sighing, he cast his line out into the tranquil water.

Sometime later, it struck him that his fishing spot was not casting its usual magic. His thoughts still lingered on Sara. Her quick and adamant rejection of his plan had gutted him. He'd thought it the perfect solution—she would be safe from Stinky, she wouldn't have to work anymore, and he'd make wild passionate love to her every night. He would even pay off her husband's gambling debts. What more could she want? Miranda had always begged to stay in his townhouse.

His feelings frightened him, especially since he cared more about losing Sara after one night than he had about Caroline leaving. Perhaps a few passionate nights with her would cure him. Yes, that was the solution. He just had to convince her to spend time at his townhouse. Even after it was over, he'd take care of her. Make sure she was safe.

But how could he persuade her?

CHAPTER NINETEEN

WHEN SARA ARRIVED HOME, SHE was still reeling from her encounter with Philip. Her hands shook as she tried to fit the key in the lock. Once inside, she closed the front blinds and locked the door behind her. She searched her shop, making sure she was alone. There was no sign of forced entry or any intrusion into her space, so she hurried upstairs to change her clothing. She had plenty of sewing to do.

As she sat at her worktable, her mind ran over the events of last night. How could she have believed she was in love with such a man? True, the lovemaking had been wonderful, but maybe it was that way with most couples. Would she feel the same way in another man's arms?

There had to be another man she could care for who did not want to turn her into a strumpet. Even if she was now a widow, she still deserved respect, didn't she? How could he even think she would just move in there, close her shop, and be sexually available to him whenever he wanted?

Of course, her marriage had been almost the same way. The only things Duncan had wanted from her were her father's money and sex, and the sex had been totally different from last night. Her husband had only cared about his own needs.

At least the duke had taught her that women could also derive pleasure from the act. Now that she knew it was possible, she didn't think she would ever marry again unless she was intimate with the man first. She would never again be bound in a loveless, passionless marriage.

A noise sounded outside her back door. She jumped, only to realize it was an animal of some sort. Her overreaction gave her pause—perhaps it had been foolish of her to reject Philip's offer so quickly. There was no denying the arrangement would have benefits: Stinky would no longer be a threat to her if she lived with the duke. Besides which, she would no longer have to worry about money. She loved her business, but she preferred designing dresses to sewing them. Sara tried to flex her broken finger. It was improving, but what would it be next time?

Living with Philip would get rid of it all—the pain, the fear, and the insomnia.

Of course, if she made that choice, she would no longer be able to visit with his mother or his sister. What would Mary think? Or worse, what would her mother and father think of her? Even though they were both dead, she hoped to reunite with them in heaven someday.

Since she was an only child, both parents had fussed over her. Although she had no strong memories of her mother—just a sense of warmth and love—her father would always praise her whenever she did something particularly well. He'd smile at her so broadly the edges of his eyes would crinkle. "That's my girl," he'd say, patting her on the shoulder, "I'm so proud of you."

What would they think of her if she moved in with the duke?

The tears finally came.

A few days later, Sara sat cleaning the front room of the shop when the bell alerted her to customers. She turned to see the duchess and Emma enter with the duke directly behind them.

"Good morn, Your Grace. How may I help you?" Sara

gave a deep curtsy. Even though her stomach was full of butterflies at the sight of Philip, she vowed not to give in to her feelings.

"Good morning to you, Lady Downey." The duchess smiled as she advanced toward her. "We are here to see if one of Emma's walking dresses is ready."

"Why, yes, Your Grace, I just finished two yesterday."

"Goodness, my dear, how do you do so much in a day?" Mary asked.

"Oh, it was nothing. I enjoy sewing. It relaxes me." Sara stole a glance at the duke over Mary's shoulder. Blast it, did he have to be so devastatingly handsome? His dark hair curled slightly at his neck. She longed to run her fingers through those locks the way she had the other night. However, when she gazed into his eyes, she saw the stark coldness had returned. There was no sign of the warmth she'd savored in his townhouse.

Ah, so this was how the world worked. Sweet smiles, warm caresses, and soft words until the act was done. Then everything returned to the way it was before. Why did that upset her? Had she really thought he would stroll up and kiss her in front of his mother? No, of course not, but at least he could have smiled at her. His face was grim as ever. His coldness confirmed she had made the right choice. If this was how he would treat her after making love to her, she did not want anything to do with him.

She dipped her head to hide her blush. To prevent herself from feeling any more awkward, she quickly turned away, saying to the St. James women, "Follow me, please. I will gather the gowns from the other room."

Philip paced in the front room. He was glad Sara had taken his mother and sister to the other room. Bloody hell, but the woman made him hard instantly. He'd forced himself to think of Caroline just to get himself back under control.

Damnation, he and Sara had been fabulous together. He pulled on his cravat. He hadn't expected to have this response. His desire for her should be lessening, not increasing. Why did she have such a profound effect on him?

"Lady Downey, the gowns are absolutely fetching. Thank you so much for your hard work," his mother said as she returned to the front room.

"I especially love the pale blue gown. The pastel ribbons across the skirt are beautiful. I have never seen anything so clever!" Emma remarked. "Oh, Your Grace, wait until you see the designs Lady Downey has made for me. I don't ever want to go to another dressmaker. She is by far the most talented. I'm sure you agree with me, don't you, Mother?"

"Yes, my dear." Mary ushered her daughter to the door. "Philip, we'll be outside in the carriage. Please take care of everything for me, won't you? Thank you again, Sara." She nodded to Sara as she exited the shop.

Philip paid Sara what he owed her for the gowns, and when their fingers brushed, she jerked her hand back as if she'd been burned.

He gazed into her eyes. "I did not think you minded my touch, Sara." His voice was husky, his words soft. He breathed in her scent and his mind reeled with all the sensations that one breath brought him. He thought of how wonderful she had tasted, about how good they had been together. He wanted her again. No, he *had* to have her again.

Her cheeks flushed as her eyes lowered. "I didn't mind your touch the other night, Your Grace, but things have changed." She brushed a stray hair away from her face.

Philip reached for her face, intending to stroke his fingers across her cheek, but stopped. "Have you given my proposal any more thought? It does not have to be this way.

You know we're fantastic together. Come to my town-house tonight." He ached to run his hands down her arms again, to cup her breasts. To kiss her.

Sara stepped back. She looked up at him then glanced away. "I'm sorry, but I cannot do that. Thank you for your kind offer, but I think it best that I stay here." She swallowed as her hands fisted in her dress.

He needed to touch her, taste her, but propriety held him back—that and the fact that his mother and sister were watching their every move through the window. Instead, he said, "Sara, you're not safe here."

"I can't do it. I need to stay here and finish my work." Playing with a thimble, Sara added in a whisper, "I don't wish to lose my self-respect, even though a small part of me wishes I didn't care so much."

She'd refused him again. He'd hoped she would change her mind once she had the chance to consider his offer, but she'd trampled on his heart, just like Caroline. "Ah, the little modiste is above me, is that it, Sara?" he said, barely recognizing his cold, distant voice. "Do you forget your station?"

He stared at her quivering chin as the tears gathered in her lashes.

Guilt stabbed into him—since when did he give a toss about stations?—but he couldn't take it back. He couldn't grovel. She'd made herself quite clear, hadn't she? Suddenly desperate to get away, he turned on his heel and slammed the door on his way out.

CHAPTER TWENTY

PHILIP WAS QUIET IN THE carriage, his mind firmly fixed on Sara. Why the hell had he treated her so poorly?

Finally, his mother spoke. "Why don't you drop Emma and me at the orphanage? You can pick us up later."

"Mother, I can wait if you need me to." He stared blankly out the window.

"No need. Lady Downey gave us all these new outfits for the children at the orphanage."

Philip turned his head sharply to stare at his mother, only then taking in the two large sacks she'd carried away from the dressmaker's shop. "She what?"

"Sara cannot bear to throw out good material so she puts scraps of fabric together for the children. She asked me to take these outfits to the orphanage. There is quite a bit of clothing here, and it will take us some time to sort through it all."

He stared at his mother in shock.

"Philip, are you quite all right?" Emma asked.

"Yes, of course. I will return for you in two hours. Will that be sufficient?"

"Oh, certainly. That would be wonderful."

After leaving off his mother and sister, Philip made his way into White's and strode into the far room. Ardleigh sat at his usual table, thumbing through the newspaper.

"Greetings, Brentwood. What has put you in such a sour mood today?" Ardleigh queried with a smile.

Philip sat across from his friend. "It certainly isn't any of your business, but I was hoping to move a certain widow into my townhouse."

"Ah." Ardleigh nodded. "Lady Downey turned you down. Perhaps you are going about it in the wrong way. Women do expect to be treated with care. You two must have had quite a night together after the ball."

"As it happens, it was an excellent night. At least, it was for me. Apparently, not so for a certain widow."

"Brentwood, you've lost your charm, have you?" Ardleigh said with a chuckle. "Did you ask her kindly or order her to do your bidding?"

"It isn't important how I asked her, what matters is her refusal. Why ever would a dressmaker refuse a duke? I could take care of her and protect her from the threats to her safety. What is her problem?"

"Since I happen to be familiar with the lady in question, perhaps it could be self-respect? Perhaps the lady doesn't wish to be known as a mistress. She's very intelligent, Brentwood, not your usual twit. I doubt she would be happy in your townhouse."

"She can spend my money and never have to work as a modiste again. What more could she want?" Philip loosened his cravat. "That was all Caroline cared about, jewels and more jewels."

"Fortunately for you, I see no similarities between your ex-wife and Lady Downey."

Philip grunted. "She is nothing like Caroline," he agreed, "or I would not go near her."

"Ah, the truth finally. Then why are you treating her as you did Caroline? Perhaps Lady Downey would prefer to keep her business running. She is very good at it, you know. I also think she might prefer to be able to hold company with your family and with Phoebe. She couldn't do that as your mistress."

"I know that, but she doesn't need to stay in touch with my family. As for Phoebe, you wouldn't stop your wife from seeing Lady Downey. I know you better than to think that."

"No, I would not, but I suspect Lady Downey would stay away from my wife. She knows how the *ton* is, and I suspect she would stay within the guidelines of acceptable behavior."

Philip stared at his friend. "Then there is no solution."

"I think there is one, but you are neglecting to mention it."

"What?"

"You've learned the lady is a widow. Why not marry her?" Ardleigh leaned over the table as if relating a secret. "You will not regret it."

"You cannot be serious. I am a duke. My wife must have noble blood. She is to be the mother of the next duke."

"It would seem to me you are inventing reasons to keep you two apart. No one knows much about Lady Downey's family. Perhaps she does have noble blood. Regardless, she has already married into the *ton*. She's just down on her luck because her first husband was a beast."

"And you think my mother would tolerate such a thing?" Philip ground out. Even as he said it, he recalled how much his mother seemed to favor the lady. How protective she always seemed of her.

"I think your mother wants to see you happy, and she's much wiser and more forgiving than you give her credit for. She will welcome anyone you love into her home. After all, she accepted Caroline, and she knew from the start that it wasn't going to last."

"Who said anything about love?" Philip burst to his feet, no longer able to sit still. "I am not in love with Lady Downey," he added, looking out the window. "I will never allow that to happen to me again."

Ardleigh clucked his tongue. "So sad what Caroline has done to you. I thought by now you would be beyond her, but you're as sour as ever. You think you can always control everything, Brentwood. Well, you can't always control your heart."

That was where Ardleigh was wrong. Philip was quite sure he could, although he had not given up on Sara just yet.

CHAPTER TWENTY-ONE

SARA SORTED HER RECEIPTS CAREFULLY at the front counter. A few days had passed since she had last seen Philip, yet he was always lurking somewhere in her mind. She forced herself to focus on the task at hand, however, and a triumphant smile surfaced on her face as she finished.

She had one customer who was expected to pick up several gowns today, and then she should have more than enough money for Stinky. She hoped to have enough money left over to buy food for the week. She took a few coins and hid them in a separate place for safekeeping.

She had returned to her worktable in the back when the front door slammed, sending her vaulting out of her seat. It was too early for Stinky, but he'd already come by once, hadn't he? She rubbed the palm of her good hand down her dress to wipe the dampness away. Her heart sped in her chest as she proceeded to the front. She held her breath and stepped around the corner, grabbing a pair of scissors for protection.

A liveried footman stood just inside the door with his arm outstretched. "A package for you, madam. Lady Ardleigh instructed me to wait until you open the package. If they're not quite right, you may return them."

Sara's curiosity piqued. What would Phoebe have sent her? She accepted the package with a smile and slid behind the front counter to open it. Her heart pounded in anticipation. How long had it been since she had received a surprise gift such as this?

Untying the ribbon, she carefully pulled the wrapping back until her eyes fell on the assortment of blue and ivory beads inside the fabric pouch. Sara couldn't stop herself from uttering a small moan of appreciation. "Oh, they're so beautiful."

She fingered each bead individually as she peered at them.

"I think they just might be perfect."

She knew Phoebe's messenger was not interested, but she announced her satisfaction anyway. Running into the back room, she retrieved her mother's bag, slammed the drawer, and rushed back to the front room to determine if the beads matched.

Her entire body bursting with joy at the prospect, Sara placed the edge of her mother's bag next to Phoebe's package.

"Oh, no! The shape and coloring are a perfect match, but they are too small. If only they were a touch larger." Sara rolled the pale beads between her fingers with a sigh.

Addressing the messenger, she said, "Sir, if you'll please wait one more moment, I will write my response to Lady Ardleigh."

What a blessing it was to have one good friend in her life. She quickly penned her note, thanking Phoebe for her kindness and asking her to keep an eye out for any beads that were the same color and style but a little larger. She was about to hand it off to the messenger when the front door flew open again. Startled at the sound of the door banging open, Sara dropped the letter and placed a hand on the package of beads.

Miranda Montrose barreled through the entranceway. Coming to a stop directly in front of Sara, she glared at her and locked her hands on her hips.

Fire flew from her eyes as she thrust her face at Sara's.

"So, you little trollop, you thought you could just walk into the ballroom and steal my man, did you?" Miranda's chest heaved as she spoke.

"Lady Montrose," she said, staring into the woman's wild eyes, "I don't know what you're talking about."

"Oh, isn't that convenient, Sara. Steal my man and act like an innocent. How dare you! You will not win. Brentwood loves me. You are to stay away from him. I knew you were nothing but a whore. Is that what you really sell in this shop?" Her arm waved in a semicircle around her. "Of course, you pretend to fool everyone by claiming to create these hideous gowns. Oh, and you should know the gown you wore the other night was just atrocious." Miranda made her way around the inside wall of the front room of Sara's shop, fingering the gowns she had made that were awaiting pickup and customer approval.

With a giggle, she sneered at Sara. "This is not what you really sell, though, is it? It's all just a cover? You actually sell yourself."

Gasping at Miranda's implication, she left the counter and took a step toward the woman.

Miranda tipped her head back and ran her eyes down the length of Sara. "Not that you would find many buyers for your boyish figure, but some men do like to try a wide variety. Since the duke and I were having a little disagreement, he must have wanted to find a woman as unlike me as possible.

Miranda laughed as she tossed her head, her hand going up to the back of her hair where a few upswept strands had fallen out. "He was looking for a cheap little strumpet. And so he found you for one night."

Sara forced her mind out of its daze. *Do something.* The woman was obviously out of her mind, however, and she did not wish to set her off.

"Please leave, Lady Montrose. I have no designs on the

duke. I promise you that you'll not see us together again. I had a terrible fright that evening, and he was consoling me. That was all." Sara pulled her hair out of her eyes as she searched the room for the scissors she'd set down nearby. The footman seemed completely unmoved by the exchange. He simply stood there, awaiting her message. Couldn't he help her a bit? That would be the honorable thing to do.

"I know he'll never be with you again, because I will kill you if you're seen with him again. Do you understand me? I want to be clear on what will happen if you entertain the notion of spending time with him again." Miranda grasped a yellow day gown in her hand, rolling the fabric between her fingers.

"Why this is quite ugly, Sara. Did you design this?" As soon as the words left her mouth, Miranda pulled a small knife from her reticule and sliced it down the front of the gown.

Sara gasped in shock and horror. "What are you doing, Lady Montrose?"

"Why, Sara, it's my job to make sure no one decent wears any of these monstrosities."

She wished to stop Miranda, but the woman's twisted grin frightened her. Instead, she watched in horror as Miranda grabbed the next gown, tore one sleeve off, and ripped a hole in the middle of the bodice.

Sara fought for control. "Lady Montrose, please. I beg you to stop!" She immediately thought of Stinky and how she needed the income from the gowns to pay him.

Miranda didn't stop, however. She continued on her path of destruction, smirking as she did so.

"Stop? Why should I stop when you clung to my man at the Ardleigh ball the other night? I told you before to stay away from him, and you did not listen." She grabbed a fistful of material from a third gown.

The messenger finally awakened from his stupor. "Please, madam. What you're doing isn't right."

Miranda pointed the knife at his throat. "This is none of your concern, so do not interrupt."

Sara's skin turned cold, her mind flooded with visions of Stinky. "Please, Lady Montrose. I'm not interested in the Duke of Brentwood," she repeated, her tone adamant.

"Why, I think you looked very interested the other night. You couldn't have gotten any closer to him had you tried. I watched you, you see. I saw the sweet, innocent smiles you gave him to entice him to your bed. Are you going to tell me he did not come to your bed that night? Because I'm sure he did. He was supposed to come to me, but he went to you instead." She grabbed the skirt of another gown and shredded it. "It's all your fault. You are a trollop. You must have hypnotized him. Or did you put something into his drink?" Miranda turned back to Sara with a condescending smirk. "Truly, what could he possibly want with you?"

Sara was frantic. Each ruined gown brought her closer to another altercation with Stinky. Her voice broke as she begged Miranda, "Please, Lady Montrose! I'll stay away from him. That was the only time we danced. I'm not interested in him."

She rushed toward Miranda, hoping to grab the knife out of her hands, but when she reached for her, Lady Montrose swung out with her knife and caught the edge of Sara's arm. Blood spurted across the surface of the gown Miranda held and dripped onto the floor.

Miranda's eyes brightened. "You see, Lady Downey, what terrible taste you have? Why that red color is horrid on this lavender gown. Here, let me cut out that stain for you." She cut out a portion of the dress and threw it on the counter, then tossed her head back and laughed.

The door banged open again and another messenger entered. "Heavens, what are you doing with that weapon, madam?"

The first man, who'd watched the scene unfold with mounting horror, shooed him away. "Leave her be, she has gone mad." He reached for the door. "Let's get help. I'll look for the horse patrol."

"Stop right where you are!" Miranda's large bosom heaved as she swept her gaze across both men. The knife was still clutched in her hand. "Never mind any of this." She turned to Sara. "Did you get my message, Lady Downey? Next time, I'll be cutting more than the gowns." With that, she tucked the bloody knife into her reticule and calmly strode out the door.

As soon as she left, the second messenger stepped forward. "Miss, are you all right? Can I fetch the doctor for you, or perhaps the authorities? I shall search for the magistrate, if you wish."

"No!" she said at once. "Thank you, sir, but there's no need. I'm a little out of sorts. She left quite a mess." She fussed over the items sent astray.

The Ardleigh's messenger said, "I'll return in a moment." He murmured something to the second messenger—the only word she made out was "help"—and ducked out of the door.

"Well, if you care to see it, Lady Downey, I have a package from the duke for you," the second man said. "He asked me to await a written response."

She shook her head as she stared at the outstretched hand holding a small package. She glanced up at the messenger, blinking back tears. Too much had happened in too short a time. Just like that, her life was a mess again. Half of the gowns she'd prepared for her client were destroyed. She wouldn't be able to pay Stinky after all.

Confusion washed through her mind. "What?"

"For you, my lady, the duke sent it for you."

Another package? She stepped behind the counter again,

and brushed Phoebe's package and her return note off to the side. As she opened the package from Philip, she could feel the messenger's eyes on her.

When she removed the cover, her pulse stopped. Inside was a beautiful necklace made of large rubies and diamonds. The light danced off the gems as she removed it from the package. It was worth a fortune.

She looked up at the messenger. "I am sorry, but I cannot accept this."

"The duke says you must, Lady Downey. He told me I was not to bring it back."

The first messenger returned to the shop and let himself in. His eyes widened when he caught sight of the necklace. "Forgive me, madam, for interfering, but it would pay for all those damaged gowns there on the wall." The man nodded his head toward the ruined gowns. "The magistrate is on his way."

If only he'd interfered earlier and saved her from this whole situation. All the same, he was right. This one piece of jewelry could put an end to all her troubles. She could take it to the jewelers for cash and give whatever she needed to Stinky. Or she could simply give it to him. He would be happy to take such a valuable item. It was certainly worth more than what her husband owed his debtors.

Her head ached. She reached up and rubbed a spot on her scalp, closing her eyes for a moment as she considered her quandary. Oh, what to do! This was too much to handle.

Except she already knew she couldn't accept the necklace. If she did, she'd be no better than Miranda Montrose. She would be a trollop, accepting payment for services provided.

A whore. This would make her a whore.

No, she couldn't do it.

She returned the necklace to the package. Grabbing

the pen, she retrieved another note card and started writing. She told Philip what she thought of his gift and why she could not accept it, keeping her tone civil in case the messenger read it. As she wrote, she noticed her arm had begun to bleed again. She slipped in the back to retrieve a cloth to hold on her wound. When she returned, she noticed Phoebe's messenger still standing there.

"Oh, sir, I am sorry to keep you waiting." She ran to the counter, grabbed the note and handed it to him. "Thank you. Please inform Lady Ardleigh that I will be in touch."

Sara grabbed her head after he left as she felt a wave of dizziness come over her.

"Here, miss, sit on this stool." Philip's man said, rushing forward to help her. "Are you sure I cannot reach someone for you? You don't look so good right now."

Sara held her head until the dizziness subsided.

"No, I am fine, sir. Thank you kindly for your assistance. I have finished penning the note. Please take the package and the note back to the duke for me."

"Are you quite certain?" The messenger was concerned, but she could tell he was also nervous about the position she'd put him in. The duke wouldn't take kindly to her response, but there was nothing she could do about that.

She dismissed the man with a wave and a smile. He bolted out the door with the package and the note, and as soon as he was gone, Sara collapsed on the floor and sobbed.

Philip paced in his room. What was taking his footman so long, anyway?

Part of him feared Sara would not react to the necklace as he hoped. She'd rejected his offer of financial help, after all, and she was not like other women. And yet, every woman enjoyed jewels, especially a piece as fine as the one he'd sent.

Perhaps it would be enough.

Perhaps she would be in his bed tonight.

Lady Downey had been on his mind all week. He wanted to taste her again, run his tongue down the soft skin of her neck.

Of course, Ardleigh's suggestion was ridiculous. He was a duke; he couldn't marry a dressmaker.

Even so, he couldn't deny he liked the thought of having such an intelligent woman on his arm. Looking into her warm green eyes across the breakfast table. Savoring her each and every night. His cock was rock hard again at the thought. Damn! It shouldn't be like this. He didn't even glance at other women now. She had ruined him.

It only made matters worse that his mother kept mentioning her. Why did she torment him so? She had to know nothing could ever come of their relationship.

Or did she?

Hellfire, where was his valet? He opened the door to his chamber and bellowed down the hallway, "Charles? Where are you? Let's get this done!"

Charles appeared out of nowhere. "Yes, Your Grace, I'm coming. I was starching your neck cloth."

"Damnation, Charles, I need a shave. I expect to have company tonight. Let's get on with it."

"Yes, Your Grace." Charles hurried Philip into a chair and wrapped a warm towel around his face.

He continued to mumble through the towel. "I expect Eli to return any minute. When he does, I need to be ready to go out immediately." Then, realizing how out of sorts he sounded, he hastened to say, "Forgive me, Charles. I appear to be on edge today for some reason."

His valet answered with a stiff, "Quite."

Philip heard the door close downstairs. He threw the towel off his face and yelled, "Eli?"

No one answered, which only made him more anxious. He raced down the stairs in search of his messenger. His mother came out of the sunroom. "Philip, what is the problem? Why are you yelling and running about?"

"Nothing, Mother. I apologize." He leaned down to kiss her cheek. "Did Eli pass through here a moment ago?"

"Why, yes, he did. But what is your problem?" She pursed her lips. "You are acting like a lovesick schoolboy. Control your behavior as befits a duke, would you please?"

"Your pardon, Mother, I must find Eli." He pushed past her and headed out the side door to the stables.

"Eli!" he yelled, catching sight of him from behind. He chased the man down in the stables.

"Ah, there you are, Your Grace," his footman said, turning around. Something was gripped in his hand. A note. And a box. The one that had contained the necklace. "Stevens thought you had headed to the stables. I feel I must inform you of the lady's condition, as well."

"What? Damnation, Eli, can't you see I need to read the bloody note?" He took it from him, tugging it away, and read it right there in the stable. The duke's eyes raced over the letter twice before he froze. Fury exploded inside of him.

He couldn't believe it. Sara would never say such a thing. She wasn't enterprising like Caroline. Except...

He read it again, his knuckles tightening around the paper, and growled. No, there was no misinterpreting such a message. He'd been wrong about her. Badly wrong. And he was ashamed to admit that it hurt. He'd let her get to him after all. And she'd gotten to his mother, too. His sister.

Philip grabbed the package from his messenger and strode back into his house, intent on his mission. "But Your Grace, I need to tell you something about the lady."

"Later, Eli, later!" he yelled back over his shoulder. A few steps into the house, he called out, "Mother? Mother, where are you, blast it?"

His mother stepped into the hall and hastened toward him. "What is it this time, Philip? Must you continue this rowdy behavior?"

"This!" He shoved the note into her hands. "I need you to see this. See it and read it."

Philip raked his fingers through his hair, hoping to calm himself, although it was a doomed mission. The blood pounded through his veins. Clenching his fist, he searched the room for something to hit. He hadn't known it was possible to feel this angry with anyone.

He'd never felt like this about Caroline.

Calm down, he reminded himself. *You promised yourself after Caroline left that you would never allow another woman to get under your skin.*

"Philip, I don't understand," his mother said, looking up at him in confusion. "What is Lady Downey talking about?"

"This, this necklace I gave her—" he brandished the box, "—she returned it. I wanted you to see her words with your own eyes so you'll understand why I can never be with Lady Downey."

He opened the package and let the necklace cascade into his mother's hands.

"This is not good enough for her. Do you see why I will never marry again? I thought she had a good heart, a kind soul. She makes clothes for the orphans, but this necklace isn't good enough for her. Have you seen a finer piece?"

"Are you sure she's talking about the necklace, Philip?" his mother said, her brow furrowing. "It doesn't sound quite right to me. When did this happen?" She placed her hand on his arm. "And please calm down."

"Calm down? I send her a necklace and she tells me it's not big enough? She needs larger stones? How bold can she be?"

"But there is something about this note that does not quite fit the situation. She talks of 'beads,' not gems. Ladies don't call gems 'beads.' I don't think she's talking about the necklace at all. Perhaps you're misinterpreting the situation. Please reconsider, Philip, before you have a true apoplexy."

"Gems, stones, beads. What difference does it make?" He poked his finger at the middle of the note. " 'If you have any larger, please save them for me.' It is not good enough for her. She needs a larger necklace. And more than one. 'Them,' she says. 'Them!'"

Philip needed to regain his control so he stomped out of the house. "I'm going riding, Mother. Just so long as you understand the subject is dropped. I will never remarry! And I don't ever want to hear Lady Downey's name again in my presence."

He tore across the lawn, bellowing, "Saddle my horse!"

Before he mounted, he thought of one more thing. He went into the cupboard and collected the toy sailboat his father had given him.

As he galloped fiercely by the lake, he catapulted his beloved boat into the water. His dream was dead.

CHAPTER TWENTY-TWO

SARA MANAGED TO GET HERSELF back onto the stool. She grabbed the bag of coins and emptied them into her skirts. Not enough. Returning them to the bag, she strode over and locked the front door. She stopped and turned to stare at her ruined creations.

The tears flowed freely down her cheeks. How much more could she handle? After all the days and nights she'd sat up late sewing, all her work had been ripped up by a jealous woman.

Fear of Stinky overpowered her. What could she do now? Although she had nearly enough money, it would be several days before she could complete the work that would earn her more. Maybe she should have kept the necklace. Better to be a whore than dead, right?

She was rolling the bag of coins around in her hand when the click of a door handle forced her to swing her head around.

She smelled him before she saw him. An eternity passed before he crept around the corner from the back of her shop. He approached her with his hand held out, a knowing grin revealing his black teeth. "You thought a larger lock would keep me out? I have all the necessary tools, my dear. You can try to lock me out, but it won't happen."

It was almost like he already knew she wouldn't have enough.

You fool, she thought to herself. *Did you really think money would entice him to leave you alone?*

She dropped the bag into his hand.

He sneered at her, then glanced into the bag for a quick moment before his head came up. "Not enough, Lady Downey."

"It will never be enough, will it?" Her shoulders slumped as she dropped her gaze to her broken finger. "You'll always be back for more, won't you? That's why you've never told me the exact amount."

"Ah, but can you blame me?" he said with a sick smile. "There is so much more you have to give." He grabbed her chin, but she pulled away. "Ah, I'm not good enough for you?" He cackled. "We'll see." He pocketed the coins and then clutched her left arm in a vise-like grip, wrenching it painfully. "I see you are already bleeding. Maybe I can fix that."

Instinct took over. She kicked him in the shin as hard as she could.

"You stupid bitch!" He slapped her hard across the cheek. Her knee flew up toward his groin but missed. Eyes filled with rage, he punched the other side of her face and grabbed a finger on her left hand, yanking it until it nearly snapped, but he lost his grip. Screaming and yanking, she cradled her arm. Did he mean to kill her? She kicked defensively again, but he shoved her to the floor and kicked her hip, sending a wave of pain through her body. She squeezed her eyes shut, waiting for the next blow.

But it didn't come.

When she opened her eyes and searched for him, he was gone.

The noises outside the door must have interrupted him, but she didn't have the energy to look out there and see what was going on. She didn't have the energy for anything.

She laid her head back as her vision dimmed.

Sara awoke to darkness. How long had she been there? She noticed blood had splashed the floor around her. Another finger was possibly broken and maybe her arm from the wrenching. Worst of all, her spirit was broken. Hopelessness beat down on her. She had nothing. Stinky stole every cent she could make, and if he continued to injure her, she wouldn't be able to sew at all. And then there was Miranda, who'd made it clear she would attempt to harm her, too, if she persisted in seeing the duke. The duke only wanted her as a whore, and she had only one friend, Phoebe.

Perhaps she should accept Philip's offer. Pride and self-respect wouldn't get her very far if Stinky came for her again. She could no longer stay here by herself.

Let's see, she thought, *raped, dead, or a mistress. Which should I choose?*

A banging sound off in the distance caught her attention. What was that racket?

The sound of splintering wood broke through the fog in her brain. She managed to raise her eyes enough to see Phoebe's messenger and the Earl of Ardleigh standing just inside her door. Phoebe pushed past them and was at her side in an instant. She took one look at Sara's arm and gasped. Her eyes darted around the room, taking in the chaos and destruction Miranda and Stinky had wrought, and then settled on Sara.

"Sara, I am taking you home with me," she said. "I'm afraid I won't take no for an answer. My footman informed Ardleigh and me of the problems you were having, although he forgot to mention someone had broken your other finger."

Sara attempted a smile. Phoebe, the only person she could trust, had come for her. She managed to nod. It happened quickly after that. Ardleigh and Phoebe helped her to stand, then Phoebe ran upstairs to grab a few of Sara's things. They left the ruins of her shop behind.

Philip slowed his horse to a canter. He noticed the foam at the horse's mouth and decided to take him to the creek for water. It had been wrong of him to take his anger out on the horse.

At least he was thinking coherently again. He understood why his mother had questioned the situation. He was still stunned. Sara was different, he could feel it in his gut, and that note truly didn't sound like it had come from the woman he had grown to—to what?

How did he feel about her? He rubbed the side of his face. Sara had given him hope again. Making love to her was unlike any other romantic experience he'd had. They had actually laughed together in bed. Shouldn't lovers be able to laugh? He never had before. Not with Miranda. And certainly not with Caroline.

Maybe Sara had only returned the necklace to make him angry. To get back at him for not proposing to her.

What was his next move? He certainly wouldn't buy her a larger necklace. Maybe it would be best to talk to her in person. Set her straight. Yes, he'd tell her to her face what he thought of her note.

CHAPTER TWENTY-THREE

P HILIP DROVE HIS PHAETON INTO the city, intent
on confronting Sara as soon as possible now that he'd
decided to do so. Except his determination bled out of
him the moment he saw the front of her shop. The door
was destroyed. Someone had broken into her shop.

Stinky, it had to be Stinky.

He found his way through the splintered wood and
searched the front room. Cold sweat poured down his
neck and his forehead as he stared at the destruction. Torn
gowns and ripped material covered the floor. Blood speck-
led both the floor and the gowns. Whose blood?

Someone yelled at him. He jerked his head around to see
who was there.

"Brentwood, that you, Your Grace? What happened
here? Someone reported a break-in. Seems they have it
correct." A gentleman from the horse patrol stood in the
entranceway.

"Shouldn't you know, Officer? Someone breaks into a
woman's shop in broad daylight and you don't know anything about it?" He struggled to rein in his temper.

"Well, we heard the commotion, but we didn't get here
in time to talk to the gentleman firsthand," the officer said,
his tone a touch defensive. "There were so many people
strolling about the crowd held us back. We saw your arrival
from across the street. Thought you might know something." The officer stared into his eyes, waiting for him to
speak.

"What man? What man did you see?" His voice trembled as he battered the officer with his questions.

"Ardleigh, Your Grace. The Earl of Ardleigh's carriage was here. He broke the door down to get to Lady Downey."

"What do you mean he had to break the door down?" It felt as if a hand had reached into his chest and was squeezing his heart as he waited for the answer to his question. It was entirely possible he was about to vomit or have an apoplexy.

"I don't know any details, but Lady Ardleigh swept her off to her house. She said she needed to get a physician for her. That was all she said." The officer studied him a little too hard. "Any idea who might try to hurt Lady Downey, Your Grace?"

Philip flew out the door and jumped into his phaeton.

"No, I don't know who did this," he tossed back over his shoulder.

He hated lying.

But Stinky was his.

The trip to Ardleigh's was the longest journey of his life. He'd spent so much time thinking of how to proceed with Sara that he hadn't stopped to consider the possibility that she might be plucked from his life. Why hadn't he made her safety more of a priority? When was the last time he had spoken with his private investigator? He berated himself over and over again.

He had broken one of his own caveats. *Always rely on logic before lust.* Bloody hell, why hadn't he followed his own edict?

He knew why—Sara made him lose the ability to think rationally.

When he reached the Ardleigh residence, he barged in past Ardleigh's butler, yelling for Edward.

The earl and the countess both stepped out to greet him, although he didn't care for the expressions on their faces. The hand clutching his heart squeezed harder.

"Where is she? I must see her. What happened? Is she all right?"

Ardleigh ushered him into the library.

"Brentwood, have a seat," his friend said, gesturing toward a chair.

"A seat? I cannot sit! Where is she? Ardleigh, stop playing games and speak!" he shouted. "I saw the destruction and the blood all over her shop. What happened?"

Phoebe, who'd followed them in, stepped up beside him and placed her hand on his arm. "Physically, she is fine, Your Grace. The physician is bracing her finger as we speak, though he's uncertain as to whether it's a break or a sprain. Emotionally, her condition is more questionable. We don't know the whole story yet."

"Setting her finger? More broken bones? Blast it, I need to be with her." He bolted out the door and up the stairs. A maid at the top of the landing pointed him in the right direction.

He vaguely heard Phoebe yelling up the staircase, her tone angry now.

"Your Grace, you have no right!"

"I have every right. She's mine," Philip declared for all to hear.

He stopped in the doorway and stared at Sara lying in the middle of the bed. The physician probed her arm as he talked to her. His heart sank as he noticed how slight she looked in the bed. He stepped into the room as softly as he could.

The physician's head jerked up.

"Your Grace, this is not proper. You can't stay. You have my word that I'll take care of Lady Downey." The man's straight-backed posture was formidable, but nothing would stop Philip. He belonged at her side. He should have never left.

"Sara?" He approached the bed cautiously. Her head turned to find his voice, but her eyes were blank. There was no recognition in them.

"Sara? It's me, Philip. Can you hear me?" His voice faltered as he took in her bandaged arm, her swollen fingers. He pushed past the physician, only to stagger to a stop. The bruising on her cheek was evident along with the swollen black eye on the other side of her face. He fought to unclench his fists and slow his breathing to normal. He didn't want to upset her anymore.

She didn't respond to him at all. Her eyes found his, but they looked…empty. Oh, saints above, what had happened? He'd never seen eyes like hers; they unnerved him.

"Dr. Newberry, how many broken bones?" Philip whispered to the doctor while holding Sara's gaze.

"Possibly one more finger, same hand. I can't be certain because of all the swelling. Brutal man she was accosted by. Thought the arm might be broken, too, but after examining it, I don't think so. Will bother her for a while. You can see the damage to her face; she also has a bruised hip. Someone needs to help this poor woman." He peered over his glasses at Philip as he held Sara's arm. "I don't care to see what comes next."

"I'll sit with her while you set her finger."

The man studied him for a moment, then said, "I cannot bodily remove you from the room. I have given her enough laudanum to make the pain tolerable. Please sit and don't aggravate her. She's very fragile right now."

Philip moved to the other side of the bed. He pulled up a chair close enough that he could take her hand. Sara's eyes followed him, completely void of emotion. He kissed her fingers and whispered, "I'm sorry, Sara. I am so, so sorry. I should never have let this happen to you."

Dr. Newberry gave him a perplexed look, but Philip ignored him.

"Hold her tight, Brentwood, she may scream and come off the bed. I just wish to probe it a bit to determine if it's broken. With all the swelling, it could be quite painful."

Dr. Newberry gripped her hand and moved her injured finger back and forth.

Sara never flinched. She stared into Philip's eyes and didn't blink.

Philip dropped his head to the bed to hide his tears.

Philip entered Ardleigh's library after Sara had fallen asleep.

He ran his hand down his face and stared at Ardleigh. "What happened?"

Phoebe followed him in moments later, quickly enough that he wondered if she'd been watching the stairs, and closed the door. "We're uncertain as to what happened. Sara wasn't coherent enough to tell us everything. I might ask you why you are here. How did you know where to find her?"

Phoebe's eyes locked with his. She wasn't going to make this easy, but perhaps he didn't deserve for it to be.

He stuck his hands in his pockets and paused for a moment, feeling the crumpled paper inside. Confusion danced through his mind. He strode over to the window to clear his head. He'd forgotten about the letter. The fear he'd felt upon seeing her door broken in…it had erased everything that had come before. But when he reached in his pocket, the paper was still there. Needing to steel himself, he unfolded it and silently read the words.

The message rekindled some of the anger he'd felt. Hellfire, how was he going to explain this to Ardleigh and his wife? Perhaps he'd do best to be honest.

"How close are you to Sara?" he asked.

"I'm quite close to her, Your Grace," Phoebe answered, "but with all due respect, I would like to know your business with her. I know some of the events that led her here, but perhaps you can fill in a few voids."

Phoebe's stare did not soften. Fine, then he would tell her.

"All right. I'll give you the events as I know them. I sent Sara a necklace, a very expensive necklace. She returned it to me with this note." He yanked the note from his pocket and attempted to smooth out the creases from the way he had crushed the letter in his hand. His temper flared again, and he relinquished his ministrations and handed the note to Phoebe.

"I wouldn't have believed it of her—" the duke shook his head as he paced around the library, "—but it would seem she's quite enterprising, our Sara."

Phoebe scanned the note and handed it back to the duke. A small smile crossed her face. "Is that what you believe? You suggest that Lady Downey is the type of woman to be bought and sold?"

"Humph!" was the only sound he could express in Phoebe's audience.

"Shall I tell you the events as I understand them, Your Grace? Or perhaps you are afraid to hear the truth?" Phoebe settled herself in a chair and folded her hands on her lap.

Philip crossed his arms. "Go ahead, Lady Ardleigh. Please try to convince me of her innocence. I will gladly change my opinion."

"Very well, I'll tell you what I know. I sent my footman to Lady Downey's to deliver a gift. Lady Downey's mother died many years ago, leaving her with a special bag. She has been hoping to make a dress to match for many years, although she needs to first find the right beads. I believed I had found the perfect match and sent them to her for her perusal. I instructed my footman to wait for an answer to my note. Actually, I believe I will ask Frederick to repeat the events as he observed them."

At the mention of that word—"beads"—Philip's stomach seemed to drop through his feet. Could he have gotten it wrong after all? He waited, anxious, while Phoebe opened the door to call for her footman. When the man arrived, he seemed almost as anxious as Philip, wringing his hands and glancing about the room with quick darts of his eyes.

"Frederick, if you please, explain to the duke what you saw in Lady Downey's shop." She stepped back to give the man space.

"Of course, Your Ladyship." He nodded briefly at the duke. "Your Grace, it was madness. I was waiting on Lady Downey's response, as my mistress had bid me, when this wild woman walked in. She accused the lady of stealing her man and called her some most inappropriate names. Then, before either of us could react, she took a knife out of her reticule and just started cutting at the gowns on the wall. She was acting quite mad. I didn't know what to do!"

Philip felt the blood drain from his face. "What? Who was it? Who treated her like that?" He leaned toward Frederick with fire in his eyes. "Tell me who did this to her! What was her name?"

"Lady Downey called her 'Lady Monster' or something like that. I think she recognized her. Must be she has acted like this before."

Philip glanced at Ardleigh. "Lady Monster? Who the devil is Lady Monster?"

Ardleigh spoke softly to his footman. "Could it have been 'Lady Montrose'?"

"Yes!" Frederick started. "That was it. 'Lady Montrose.' That's what she called her. Pretty woman with dark hair and big... Oh, pardon me, Lady Ardleigh." His head dropped to stare at his feet.

Phoebe patted his shoulder. "It's quite all right, Frederick. Please continue. What happened next?"

"Well, sir, I tried to interfere, but the woman threatened me with her knife, and I got a wife and kids. I couldn't stop her. Then Lady Downey reached for her and the Montrose woman cut her. The madwoman said she was going to kill her if she didn't leave her man alone. The duke, that's who she said." Frederick stammered as he peered nervously at Philip. "I think it was you she was talking about, Your Grace."

Philip's face felt as if it had been carved from stone. Not a muscle moved in his body. He recalled how Eli had tried to tell him something, but his anger had overridden his ability to listen. What a mistake he'd made with Miranda, and to think Sara had paid the price...

"And did this same person break Lady Downey's arm, Frederick? Did she push her? Is that how her face became bruised?"

"Oh no, she left. Your footman came in the door, and the woman who was attacking Lady Downey left. I ran outside to look for a magistrate, but I was only gone for a few moments. When I went back, she was staring down at the necklace you'd sent her. There were tears in her eyes. After she finished writing a note for your man, she remembered I was still there and gave me a message for the countess. I ran home as fast as I could to tell the Ardleighs what happened."

Phoebe nodded at her footman. "Thank you, Frederick. You did well today. You may go."

After she closed the door behind Frederick, Phoebe crossed the room and handed a note to Philip. "This is the note I received, Brentwood."

His stomach lurched again as he took the note from her.

I am sorry, but I am unable to accept your gift. While I understand that we have certain affections for each other, accepting this would mean that I am willing to live with you as your mistress. I just cannot do that.

I do not regret our friendship. You have taught me much that I may have never learned, but I am afraid I must put an end to our relationship.

The necklace is beautiful, but it's not for me. Perhaps it belongs with Lady Montrose.

Regretfully,

Sara

Groaning, he rubbed his forehead at his utter stupidity. What had he done? Thank goodness he'd never confronted Sara.

"Which letter do you think was meant for me, Your Grace?" Phoebe raised her eyebrows.

He sank into a nearby chair. "I beg your forgiveness, Lady Ardleigh."

"Sara is the one you must beg, not me. How could you think someone as innocent and sweet as Lady Downey could ask you for a larger necklace? I know you have known two women who might do such a thing, but Sara?" She shook her head in disgust as she turned away from him.

"Lady Ardleigh, I will beg Sara's forgiveness."

"As you should, Your Grace. Now, concerning the other issue in that note, I am not quite bold enough to discuss it with you. I will leave that to Ardleigh." Phoebe gave her husband a stern look.

The duke glanced from husband to wife. "I assume the authorities are aware of Miranda's part in this atrocity?"

Ardleigh spoke up. "Yes, I have apprised them of the situation. The magistrate is arranging for a warrant for her arrest."

"But we still don't know who hurt Sara."

Phoebe turned to glare at Philip. "Oh, I know who hurt her, but I don't know who beat her."

CHAPTER TWENTY-FOUR

SARA ATTEMPTED TO OPEN HER eyes, but the lids were still heavy. She pried one open, but the other only opened partially. Where was she? She tried to sit up, but the pain in her arm stopped her.

Memories flooded back into her mind. Glimpses of Miranda Montrose, Stinky, and Phoebe. *Oh, yes, that's right. Miranda tore up my merchandise, Stinky tried to break another finger, and Philip sent me a necklace to try to convince me to whore for him.*

Sara groaned and allowed her head to fall back on the pillow. She was at Phoebe's. It must be just past dawn. A maid stood in front of her, her eyes wide.

"My lady, are you all right? May I get something for you? Shall I get Lady Ardleigh? Are you hungry? Shall I fetch something for you to eat?"

Sara could see the woman had good intentions, but her head was pounding too much for her to carry on the simplest of conversations. "Perhaps some tea, if you don't mind."

"Yes, Lady Downey. I will return straightaway." She nodded and ran from the room.

A few minutes later, Phoebe strode in through the door.

"Sara, how are you? You must be in pain? What can I do for you? The doctor left some medicine I can give you."

"I am all right, Phoebe. I sent your maid for some tea. Then I should get my things together and head back to my shop. I have much to do."

"Don't be ridiculous. The doctor said you're to stay in bed for a few days at least. Your arm must be terribly sore as well as your face. You need to rest. You may eat and bathe today, but no more. I must insist. I know you're stubborn, Sara, but so am I. You are not leaving this house."

Sara sighed and decided her friend was probably right. She had a multitude of aches and pains right now and the thought of getting out of bed was not the least bit enticing.

"Besides, if I allow you out, the duke will have my head."

Sara's head shot up. "Philip? What does he have to do with any of this?"

"He came here yesterday after he saw the state your shop was in. He was quite adamant that you not be allowed to leave."

Sara rubbed her head. "Oh, he knows then."

"Yes, he knows about Miranda, too. He sat with you while the doctor checked your finger. You don't remember?"

"No, I am afraid I don't recall much after Stinky left. Except your face, Phoebe. How can I ever thank you for caring enough to come to my shop?" Sara turned her head to hide her tear-stained lashes.

"Sara, you do not need to thank me. We're friends, and you would do the same for me." Phoebe's voice softened as she took a seat on the bit of mattress beside Sara. "But as your friend, I'd like to know more about what's going on in your life. Don't you think it's time to tell me?"

Sara grabbed a hanky to wipe her tears. She nodded her head and told Phoebe all about Stinky.

"Oh my, you poor thing." Phoebe had reached for her hand at some point in the telling and continued to hold it as she finished. "Does anyone else know about this?"

Sara stared at her lap. "Just Philip. I haven't dared tell anyone else."

"Ardleigh and I are here for you now. What does the

duke suggest?"

"He wants to pay whomever is involved, but I don't know who's in charge. Or if they'll actually stop if they get the money. I have never seen Stinky anywhere else and he has never given me his name or the name of his boss." She paused, fighting a swell of emotion, then allowed herself to say, "I can't live like this anymore. I am tired of looking over my shoulder all the time. Of not being able to sleep."

The maid returned with tea and toast. After dismissing the woman, Phoebe poured Sara's tea and patted her hand. "Relax, my dear. You are staying here. You must focus on resting today. My husband and Brentwood will decide what to do about your problem."

Sara sipped her tea, wincing at the pain such a simple act caused. "I'd prefer not to involve the duke. Our relationship is over." Setting her cup down, she turned away from Phoebe.

The other woman cleared her throat and whispered, "I received the wrong note, Sara. I am very aware of the status of your relationship with the duke."

Her head snapped toward at Phoebe. "What note?"

"I received the note you intended for Brentwood about the ruby necklace. Apparently, in the chaos of your shop, you switched the two notes you penned. Brentwood received the note about my beads."

She groaned in embarrassment as she recalled the content of the two notes. "Please forgive me for the mix-up. I must thank you for the beads. They are beautiful, but not quite the right size." She shut her eyes, not wanting to look at Phoebe as she said this last part. "I am embarrassed that you read the other note."

"You do not need to apologize—the duke does. You made the right decision. He is a good man, but he is confused right now." Phoebe gave her hand a squeeze, and Sara forced herself to open her eyes again. "If you had met his wife, you would understand. Caroline was a selfish, demanding, conniving woman. I am afraid his…connection to Miranda Montrose hasn't improved his impression of our sex. I believe if you are patient with him, you will not regret it. He is a dear friend of Ardleigh's and you know how I feel about my husband. They've known each other for years."

Sara's hand shook as she brought her tea up for a sip.

Phoebe leaned in and placed a kiss on her forehead. "I think maybe you should sleep. You have been through so much. Relax and rest. Allow me to give you a bit of the medicine Dr. Newberry left for you." She added a few drops of the laudanum to the tea and proceeded to help Sara drink it.

As Sara's eyes fought to stay open, she murmured, "I like this medicine. It helps me forget everything."

The last thing she felt was Phoebe's hand tucking the coverlet around her.

Philip sighed as he grabbed some coddled eggs from the sideboard.

"Goodness, my dear, that sigh has some strong feelings behind it."

He turned to watch as his mother pulled out a chair and sat primly with her hands folded on her lap. Why could she always tell just the right time to barge in?

"Why, Philip, you look as if you didn't sleep a wink last night. Is that true?"

He sat down with his food and shook his napkin out. "Truly, Mother, I did not sleep well last night. I've much on my mind lately."

"Forgive me for prying, but does this thing weighing on your mind happen to weigh about as much as a certain dressmaker we know?" She offered him an innocent smile.

He decided there was no point in denying it. Why try to evade her? She would find out the truth eventually.

"You're correct. Lady Downey is on my mind." He gave his mother a brief description of the problems of the previous day, skipping the part about Lady Montrose, of course.

"Ah, so the beads were completely unrelated to the necklace you sent. You said the reticule was her mother's, yes?"

"It is one of the few possessions she has that belonged to her mother."

"Who was her mother? Have you determined that yet?"

"She has never said. I only know that she passed away when Sara was quite young. The family lived outside of London until Sara came to the city to marry."

"Hmmm. You have me thinking."

He rolled his eyes. He hoped she didn't think too hard about it, but at least it would temporarily shift her scrutiny off him.

"Why don't you just give in and court the girl, Philip? It's clear there is something between the two of you. Why must you persist in fighting it?"

He choked on the tea he was drinking.

"If it would please you, could you be a bit more blunt, Mother? What exactly are you saying?" He wiped his chin with his starched napkin.

"I am saying invite the lady to the opera or the theater. She is a widow. It would certainly be proper." She bestowed her best smile on her son as she picked at the food the servant had set in front of her.

"You must recall that I vowed never to marry again. If, perchance, I changed my mind, Lady Downey is not of noble blood. You know my sons must be of noble blood. If not, the *ton* will hold it against all of us and you know it."

"Fiddle-dee-dee, since when do you listen to the *ton?* You don't even know her mother's name, so you can't claim to know anything of her bloodline. Moreover, why should you care? I would think you would be more concerned with whether the mother of your sons could give them strength, honor, and character. I believe Lady Downey, with all her recent problems, has shown more strength of character than any other woman in my acquaintance. Certainly she has shown more integrity than a certain duchess I once knew."

He set his fork down. "You are serious, aren't you?"

"Of course I am. I cannot believe all the poor girl has had to endure by herself. She certainly doesn't carry on the way your ex-wife did. If the color of Caroline's napkin didn't suit her, she'd cry on your shoulder. Why, I didn't hear Lady Downey make a sound when her finger was probed by Dr. Newberry. Was she screaming in pain when he set her finger at the Ardleighs'?"

He gaped at his mother. He'd never seen her in such a tirade before.

Her eyebrows rose when her son refused to answer. "I didn't think so. Thank goodness Caroline never became with child. She would never have survived the pain of childbirth. And we both know she would have been a terrible mother. I bit my tongue with your first wife, but I refuse to keep my silence anymore. Lady Downey is an amazing person. You need look no further than the way she built her business without the help of anyone. The Lord has given you a gift, and you refuse to accept it. I cannot believe my own son is so ignorant as to ignore what has been given to him by the heavens above. Your insistence on never marrying again disappoints me, Philip. I did not raise you to be afraid of life. Get over your first mistake and move on." She stood up and threw her napkin down before storming out of the breakfast room.

His brothers snuck in through the other doorway, Adam followed by Ben.

"Dem, what did you do to her to set her off?" Adam asked.

Benjamin shook his head. "We weren't about to step into the middle of that."

Philip continued to stare after his mother.

Was she right?

He stood up and strode out of the room. At the doorway, he turned to his brothers, "Please be here at dinner tonight. I have something important we need to discuss."

CHAPTER TWENTY-FIVE

PHILIP WAITED INSIDE THE LIBRARY as Ardleigh's butler searched for Phoebe. He gazed out the window, thinking about all his mother had said. And his friend Ardleigh, too. Was there a possibility of a true relationship with Sara? Could he picture her sitting across from him every morning at breakfast? Would he enjoy having her on his arm at the required social affairs? He didn't need to ask himself whether he'd like to have her in his bed every night. He knew the answer to that.

His mother was right. Caroline was a shallow, scheming woman. She was not the type to be a good mother. But Sara…she was completely different. Beautiful, yes, but also intelligent and curious. Brave. Driven. Creative.

Was he afraid? Probably he was. His heart had taken a beating when Caroline had left him. At first, he'd longed for her to come back to him, to admit it had been a foolish mistake, but that time had long since passed. He dreaded any contact with her.

"Good afternoon, Your Grace," Phoebe said as she rounded the corner of the library.

"Good afternoon, Lady Ardleigh. You look radiant this morning." It wasn't a lie. Phoebe was lovely and always fresh.

"Thank you kindly, sir. My husband and daughter are such treasures to me I awake with a smile on my face every day. Forgive me, but I left Ardleigh outside with the baby. They have so little time together with all his responsibilities."

"Of course, I actually came to see Lady Downey." He was direct when he needed to be.

"Her emotions are very fragile right now. I believe it would do her good to hear your apology, Your Grace, but please do not overstay your welcome. You did say you came to apologize, did you not?" Phoebe's eyebrows rose as she questioned him.

A person would do best not to underestimate such a lady. "Of course. I'm a man of my word, and I gave you my word yesterday. Has she said anything else about the assault?"

"She could only name her attacker as 'Stinky.' She told me you're aware of him, as he is the same man who broke her finger. Perhaps you should stay and speak with my husband after your visit."

"Yes, I would like that." He followed Phoebe out of the library.

"By the way, I have medicated her," Phoebe said before she opened the door.

"Is she still in much pain?"

"Well, yes, but it isn't the physical pain that concerns me. She is very fragile right now. I fear she is hanging on the edge. Please be careful what you say, Your Grace."

Philip ran his hand down the front of his face, wishing such a simple movement would wipe away his guilt. He had wronged Sara in more ways than one. Lady Downey was a woman of integrity and principles, and she deserved to be treated as such.

He'd do what he could to make it right.

Phoebe ushered Philip into the dayroom. Sara rested on a settee facing the window overlooking their gardens and the stream that ran through the bulk of their property. His heart leapt in his chest as she turned to look at him.

Sara had been thinking about Philip, about his gorgeous blue eyes, and here he was as if she'd conjured him. Phoebe had given her a bit of laudanum to ease her pain. It had been quite difficult to walk to the dayroom, but her friend had insisted the view would be preferable, and indeed she could see the Earl of Ardleigh and his daughter playing in the lovely gardens.

Phoebe knelt in front of her and held her hands. "The duke would like to speak to you, Sara. Are you agreeable?"

Sara glanced up at Philip again. The view was more than agreeable, and so she nodded her agreement. How long had it been since she'd seen him? She tried to remember but couldn't. She gave him a quick smile as he sat down across from her. Why was he sitting so far away from her? The answer seemed to bob just beyond her reach. Her mind was too cloudy to think. Well, it didn't matter. She didn't need to think to look at him.

Philip pulled her coverlet higher on her lap, then leaned in to give her a chaste kiss on her cheek.

Oh, yes, she remembered how much she loved his scent.

"Sara, how are you? I am so sorry this happened to you. I should never have left you alone in your shop. You trusted me to protect you and I failed. I'm sorry. Can you forgive me?"

She smiled at him. He had the whitest teeth, but he seemed upset right now. What was he saying? If she could just get him to smile and look at her the way he had that night at his townhouse. The night that he had loved her. That's what she wanted, to feel like he loved her again.

"I also apologize about the necklace. It was rude and presumptuous of me to have sent it to you after you made your position clear to me."

She pointed to the window. "Philip, do you remember

the Ardleighs' baby, Abigail? She is the most beautiful baby I have ever seen." He would definitely smile at the baby, wouldn't he?

"Do you know Ardleigh said he is going to teach his daughter to fish when she gets older?"

"My father used to take me fishing," she replied automatically. "I didn't like to put the bait on the hooks, but I loved fishing with him."

He stared at her, but he still wouldn't smile. She wanted him to smile because she loved seeing him happy...because she loved him. Had she ever told him that?

She tried again. "That was my favorite time with my father, you know. When we fished together, I knew he really loved me. We didn't get to spend much time together because he was so busy."

He continued to stare. When he reached out to her, she went to him gladly. Oh, his embrace was so wonderfully warm. She felt so safe when he held her like this. She loved his long eyelashes, too. Were his left eyelashes wet? Why would that be?

She tilted her head to the side. "Do you fish, Philip?"

"Yes, Sara, I do fish. I would love to take you fishing sometime." He finally did as she'd been willing him to do and smiled.

Her heart burst. She leaned over and whispered in his ear, "I love you, Philip. Do you love me?"

He was silent for a moment as he peered at her. She thought she heard a very soft, "Yes, Sara, I love you."

She kissed him briefly on the lips and pulled back to smile at him. "Are those tears, Philip? Why? Why would you cry? Don't you really love me?"

Why would he be crying if they loved each other? Wouldn't he simply be happy to be with her?

Something was wrong. She turned, searching for Phoebe. Her hand struggled with the coverlet before it dropped from her lap. Her eyes seemed to burn, forcing her to blink several times. She turned back to the window. Where was Philip? Where had he gone?

She reached for something to grab onto, anything, but only found air. Pain seared through her.

He doesn't love me after all. A strange wetness on her hands made her glance down, only for her to see tears dripping onto her lap.

Phoebe appeared in front of her.

"What's wrong, Sara? Did Philip say something to upset you? Everything is going to be fine. Don't worry about anything. I'll take care of you." Phoebe waved toward something at the doorway. "I will take care of you, Sara," she repeated, cradling Sara's head against her shoulder.

Sara sobbed in her friend's arms. "I love him, Phoebe. Why can't he love me back?"

The Ardleighs sat in the library with Philip.

"I don't know what I said to upset her, Phoebe. Honestly. I never mentioned the name 'Stinky' to her."

Even as he spoke to Phoebe, his mind was on Sara. On those three words she'd said. She loved him. Was it the laudanum talking, or had the medicine simply released her true feelings? Moreover, he'd told her that he loved her back. Well, he did, didn't he? Or was it pity he felt?

"Never mind. I fear her mind is fragile right now. I need to know what we can do about this man." Phoebe directed her gaze from Philip to her husband.

Philip's thoughts were still a chorus of "I love you."

Stop it! he silently lectured himself. *Stop letting the ramblings of a medicated woman affect your ability to think logically.*

The sound of Ardleigh's voice broke through his thoughts.

"Philip?" he asked for what was clearly not the first time.

"Can you please tell us what the investigator told you?"

"What? Oh, yes. Pardon me. The investigator said her husband was a heavy gambler and was in debt to one of the major criminals in London. But he has yet to ascertain which one is responsible." He stood up. "Ardleigh, do me a favor, please. Check with the investigator and see if he has found any new information. I am sorry, but I must leave. I have business to attend to."

Ridley had proven himself useless so far. Philip wished to find a replacement, although the new man would need to be equally discreet. Perhaps one of his brothers would have a suggestion.

"What could be so important, Brentwood?" Ardleigh asked as his friend hurried through the library door.

He glanced back over his shoulder.

"I need to practice shooting, and my brothers, too. My focus is on what is the most important in my mind right now.

"Revenge."

CHAPTER TWENTY-SIX

PHILIP TRUDGED UP THE STEPS to his front door. Once inside, he ignored Stevens and every other servant who stopped to stare at him. They looked like they wished to speak to him, but his expression clearly put them off. Something was wrong with the estate, or perhaps one of his brothers had done something stupid. At the moment, he struggled to care. Phoebe was right, how could he have suspected Sara of dishonesty, even for a moment?

He remembered the night they had spent together. She gave herself to him completely. Her body, yes, but she'd also given him so much warmth, passion, laughter, and trust. What had he given in return? Distrust, insults, and worst of all, he had turned his back on her when she needed him most. He had known she was not safe in her shop, but he'd done nothing to press the issue.

He was about to walk into the dayroom when his mother approached him.

"I know, I know, you were right again, Mother." He held his hands up to concede victory. "I haven't forgotten our last talk."

"Oh, pah, I am always right. When will you learn? But never mind that now. You have a visitor. I left her in your library." She pointed back in the direction of his library.

"Mother, please, whoever it is, just send her away. I can't deal with anything else today." He grumbled as he thought of having to talk to some mother who was going to push her young daughter at him. The only woman he wanted was Sara.

"No, Philip, you better handle her, because I certainly won't. I will not deal with that kind of woman." Something flashed in her eyes, revealing a clear dislike of his visitor, but she didn't say anything more, instead stalking away.

He obediently turned back to his library, grumbling a bit as he did so. He opened the door and froze in shock.

"Oh, Philip. There you are. You've kept me waiting forever. I know you must be a little angry with me, but I am sure I can think of a way to make it up to you."

Caroline sat perched atop his desk with her legs crossed. Her glorious dark curls cascading over her shoulders, her large breasts nearly visible. She'd always worn her hair down in the bedroom, simply because she knew it drove him mad. She wore a slinky red outfit that belonged in a whorehouse. Her swanlike neck was adorned with the ruby necklace he'd bought for Sara.

Where the devil had she come from?

"What do you want, Caroline?" He reached behind him and closed the library door. He had to get rid of her. The last thing he wanted was for Phoebe to catch wind of this. Sara's friend likely already thought poorly of him.

"You, Philip. I want you."

He gave her a scornful look to let her know he didn't believe a word she was saying.

"I missed you. Didn't you miss me? I'm so sorry for what I did. But now I know the truth. You are the only one for me. I hope you can forgive me."

She stepped off his desk, then slid the straps off her shoulders, one at a time, and let the obscene gown slip off her body. She reached up and ran her thumbs slowly over her nipples, just the way she used to do, her guaranteed trick to make him hard instantly. He used to call them his sweet chocolates. His mouth went dry as he leaned against the door. Her voluptuous breasts overflowed in her hands, her nipples turned dark and hard. As he did, instantly.

Bloody hell, betrayed by his own body. He licked his lips as he watched her saunter over to him, swaying her hips in a perfect rhythm. He couldn't take his eyes off her nipples, his erection so hard he was in pain. Attempting to adjust himself, he struggled to calm the blood pounding through his veins—no, pounding in his groin. Sweat gathered on his brow as he loosened his neck cloth.

"I found this beautiful ruby necklace on your desk. How does it look on me?" She fingered the red gems before caressing the diamonds with her tongue. "Does it look as nice on me as the other necklace you gave me?" She offered him a sweet smile before she ran her tongue across her lips. Licking her finger, she traced it across her nipple, leaving a trail of wetness for him to see.

He gazed at the necklace and then into her eyes.

Caroline's eyes were cold, hard, and calculating. There was no warmth, compassion, or love in them. None of the things he'd seen in Sara's green eyes.

One glance into their cold depths was all he needed.

His erection deflated as fast as if he had stepped into a pool full of ice. All he felt was revulsion. She had no power over him anymore.

He rejoiced as he strolled around her to pick up her red gown. He was no longer a prisoner to her whims. Her hold on him had ended, and a great weight had been lifted from his shoulders.

"Put this on, Caroline. I am no longer interested. Better yet, where are your real clothes? Get them on and get out."

He turned around and leaned against his desk as he crossed his arms, reveling in his freedom.

She grabbed a voluminous gown off the floor, something she'd worn over the transparent red outfit, and began dressing. "You can't throw me out. I am your wife. This is my home, and I'm back, so deal with it, Philip."

"No, you aren't my wife any longer, Caroline. I divorced you. Or didn't you receive your official notice? Oh, sorry, you should have paid attention to your mail while you were with your lover." He gave her a smile as false as her own.

The comment stopped her in her tracks. "What?" Her eyes blazed as she strutted over to him. "You can't do that. Divorce is not allowed in the aristocracy and you know it. You married me for life!"

Her hands fisted on her hips. She paced in a fury, her eyes shooting sparks as her words flew at him like arrows. "You have to provide for me, Philip. It was part of our marriage vows. I have needs, you realize. You are required to fulfill them." She came at him then, pounding him with her fists.

He took a step back, dispassionately moving her hands away from him. "You're correct about one thing, Caroline. I do have money. When you have money, as you know, you can do almost anything you want within the law. I chose to use a good portion of my wealth to divorce you. Had you shown up for the proceedings, you may have been entitled to a payment, but you chose not to come. You were busy with your lover. However, I am feeling generous today. Keep the necklace. It is worth enough to pay rent somewhere for you until you can find some other fool to fall for you. I certainly don't want that necklace to touch anyone else now that it has touched your skin."

Caroline fisted her hands at her sides and stomped her foot. "Philip, you cannot do this to me!" The tears started down her cheeks.

Unfortunately for her, he was accustomed to her drama, and unmoved by it.

"I can, and I did." He stepped around her toward the door. "Gather your things, Caroline. I want you out by the time I return. Don't come back." He reached for the doorknob.

She threw herself against his body from behind, her nails digging into his arms. "Please, I will do anything. I have nowhere else to go. I know you are angry. I know I embarrassed you. Punish me. Beat me. Do what you will, but don't throw me out."

He halted at the door, although not because her offer appealed to him.

"Philip, spank me. Take me over your knee."

He jerked his head around to look at her. Once glance confirmed what he'd suspected.

"Ah, the truth comes out at last," he said. "I wasn't enough for you in the bedroom?"

"Philip, please, I beg you. Duncan was the only one who knew how to satisfy me, but I can show you." Her breathing turned ragged, her teeth nipping her bottom lip.

Philip pulled away from her.

"Get out, Caroline. You disgust me."

Philip closed the door behind him and leaned against it. He ran his hand down his face to steady himself. All his remaining questions had been answered in less than an hour, and his ex-wife would never clutter his thoughts again. He didn't care what she did. He hoped he never saw her again.

He gathered himself together and headed down the hallway. His butler awaited him in the entryway. "Stevens, make sure my ex-wife leaves the house within the next few minutes. Do not allow her to wander around. In fact, have Eli take her to a hotel and pay for the night. Arrange for a week's stay to be billed to me. Let her know it shall be the last of my generosity."

Stevens nodded, a slight twitch at his mouth. "Yes, Your Grace, I will handle everything discreetly, as usual."

Philip retreated and headed for the dining room. His mother gave him a questioning look from her seat at the end of the table. "Everything is taken care of, Mother. May I take this moment to remind you how much I love you?" He smiled and leaned down to give her a kiss on the cheek.

His mother offered her cheek with a puzzled expression. "I suppose so. You may expand upon the details later."

He continued on his way, but then turned back. "Mother, would you do me a favor and ask Benjamin, Graham, and Adam to meet me outside on the shooting range in about an hour? We need to practice, make sure we can each handle a gun and even a dagger. In fact, I will make sure I'm proficient at both. We have work to do."

CHAPTER TWENTY-SEVEN

THE NEXT MORNING, PHILIP EXITED his carriage and bounded up the steps of the Ardleigh Manor House. He and his brothers were more skilled with weapons than he would have guessed, though they each had their preference. They'd worked tirelessly most of the afternoon. He and Adam were best at pistols, though Graham could use his fists better than any weapon. He felt better prepared to handle whatever scum was pursuing Sara.

The butler let him into the foyer, and when he heard his friend moving about in the library, he boldly intruded rather than waiting to be introduced.

"What have you discovered, Ardleigh?" he queried.

Ardleigh's eyebrows rose. "Ah, Brentwood, nice to see you. What brings you here so early?"

"Honestly, Ardleigh, let's not bandy words. What did the investigator have to say yesterday?" He stuffed his hands in his pockets as his foot tapped a beat on the carpet. "I would prefer to hire another investigator, but I've been unsuccessful. Has Ridley discovered anything useful?"

"Nothing that pleases me. He believes one of the two most powerful crime lords is involved. It would seem Lord Downey borrowed quite a bit more money to try to keep your ex-wife happy. That is why he is bothering Sara. As long as he can get her to continue paying, he will. But we have another problem. Word has gotten out that she's alone…" Ardleigh's mouth formed a grim line. "My man tells me there's a major boss who preys on young widows.

He forces them into the business, if you get my meaning."

"What? They just take women to whore for them? How can they get away with such aberrant behavior?"

"They choose carefully and have been lucky thus far. They seek out beautiful women who lack any connections. Ones who won't be missed. Unfortunately, Sara fits the requirements. No known family, no strong connections. We need to keep her here with us to convince these people she will indeed be missed should anything happen."

"She will go home with me! I have connections. I'll protect her. Have your servant gather her things." His hands flexed as he paced.

"No need to raise your voice, Brentwood. I don't think Sara is ready for that yet."

"I don't care if she is ready. I can keep her safe!" Philip's mind reeled at the possibility of Sara being kidnapped. As a prostitute? He could hardly restrain himself from punching a hole in the wall at the thought of such a thing. "Ridley knows it's a major man from the underworld, but he doesn't know which one? How does that help us?"

Ardleigh simply shrugged in response to his last question. "When he learns more, I suspect he'll tell us more. In the meantime, I think Lady Downey would do best to stay here," Ardleigh said calmly. "I will keep her safe, and she is comfortable with Phoebe. These men will stay away from her once they realize she has our protection. Besides, if you recall, the lady is not interested in moving into your townhouse, Brentwood."

The words felt like a blow, but Philip shook them off and continued his pacing. "We have to do something. I need to know who's behind all of this. I'll break the man's neck with my bare hands!" He knew he was losing it. His nails were close to drawing blood from the flesh of his palms.

Ardleigh calmly continued, "I have involved the authorities. Give them some time. They will solve this, and we will keep Sara safe in the meantime. Now, why are you here, Brentwood? You did not come here in your carriage to discuss the investigator, did you?" Ardleigh stared out the window at his carriage, the largest in all of London. His family's golden crest was blinding in the sun.

He shook his head. "No, of course not. I came to ask Lady Downey if she would come with me for a ride in Hyde Park today."

"Zounds, surely you do not mean that, Brentwood? Of course, you understand what people will think?" Ardleigh's lips curved into a smile.

"Yes, I believe I possess the intelligence to understand the statement I'll be making, Ardleigh. Now, may I speak to Sara or not?" He tugged on his neck cloth as he spoke. If he took Sara into Hyde Park with him, he would be declaring her off limits to all others. He would be announcing their courtship essentially. Which was well and good. He wanted others to know she was taken, and he really wasn't concerned with the realm right now. His primary concern was Sara. He needed to talk to her privately. She was a widow. It was certainly acceptable for them to be alone together.

He must have made quite a bit of noise, for Lady Ardleigh entered the library just then. "The ducal carriage, Your Grace? What is the occasion?" But his attention was fixed on the woman following her. Sara. She lingered in the doorway.

He cleared his throat. "The occasion is that I have come to ask Lady Downey if she would do me the honor of accompanying me for a ride through Hyde Park this morning. It is a beautiful morning, is it not?"

Sara finally stepped inside, holding her arm next to her body. A sling had been fashioned to hold it in position for her.

She curtsied with a blush. "Good day to you, Your Grace."

He almost lost the ability to speak. Sara wore a yellow day

dress that made her more beautiful than he had thought possible. Why did she grow more stunning every day? Was that possible or was he a hopeless romantic? Damnation, he was acting like a besotted schoolboy.

Was she still medicated today? Would they be able to converse?

It struck him that he'd never before looked forward to speaking to a woman who interested him. In the past, he'd wanted one thing, but with Lady Downey, he wanted everything.

"I would be honored to accompany you," she said.

Sara stared at Philip. Was he angry today? No, his eyes were a soft, warm blue, not even a touch of ice to them. Oh, how she loved it when he looked at her this way. It made her want to stay close to him, always.

Her mind was not cloudy today as it had been yesterday. When she'd awoken this morning, she had asked Phoebe to lighten the amount of medication she was given for pain. She wanted to be back in control of her faculties, of her life. Customers awaited their garments, and there was no one else to sew for her. Although it would be hard with her fingers in their condition, she would find a way. She always found a way.

Phoebe wrapped a shawl about her shoulders, and before she knew it, Philip was escorting her to the carriage and helping her inside. Was she doing the right thing? How quickly she forgot about his insult to her. About Miranda Montrose and the reason for her unseemly attack.

Philip closed the door behind him and sat down next to her.

"Here, Sara, I brought this pillow for you to prop your arm. I was afraid it would still be sore today." He fussed over her, tucking the velvet pillow beneath her elbow, then rapped on the roof to get the carriage moving and settled himself across from her.

"Philip, do you care to tell me what this is about?" she asked softly. "I didn't expect to see you again." He'd come to see her yesterday, of course, but she hardly remembered what he'd said. In all likelihood he'd only come because of her injury. The situation between them hadn't changed. He wanted something she could not give him. She brought her gaze up to lock with his blue eyes. They remained warm, fortunately.

"I'm here because I enjoy your company. It's that simple. I am also worried about you. You've been through a most traumatic event. How are your fingers? Is your pain any better?"

She turned her head to stare out the window. "I'm much better, thank you." She knew it was rude to look away, but she couldn't handle being so close to him. It made her want to touch him. It made her feel lost again. How could she not love this man? When the two of them were alone, he was so attentive, so thoughtful. A quick glance at him was enough to send a swarm of butterflies through her stomach.

However, every time she thought of what he'd asked her to do, she became angry again. She'd told him she wouldn't be his mistress, and yet he'd continued to press her. She hated him a little for that.

How could you love someone and hate him at the same time? Was that possible? She needed to get her emotions under control because despite the complicated situation between the two of them, she knew the duke could likely help her out of her predicament.

Get control and think, Sara.

"Sara, why did you return the necklace?"

Her head snapped back to glance at him. Was he dense?

"I thought I explained that in my note, Your Grace. And

before. I'm not interested in your offer." She dropped her gaze to her hands as she blushed.

"I understand your feelings. I must apologize for insulting you by repeating my offer. It was not my intention."

Sara glanced at him but then turned her head to stare out the window again. What did he want from her?

Philip reached over and took her chin in his hand. He gently turned her face back to him. "Why didn't you give the necklace to your attacker? You could have paid him off."

She pushed him away with her good hand. "Because it would have been wrong, Philip. I was not willing to accept your terms of the agreement. If I couldn't uphold my end of the bargain, I certainly couldn't keep the necklace."

"You could have paid him off, and we could have worked out the terms at a later time. If you had kept it and given it to him, it may have been enough for him to leave you alone for good. Why would you risk what happened when you had a way out? Help me to understand."

They were almost to Hyde Park. Silence descended in the carriage. He just didn't understand her. He would never understand her. How could she explain how much she valued her dignity? Her self-respect? It was the one unshakable thing she had left.

"You would have preferred it had I kept the gift without intending to do as you wished?" She pinched the ends of her good fingers with her gloved hand. If she pinched really hard, it took her mind off the pain in her broken bones. It had become intolerable again, although she wasn't about to tell the duke.

Philip crossed his legs as he continued, "No, but you're certainly intelligent enough to have seen it as a potential solution to your problem."

"Intelligent enough? Are you implying that I am stupid because I did not accept your gift?" She bit back all the insulting words she wanted to throw at Philip.

"No, of course not. But surely you can see my position."

"What position? Your position to insult me?" Sara made no effort to disguise the anger in her tone.

"No!" The level of his voice rose as he continued, "But you knew he would come back. Why wouldn't you do the reasonable thing and move out of the shop? I would have helped you find somewhere safe to stay even if you didn't wish to be in my townhouse. Lady Ardleigh would have happily given you a home. What are you trying to prove?"

"Trying to prove?" she asked, anger spreading through her like fire rising in a hearth. "Perhaps I am trying to prove that I have a shred of decency left. Perhaps I'm trying to prove that I can support myself with my own business sense and hard work. Surely you can see that being dependent on a man has not worked out for me in the past. Duncan almost ruined me." Her voice rose with every word as they entered the park. "My husband kept me hidden away, and you want me to hide in your townhouse, away from your mother and sister, away from the *ton*. Perhaps I would like to be able to talk to someone in my shop without being embarrassed about what I do when I walk out the door. You're not the only one who has pride, Philip! Someday, when I move on from this world, I hope to meet my mother again. And when that happens, I will not allow myself to be in a position to regret any of the decisions I made while I was here. Take me back to the Ardleighs, please!" The pain in her heart bothered her now more than the pain in her arm and hand. How could he think she was so shallow?

"No, Sara, I will not take you back yet. Not until you can see the danger you are putting yourself in. Do you think I want to spend every minute of my life worrying about whether that man is coming back to hurt or kidnap you? You won't let anyone help you. What else should we do?

Tell me, because I have no idea how you'll let me help you. You push away everyone who loves and cares about you!" Philip's bellow was loud enough to attract attention from others outside, but he seemed oblivious.

Sara had never seen him so carried away before, and her own heart hammered in her chest.

"Goodness," someone said from outside the carriage. "Your Grace, who's in the carriage with you that you love and care about so much that the whole park can hear you yelling?"

Philip and Sara turned their heads in unison to see Cora Applebey, the gossip of the *ton,* smiling at them from just outside the window.

"Why, who is it? Who is the lucky woman who has finally cracked the ice and caused you to feel emotion again?" Cora beamed at them as if she had just discovered the secret of the decade.

Sara froze, turning her head away from the window. This woman was bold as brass to speak to the Duke of Brentwood in such a manner.

"After the cruelty the duchess inflicted on you, I didn't think you would ever be able to love again. Any woman capable of making you yell that much must be quite special."

Philip answered Cora with an icy glare.

"Oh, begging your pardon. I am interrupting. I will move on and let you finish your argument. And please do let the young lady win. Why, is that Lady Downey with you? What a fortunate young lady. It's so good to see you engage with life again." Cora snickered and waved as she moved on.

Sara thought about what the busybody had said. Did she speak the truth? Had Philip shut himself away from life since his wife had left him? Was that why he was so cold all the time? Had she, indeed, broken through his shell?

It struck her that perhaps they weren't so different. Philip was right—she did push people away—and so did he. But he had admitted that he loved and cared for her, had he not?

It struck her that there was one topic they had not discussed. And she could not leave it unsaid.

"Are you sure you are not speaking of Miranda Montrose, Your Grace? She came to my shop to warn me away from you. She said that you belong to her." There, it was out in the open. He had to acknowledge his mistress now.

"Miranda Montrose?' he growled. "I am done with Miranda Montrose. You're the only woman I want."

She jumped as he reached across the seat, tugging her onto his lap. He pulled the curtain shut to give them privacy, and before she knew what was happening, his mouth descended on hers in a crushing, spine-tingling kiss that spoke of possession.

He broke the kiss and stared into her eyes as he slowly caressed her cheek. "I want you, Sara. I *need* you." He kissed her again, softly tasting her, and when their tongues met, he groaned deep in his throat. Sara gave in and melted against him, kissing him back without reservation. His touch, his taste unleashed her passion and shook her to her soul. She wanted more.

He pulled away and kissed her forehead. "Do you know how frightened I was?" he whispered. "Do you know how I felt when I came upon your shop and saw the devastation inside? You bloody well scared the hell out of me, even though I know this was not your fault." He wrapped his arms around her and pulled her closer. "I can't go through that horror again."

She could feel his heart pounding through his coat. She knew her heart was lost to him, and it frightened her. She sighed as his hand massaged her neck, and she fought to control her breathing. There was no place that felt better than in Philip's arms.

"Philip, I cannot move in with you," she whispered against his shoulder.

Philip sighed as he ran his thumb along her jawline. "I know. I'm not asking you to. I respect your moral conviction. Can we take it one day at a time?"

She closed her eyes. "Yes, I would like that."

"Will you promise me to stay with Phoebe until we can solve this?"

"Yes, Philip, I will."

For the first time in a long, long while, she felt hope.

CHAPTER TWENTY-EIGHT

PHOEBE FUSSED WITH SARA'S HAIR one last time, tucking her stray curls into the elaborate upswept hair style her maid had created for her. Smiling at her in the looking glass, Sara swatted her hand away. "My hair is fine. Why, you would think I was about to get married. Why do you persist so?"

"I cannot help myself. I am excited for you and for the evening we are about to share. You do look ravishing, Lady Downey." Phoebe couldn't stop herself from tucking another lock of hair behind her ear as she rambled. "I haven't been to the opera for some time. Did Duncan ever take you?"

"I think we attended twice, but it was a disaster because he never approved of my wardrobe choices. I don't think my husband was proud of me."

"He was a fool. I still cannot believe the duke has invited us to sit in his box," Phoebe said, making another minor adjustment. "I am happy for you, Sara, but please be careful."

"You don't care for the duke?" She turned away from the looking glass so she could look Phoebe in the eye. Philip had come to see her several times over the last few weeks, and she savored each and every visit. Even so, her friend's judgment meant a great deal to her. In her last crisis, she'd turned away from Phoebe—in the future, she intended to turn toward her.

"Please do not misunderstand me. Philip is a wonderful

man in his heart, but I am not sure he has healed yet. It will take time. What his wife did to him was unforgivable."

"He really had no idea she was interested in another man? I certainly suspected it of Duncan. He was very cold toward me."

"Caroline was a very good actress. She was beautiful and spoiled, and he always did her bidding. He was so in love with her, but I believe he was blind to the real Caroline. I think he saw her beauty and not her character." Shaking off the subject as if it were a fur stole she did not care for, Phoebe reached down to fuss with Sara's skirt. "You are a vision in this green dress, my dear. I knew when I saw it that it was meant for you. Fortunately, Miranda's knife missed this one in her tirade. You did make this for yourself, did you not?"

"I admit that I had hoped to wear it someday, but I never had the occasion. That's why I finally put it on display for my customers. You chose well for me when you returned to the shop." She leaned over and kissed her friend's cheek. "Thank you—for everything. I'm not sure what I would have done without you. I must say you look lovely in that deep purple gown. What a wonderful color on you."

"You are too kind. This is one of Ardleigh's favorite shades so I wear it often. Just promise me you will guard your heart, Sara. Do be careful. I want you to find the same happiness I've found."

"I'm not a foolish chit in my first Season. I promise to be careful, but I can't deny I have strong feelings for him."

Phoebe smiled a little at that. "How could you not? He is so handsome. Every female in the realm wants to catch his eye, and you're the only one who has managed to do so." With that encouraging comment, she turned and opened the door so they could descend to the foyer. "I suspect Ardleigh awaits us. We should go down."

Ardleigh stood at the foot of the ornate stairway. He

smiled as he gazed up at his wife. When she reached the bottom step, he leaned over and gave her a kiss. "You look lovely tonight, my dear. My favorite color."

"Thank you, Ardleigh. Is the carriage ready yet?"

"Ready and waiting. We should hurry along. You know how the line is at the opera." The butler opened the door for them, attentive as ever, as Sara put on her gloves, one easily and one carefully. While her arm was much better and she'd stopped wearing the sling, her fingers still pained her. Only one of the fingers, it turned out, had actually been broken. The other injury was just a sprain and was healing faster.

They heard the thunder of hooves before the pair of matched grays reached the entrance.

"What the devil?" Ardleigh turned to gawk at the interruption. "What is Brentwood doing?"

They all hurried out of the foyer to have a look. The ducal carriage had pulled in behind the Ardleigh carriage. Once it came to a stop, Philip stepped out and bowed. His attire tonight reminded her of the night they'd danced together. The night they'd done *more* together. She had to admit that memory had become one of her favorites. He was so regal when he was in full dress. His cravat was always just so, and his coat was black this evening. His blue waistcoat and dark hair were arresting together, bringing more attention to his blue eyes.

"Ladies, you are both stunning tonight." Philip's blue eyes danced as he took them in, his eyes lingering on the green dress. "I'm afraid I could not wait."

Sara and Phoebe both curtsied as he approached. He brushed his fingers on Phoebe's gloved hand and then reached for Sara's good hand and tucked it through his arm. She could feel his warmth through his jacket.

The duke smiled at her, a smile full of promises, and turned to his friend. "Ardleigh," he said, raising an eyebrow, "you don't mind if we follow you?"

"Of course not, Brentwood, but it really wasn't necessary."

Philip's gaze locked on Sara's again. "To me, it was necessary. Shall we go, Lady Downey?"

She turned and smiled at Phoebe. "Do you mind, Phoebe?"

"Of course not, go and we'll see you there." Her friend kissed her cheek and waved her off, giving her a saucy wink as she stepped away.

Philip escorted her to the carriage. After his footman opened the door, he wrapped his hands around Sara's waist and lifted her into the carriage.

"Oh!" Sara placed one hand on his broad shoulders, guarding her other arm, and gazed into his eyes. When she was this close to him, she became totally unnerved. The pounding of her heart threatened to burst through her chest. She was surprised when he sat next to her instead of across from her.

At a loss for words, she cleared her throat to fill the silence. "This was unnecessary, Your Grace, I would have been happy in the Ardleigh carriage." She peered at him from under her lashes, feeling his leg pressed against her, the contact burning into her. Why did this man upset her senses so?

"I wanted a few moments alone with you, Sara. Please call me 'Philip' when we are alone." He reached for her chin and brushed a quick kiss across her lips.

He tasted of brandy: sweet, soft. Oh, how she loved his kisses. She watched as he reached across the seat for a small package.

"I wanted to give you this." He held a black velvet case toward her. "I didn't want an audience." He opened it and held it up for her inspection.

Inside sat the most beautiful necklace she had ever

seen. Resplendent with emeralds and small diamonds, she couldn't even imagine the value of such a piece. She couldn't stop herself from removing her glove and fingering the cool gems. Tears gathered in the corners of her eyes.

"Oh, Philip, it's lovely. I've never seen anything so beautiful."

"Do you like it, sweetness?" He held her gaze as he asked the question, his eyes full of hope. How could she turn him down?

But she must.

"Philip, I love it, but I cannot accept this. It's inappropriate. It's too much," Sara stammered.

"Nonsense. I insist, Sara. I won't take no for an answer this time." He turned her shoulders. "Here, let me see it on you, please."

His fingers caressed her neck as he fixed the clasp. He reached down and brushed a trail of kisses along her shoulder. She shivered instantly and swallowed a nervous lump in her throat. Words were not forthcoming as he set her back to admire the effect.

"I'm sorry, but clearly this was meant for your skin. The emeralds match your eyes. You are the reason I purchased this necklace. It reminded me of your eyes." Philip brushed her cheek with his thumb.

He was so gentle with her. Why? What did this mean? She was so confused by this gesture. She reached up and rubbed her fingers across the cool gems. This necklace meant something different than the other, didn't it? Or was she reading him wrong again?

"Sara, I apologize for my coarseness before. I was a desperate man. I wanted to keep you in my townhouse, hidden away from everyone. I wanted you all to myself, but when I came upon your shop the other day…when I saw what had happened…I realized I want more. Can we start anew? You helped me to realize that I would like to start my life fresh." He paused for a moment, his eyes contemplative, then added, "I saw Caroline this week. I hope I never see her again. My feelings for her were shallow. It's time for me to move on. I would like to spend more time with you. Will you allow me that pleasure? Can you forgive me?"

Sara could not help but think of Phoebe's warning. What if Philip wasn't ready to love again? What if the ice in which he'd encased his heart never fully melted? And yet, her heart would only allow her one answer. Reaching down to touch his hand, she said, "I would like that, Philip. I forgive you. Let's start fresh and see where this takes us." She smiled as she nodded in agreement. "I will accept this necklace as long as you agree not to give me any more jewels. This is beautiful and I will treasure it, but it's enough. Thank you." She leaned over and kissed him full on the mouth.

It felt like the beginning of something beautiful.

CHAPTER TWENTY-NINE

PHILIP SLIPPED HIS HANDS AROUND Sara's tiny waist and lifted her down from the carriage. He turned her toward the entrance, where a throng of people awaited the opera. The footman at the door beckoned him to the side and ushered him past the crowd. Philip placed his hand on Sara's waist and kept her in front of him slightly to the right. He wanted to protect her injured arm from being jostled.

Of course, they drew quite a bit of attention, as he had expected, but he was astounded at his own protectiveness.

Decorum stated she should be on his arm, but he needed to protect her arm. He could tell it still pained her from the way she tensed every time it was jostled. She moved back into him whenever it happened, and he quite liked her there. The closer she was to him, the happier he felt.

A slow realization struck him as they made their way through the lobby. Men were staring at her, the look in their eyes familiar. Men had thrown lustful glances Caroline's way too, of course, and she'd reveled in it. He had even seen her bend over to give a handsome man a better view of her bosom. It hadn't bothered him overly much, but he hated the way these men were gawking at Sara. She was indeed ravishing, but must they stare at her so?

Sara took it in stride. Her posture was regal, her smile beautiful. She continued on as if quite unaware of the stir they were causing, although he suspected she noticed she was the center of attention. Glancing about the theater,

Philip was struck by the way the ladies of the *ton* were regarding Sara. He'd expected some of them might mistreat her, especially after the regrettable scene Miranda had made many weeks past, but these ladies clearly admired her. It struck him that perhaps they'd learned what he himself had discovered. Lady Sara Downey was a woman of character, a young woman who'd shown remarkable strength and perseverance these last months. Everyone in town knew of the attack at her shop. Few people could weather such a storm with grace, but grace was effortless for Sara. She was a true genteel lady, and the *ton* was finally recognizing it. He smiled in response.

Lady Applebey passed by and said, "I have not seen you this happy in a while, Your Grace. She is lovely."

He nodded to Lady Applebey and leaned down and whispered into Sara's ear, "Just keep moving, Sara. We are almost there." He continued to guide her lightly toward the entrances to the boxes.

"Well, Philip, so this is my replacement."

The familiar voice made his blood go cold. He turned and glared into Caroline's eyes. How dare she interrupt them?

She wore a slinky dress, toeing the rules of respectability, and stood arm in arm with a viscount of questionable ethics.

"I see you have found another friend, Caroline. I wish you happiness." He nodded with a smirk to her escort.

Rather than introduce him to her escort, as decorum dictated, Caroline glared at Sara and said, "Aren't you Lord Downey's widow? That explains a few things to me. Beware of the man you've chosen. He is quite boring in the boudoir, if you understand my meaning. But I see you know what he's worth. He must have given you that necklace. It looks like his taste." She chuckled as she stared into Sara's eyes.

Sara blushed but held her head high. "Pardon me, but our relationship is none of your concern."

Her eyes never wavered from Caroline's, and Philip could not have been prouder of her. He tightened his grip on Sara's waist and tugged her closer. "Caroline, you wanted your freedom, you have it. Please be on your way." As he guided Sara away from her, he could hear his ex-wife prattling on. Talking about him and Sara. But he found he didn't care at all. She was a relic of his past, nothing more.

He leaned into Sara and whispered, "You handled yourself well. Please don't allow her to disturb you."

She glanced back at him. "We are creating quite a stir, Your Grace."

Philip raised one eyebrow as he ushered her into his box. "It's of no concern to me. I'm more worried about you. Are you all right? Is your arm causing you much pain? I apologize for the crowd."

"I'm fine, Your Grace, thank you."

Sara noticed the box was almost completely full. She had expected it to be large, of course, but she had not anticipated there would be so many people. Phoebe and Ardleigh had already arrived. When she glanced past them, she was surprised to see both Philip's mother and his sister, Emma. Both ladies stood to greet them.

Sara quickly curtsied to his mother. "Good evening, Your Grace, it is lovely to see you again. Lady Emma, it is wonderful to see you as well."

Emma took her hand and squeezed it, nearly dancing in place with excitement. "Oh, Lady Downey," she said. "I was so happy Philip, I mean, His Grace invited us tonight, especially when I found out you would be here. I'm wearing your gown! Or rather the one you made me. I've had so many compliments on it already. I think it's my favorite. This is the most beautiful shade of blue, I believe. Or do you think a pastel shade would have looked better?"

The dowager gave her daughter a quick tug. "Emma, please, you will wear everyone's ears out the way you prattle on. Please, allow the lady a chance to breathe."

Mary St. James leaned over to embrace Sara. The position brought her close to Sara's ear, and she leaned in and whispered, "I am so sorry for all of your troubles. Please trust that we shall help you in any way we can. You can trust my son as well."

Sara's eyes misted as she thanked the duchess. Philip's mother was so wonderful—she was all the things she had imagined her own mother to be. Overcome with emotion, she was barely able to manage a quick "thank you."

Philip leaned over and kissed his mother's cheek. "Please, Mother, I would like to get Lady Downey seated. It was a bit busier than I anticipated. Perhaps we should have gotten here earlier. I fear her arm must be bothering her from all the jostling she suffered on our way here."

"I assure you, I am fine, Your Grace." He showed her to her seat, next to Phoebe and Ardleigh, and she quickly got settled.

Phoebe leaned over and exclaimed, "Sara, that necklace!"

Sara blushed as she fingered the gems. "Yes, is it not stunning? A gift from the duke tonight. He wouldn't allow me to refuse it."

"As you shouldn't," the duchess cut in. Philip sat between Sara and his sister, and the dowager duchess was next to Emma, in the preeminent seat in the box. "It appears to have been made just for you, Lady Downey. It is quite beautiful with your green eyes." Smiling with something that looked like satisfaction, she turned to address her son. "Philip, you do have exquisite taste."

As the orchestra started, Emma leaned around Philip, beaming with excitement. "Do you like the opera, Lady Downey? I love it. It's so romantic."

"I shall let you know, but I'm sure it will be wonderful.

I haven't been in a long time." She smiled at Philip. "I'm excited to share this with you."

She glanced at the crowd in the seats below them, marveling again at the size of the crowd. Rarely had she been around this many people. But her attention was quickly engaged by the performers. She found herself in awe—the costumes, the lighting, the arias. She couldn't help but smile at Philip every so often.

Of course, the best part of the night was being close to the duke. When she did lock gazes with him, she was amazed at the warmth in his eyes. He didn't try to hide his concern for her in front of his family and friends. During the intermissions, he made sure to include her in the conversation, and he was ever so attentive. She'd never seen him so relaxed or affable.

A trifle belatedly, his brothers showed up. They didn't admit to where they had been, but she was pleased to see the natural affection between the brothers. Philip's ice was gone, melted for the night at least, and she'd never been happier.

Even though it was spring, the nights were still cool. Sara huddled close to Philip as they awaited the ducal carriage. The duchess and Emma were still with them, but he'd sent his brothers ahead to find their carriage and their footmen. The Ardleighs had moved off to await their own carriage.

"Philip, I don't understand what the problem is tonight. Why is everything moving so slowly?" the duchess asked. Quite some time had passed, and there was still no sign of Graham, Adam, or Ben. Many other members of the *ton* had gathered outside, awaiting their carriages too. Sara found she didn't mind at all. The air was a little crisp, but Philip was beside her, they were with his lovely family, and they'd had a most splendid night.

"I'm not sure, Mother," he said softly, glancing at Sara as if to gauge her mood. She smiled at him and he continued, "There seems to be some commotion going on down the block that is holding everything up. I sent Graham in one direction and Ben and Adam in the other. One of them should return soon, no doubt."

Emma beamed as she stared, quite openly, at the crowd gathered in front of the theater. "I don't care, Mother. This allows us the chance to look at everyone. I like to see if I can guess which ladies are wearing Lady Downey's designs. I think that red satin gown must be yours, is it not?" Emma pointed to a beautiful lady across the street from them.

"Yes, you are correct."

Emma clapped her hands together and continued searching for another gown she guessed to be her creation.

Philip glanced around him and said, "That one. It has to be yours."

"It is, but how could you tell?" She had to wonder how a man would see her designs.

"Your work stands out among the others. I have to agree that you have an unusual talent."

"And that one in dark blue must be yours, also," Emma added, her eyes widened.

"Yes, it is mine, Lady Emma. I so enjoyed creating it for her, she is...oh!"

That scent...it could only come from one person. The person she'd thought she no longer need worry about. Sara swiveled around quickly, grabbing Philip's lapel.

"What?" He searched her face, sheer terror etched there. "What is it, Sara?"

"He's here." She buried her face into his chest.

"What's wrong, Philip?"

The duchess had posed the question, but Philip's attention was completely on Sara. "Who? What are you talking about? Where?" He leaned down close while still casting his eyes about their surroundings.

"Stinky. I can smell him." Her voice broke, but she forced herself to keep talking. "Philip, he's here." She frantically searched the faces around her. "I don't see him, but I smell him." She tightened her grip on him. "Please don't let him touch me!"

Philip's gaze searched the area. "Sara, I don't see anyone unusual here. There's no one dirty or inappropriately dressed. I don't see anyone who would fit his description. Are you sure?" He leaned down into her ear as he tugged her in closer. "I won't let him touch you, Sara. I am here." He rubbed her back to console her.

"Now, tell me again what he looks like," he instructed.

Tears threatened to spill down her cheeks. She had to get herself under control. The last thing she wanted was for the dowager duchess to think she had lost her faculties. Although the smell was so distinct, so horribly familiar, she could be wrong. She could be imagining it.

She turned her face up to him and said, "I'm all right. I must have been mistaken." She took a deep breath, then moved a bit away from Philip, just enough to turn and smile at the dowager duchess. "Forgive me, I don't know what came over me."

"My dear, you've had a terrible fright." The duchess turned to her son. "Philip? Can you not see what is happening? You need to get her away from here. I'm sure she is quite uncomfortable."

"I'm doing everything I can, Mother. There! I see one of my footmen." Philip lowered Sara's hands, his touch gentle. "Just a moment, my dear, I see Eli." He turned and shouted to Eli and moved a few feet away to talk to him.

Don't leave me, Philip. Please. He could be here somewhere.

But it would be ludicrous to say the words aloud. No one else had noticed the strange smell. Even so, she kept surreptitiously searching the area to make sure Stinky was not nearby. Her gaze darted back to Philip. He was still there. She urged herself to calm down. The last thing she wished to do was to let Stinky—or the specter of Stinky—ruin her lovely night.

Philip turned back to them. "It's just as I thought. There's something blocking everything up ahead. Eli doesn't know what, although he suspects someone's horses might be injured or something. I told him to locate our carriage quickly and lead us to it. We'll sit inside and wait if we must. Pardon me." He leaned in close and kissed her cheek. "I will return quickly, love." He turned again and strode away to catch Eli.

Sara's blood rushed to her head as soon as Philip left. The dowager reached for her hand, giving her a comforting squeeze. She realized how ridiculous she was acting, but she couldn't help it. Something was wrong.

No longer able to take it, she stepped away from the dowager, intent on walking over to Philip, when she was grabbed from behind and pulled away from her group. She floundered to keep her balance, that awful stench invaded her senses again. She heard a scream but didn't know if it was hers or Emma's.

"Philip! Philip, help me!" she shouted. There were at least four hands on her as she fought. Stinky had a friend. She caught Philip's gaze as she was being yanked in the other direction.

"Hey now, what is going on?" one stranger bellowed.

Stinky's companion produced a knife, brandishing it at anyone in his path. "You want to get hurt? I'll stab anyone who tries to stop us." The crowd parted at the appearance of the weapon, people shifting away from the threat.

"Leave her be, man. How dare you touch her?" another stranger shouted. He attempted to grab her attacker, but the man with the knife moved too quickly, catching the man's wrist with the blade. Blood dripped from the wound.

The people of the *ton* were not accustomed to physical violence, and it showed.

"He's got a knife!" a woman screamed. "A knife!" Her words echoed as the crowd opened up for the villains. Stinky now held a dagger of his own.

"What are you doing? Help! The lady needs help!" a woman yelled to everyone around her.

Sara's ears rang with all the shouting going on. But nobody was stopping her kidnappers. A couple of other people had tried, but each effort had been met with violence, either a fist in the face or a knife wound. Her kidnappers were moving more quickly now, spiriting her away as fast as they could. Fingernails dug into her skin, and Stinky had twisted her arm painfully. She screamed at the top of her lungs, but he only tightened his grip.

"I told you, gel, not to tell anyone. You'll pay for this, you will. You went to the duke? I told you, you were gonna be mine before I sell you to me boss. And I take what I want."

Sara kicked as hard as she could, and she finally connected with flesh. He slapped her face hard, nearly cutting her cheek with his weapon.

Another voice ahead of them called out, "You can't control a tiny female?"

"Dumb bitch, don't you be touching me!" He yanked her hair and she screamed louder. "Just for that, after I collect me pounds, I am going back to your shop to tear it apart. Yeh, I'll start it on fire, I will. I don't like dollymops that hit. Your new boss will be breaking you of that, he will."

Bloody hell, of all nights to have a jam of carriages. He knew Sara was losing control. Was she right? Was Stinky in the area? He was tall enough to see over most people's heads, and there hadn't been anything—or anyone—

unusual around them. Still, she'd trembled with fear. Even if her attacker wasn't anywhere near them, Philip needed to get her inside a carriage, away from the crowd.

He finally spotted Eli again. He hurried toward him, eager to get back to Sara's side. The longer they were out in the open, the more he would worry about her. He was falling hard and he knew it.

Falling hard? Hellfire, he had already fallen. The most shocking part of it was that he was happy, dem happy, as Adam would say. He liked having her at his side. This was the best night he had ever spent at the opera, and he knew it was because of her. She was vivacious, beautiful, and intelligent. What more could he want in a woman? At least he finally had his priorities straight. He would have to thank his mother again.

"Eli, I hope you have good news for me. I want the ladies in the carriage as soon as possible," he shouted to his footman.

"Your Grace, it's a long way back. I don't know if the ladies can walk that far. We will probably be here for a while."

"Is my mother's closer?"

"I don't know, sir, let me go check." Eli turned to head down the street.

Philip was about to go back and inform the women of what he had learned, but then he thought of Ardleigh.

He turned back away for a moment and yelled, "Eli, wait a moment! Look for the Ardleigh carriage as well. Surely they can find room for the ladies in their carriage. Perhaps it's closer."

Eli nodded and took off to do as he was bid. Philip marched back to Sara in time to see her lose her balance as two men in dark capes seized her from behind and ran off with her in the opposite direction. His mother yelled and Emma screamed, but Sara held his focus completely.

"Philip, Philip, help me!"

His world crumbled around him. He yelled for Eli and Graham, praying his brother was close enough to help him, as he tore in Sara's direction, but more and more people moved in front of him to satisfy their curiosity. He felt as if he were caught in a nightmare, because the crowd was parting for the villains but closing in around him. Then he saw a man with a handkerchief wrapped around his bloody wrist, and he realized what was happening. The bastards who'd taken Sara had knives.

She was in even more danger than he'd feared.

To his horror, he lost sight of her. He could only track her by following her terrified screams. Time moved in slow motion as he grabbed and shoved his way through the crowd. Men yelled at him as he pushed their wives out of the way, but he didn't care. He *needed* to get to Sara. Nothing would stop him. He finally caught sight of the kidnappers again as the men flung off their dark capes before continuing.

"Stop them," he shouted. "They're kidnapping her. Help! Someone stop them!"

No one ventured near the two criminals, but at least they stepped aside for him.

He was gaining on them. She fought, kicking and screaming, and one of the men slapped her brutally across the face. Rage and panic consumed Philip, but he forced himself to shout, "Don't give up, Sara! I am coming. Keep fighting."

He stumbled and almost fell, managing to right himself at the last moment.

"Help! Stop those men! Get the Bow Street Runners. Where are they?"

But there was no sign of them, and the men kept running, hastening Sara away from him. He finally understood what it was to love, really love, and now he was going to lose her? Absolutely not! He continued shouting to her and Eli and his brothers as he pushed and shoved his way toward her. He raced so hard he felt light-headed, but he wouldn't stop. He couldn't stop.

Graham suddenly appeared behind the kidnappers. Philip, almost upon them, could only watch as his brother grabbed a cane from a bystander and swung it across the knees of the man in front. The man's resulting stumble gave Philip all the time he needed to reach them. Grabbing Sara, he sent the man who'd restrained her flying into the air. The other kidnapper took off. Graham started to follow but stopped as three Bow Street Runners appeared in front of the criminal.

Sara grabbed his arms with both hands, hard enough to hurt. "Philip, Philip! Get them away from me!"

He sighed deeply in relief as he pulled her into his chest. "I have you, love. Everything will be fine now. Are you all right?" His heart nearly broke anew as he listened to her sob into his coat. "Sara, I have you, I won't let them get you. Please tell me you're all right?"

She nodded her head while she continued to hold him in a death grip. Hell, what more could happen to this woman?

He heard Graham shout, "Over here, Philip."

He made his way over to his brother, who'd fetched their mother's carriage. Graham opened the door and helped him get Sara inside.

"How is she?" Graham asked as they followed her inside. "Who in blazes were they, Philip? I have never seen those men before. But I supposed they are probably the chaps who injured the two horses in front to stall everything."

"I suppose you're right. I've never seen them before either." He shook his head. "One of them has accosted her before. The other must be his boss. Apparently, her late husband owed quite a bit of money, and the debtor sent one of his employees to harass her."

He brushed her hair away from her face as her sobs started to subside. "Sara, have you ever seen the other man?"

She shook her head, but she managed to gather herself enough to turn to Graham. "Thank you for your assistance, Graham," she said, hiccupping out the words.

Philip peered over her head at his brother. "Do me a favor and find the Bow Street Runners and make sure they caught them both."

Graham practically leaped out of the door. "Nothing I would rather do. I might happen to lose control of one of my fists while I am talking to them, too." His brother winked at him and departed.

CHAPTER THIRTY

TO SARA'S SURPRISE, GRAHAM STUCK his head back in the door a moment after he'd taken his leave. "You're in luck, things are starting to move."

"I am taking Sara to the Ardleigh house. After you speak to the Runners, send Mother to the ducal carriage. Wait up for me." Philip waved his brother on.

Sara's sobs finally slowed enough for her to be able to speak properly. "Thank you, Philip. I was so frightened." The carriage had begun to move, but she barely noticed it. Her attention was fixed on Philip. On the familiar lines of his handsome face.

"So was I, my love. My heart was in my throat when I turned and saw you in their hands. The look in your eyes sliced me in two." He rubbed slow circles across her back and then gently took hold of her chin. "May I take a look?" He checked her face for bruises. "Are you in pain? I've never experienced such rage as when I saw him slap you."

"My arm is sore, but I'm all right. He wrenched my arm a few times, but I was so scared, I did not take much notice. It's sore now, though not intolerable." She managed a feeble smile as she gazed up into his eyes. They'd been warm before, but now there was something more there—a glimmer of strong emotion she couldn't properly interpret.

He kissed her forehead, her nose, and then her lips. "I love you, Sara. I have never experienced such a gut-wrenching episode in my life. I fear you have captured my heart completely."

"Oh, Philip!" She threw her one arm around his neck and hugged him. "I love you, too. I am so sorry for all the trouble I've caused you."

"You haven't caused me any trouble. Stinky and your deceased husband have caused both of us problems, but none of this is your fault." He brushed the back of his fingers across her cheek. "Hopefully, this is the end of it. Stinky should be apprehended by now and behind bars. I want you to be able to put this behind you."

Sara was elated. Was it true? Did he really love her? She had so hoped he would return her feelings one day, but she'd never imagined it would happen so soon. She stared at the man she loved. Rubbing her thumb across his bottom lip, she smiled and said, "Kiss me. I want to forget about what happened and just think about us."

Philip growled as his mouth descended on hers in a hot, possessive kiss. His tongue swept into her mouth, and soon Sara was lost to everything but Philip. She loved this man with all her heart. The kiss deepened as they reveled in the taste of each other.

Suddenly, the door of the carriage flew open. Sara jumped and turned to see Phoebe's wide eyes gaping at her. They had arrived already? She hadn't even noticed the carriage stopping.

"Gadzooks, Sara! Are you all right? We heard terrible stories about you being kidnapped and beaten. What happened? Get out of the cold and inside. Your Grace, do move her, please!" Phoebe fussed.

"Thanks to Philip and his brother, Lord Graham, I am safe. I may be a bit bruised, but I'll be fine in a couple of days." Philip set Sara down from the carriage as gently as if she were a china cup.

"Brentwood, you had a most exciting evening, I hear?" Ardleigh stood to the side of the door and ushered everyone inside.

They stood in the foyer, removing their wraps as the butlers and the footmen ran to do Phoebe's bidding. She ushered them into the sitting room and covered Sara's lap with a blanket. Philip sat next to her, wrapping his arm around her and pulling her in tight to warm her. He was much more comforting to her than the soft covering on her lap.

"Oh my word, Sara," Phoebe said, still standing. Her every feature spoke of agitation. What a dear, dear friend. "What more could happen to you? Ardleigh, how can this happen? This must stop!"

"Lady Ardleigh, please sit down," Philip said softly, although the lady began pacing instead. "Fortunately, my brother, Graham, came along at the right time and helped me stop the two men bent on kidnapping Sara. They should be in the hands of the Bow Street Runners as we speak. I sent Graham to follow up on it and report back to me. I'm hopeful this will be the last we hear of Stinky and his men. We have all had a terrible fright, but we should finally be able to put this matter behind us."

"Did they say anything to you, Sara?" Ardleigh asked, settling himself in a chair across from them. "Do you know what they want? They could not have expected you to have any money on you." Something about his manner told her he had his own suspicions, but she doubted he would tell her. In his way, he was as protective as Phoebe.

Sara glanced at Philip. "I...I remember some things Stinky said. The other man never spoke. Stinky was very angry with me."

"Why? Saints above, how could anyone be angry with you, Sara?" Phoebe stopped pacing long enough to ask her question.

"He was angry because I was with you." She turned to Philip again. "Because I told you about him." As she spoke, memories of the incident cascaded back into her mind. "I…I think he said something about selling me. Yes, that was it! He said he would be selling me to his boss!"

"Did he give you the name of his boss, Sara?" Philip asked, his tone tense. All three of them stared at her, awaiting her answer.

Her hands trembled. "No, I didn't hear a name. What could he have meant by that?" He'd said it with such menace. She glanced first at Philip, then at Ardleigh and Phoebe.

No one answered her. Phoebe's hand went to her throat. "What is it?" Sara looked Philip in the eye. "What does he intend to do to me? I don't understand what he was talking about."

Still, no one spoke.

"Philip?" Tears gathered in her eyes again.

"Here now, it really isn't pertinent, is it? The man has been apprehended. He will never bother you again." Philip held her hand and leaned over to brush a soft kiss on her brow.

Phoebe ran out of the room and reappeared quickly, holding something. "Sara, I can see your arm is bothering you."

"Yes, I confess it's starting to throb." She held it gingerly in her hand, pinching her fingers again in an effort to distract herself from the sharp pain. "I was jostled quite a bit." Her headache was also about to burst through her eyes. Perhaps some medication would help.

"Jostled?" Philip said. "That awful man wrenched and twisted it several times. I'm sorry not to have asked you about it sooner." He looked to Phoebe, his expression anxious. "What can we do for her?"

"Here, I brought the sleeping draught the doctor left for you last week," Phoebe said. "I think you should take a bit. Let me put a few drops in your tea." Phoebe took the cup of tea the butler had brought at her request, offering it to her, and stood by while Sara took a few sips.

"Thank you, Phoebe, for all your kindness. You and your husband have been wonderful to me." She placed the cup back on the side table. "Philip, I thank you for a lovely night at the opera. It was wonderful until the chaos outside."

The warmth and love—yes, love—in his eyes comforted her more than the draught in the tea. He got to his feet and offered Sara his arm, then proceeded to escort her to the stairway. He must have wanted to speak to her alone, for he waved Phoebe away. When he reached the bottom step, he turned Sara back to him.

"Please try to get some rest, even though this has all been so unsettling." He gave her a chaste kiss. "Remember I love you. If you need me, just send a messenger for me. I'll call on you tomorrow."

"Thank you for everything: the opera, the necklace, and for rescuing me. I love you, too." She glanced up at Philip. The look in his eyes was so comforting. Duncan had never looked at her in such a way.

"Bloody hell! How could such a thing happen?" Philip paced back and forth across his breakfast room as he spoke with his brothers the next morning.

Graham folded his arms across his chest. "I don't know, Philip. He was in the hands of the horse patrol when I last saw him. I don't know how they lost him. The one ran off before the patrol got there. I surely don't know how they could have lost the second one."

"What did he want with her anyway?" Ben flopped down into a chair.

"Sara said something about Stinky selling her, and I don't like the implications of that."

Ben glanced at Graham before shifting his gaze back to Philip. "Sell her for what? You just can't sell a member of the aristocracy."

"If you remember, she is no longer a member of the four hundred, thanks to her husband. She is a member of the working class," Philip barked.

"You don't have to yell at us," said Ben, raising his hands in surrender. "We didn't kidnap her. We're trying to help, remember? We're all on the same side here."

"I know, I am sorry. The thought of Sara being sold for prostitution is more than I can bear. I finally find the right woman, and she could be swept out from beneath me."

"Prostitution! Hell, are you out of your mind?" Ben bounded out of his chair.

"Right woman? Did I hear you correctly, Philip? Are you that besotted?" Graham asked with a smirk on his face. "Finally found the right one, did you? I can hardly blame you, the woman is gorgeous."

The sound of a throat clearing and a foot tapping interrupted them. All three brothers turned to see their mother standing in the doorway.

"If you please, keep your yelling contained. I do not care to have to be forced to explain such matters to your sister." The duchess used her best steely gaze to get her sons in line. "Kindly fill me in on everything, Philip, although do mind your language. There is noble blood in Lady Downey somewhere. Stop talking about her as if she were a slattern. I will not allow it."

Philip sat down across from his mother and reviewed the evening in detail.

Once he finished, she stood up with her hands on her hips. "What is your plan?" she asked with plenty of attitude.

"There is no plan, Mother. Sara is with the Ardleighs. She will be fine as long as she stays there. She was exhausted last night."

"Yes, but when she awakens? You need to inform her that the man is still out there."

"I'm not telling her anything. She needs to have a few days' rest without living in fear. She has been through a horrific experience, Mother, and I will not have her troubled. She needs time to heal."

His mother marched over and stood directly in front of him. "I know that, and I see you have developed strong feelings for her, but you cannot keep something so important from her."

Philip crossed his arms. "Please do not go to the Ardleighs and tell her. I will protect her from the truth for a few more days."

"And what if Lady Downey decides to return to her shop for some of her belongings? Or a dress she needs to finish? She's a conscientious person, mark my words, and she will feel compelled to finish her work."

"Don't be ridiculous! The woman had the fright of her life last night. She'll not be able to move from her bed, much less think about traveling anywhere. You should have seen how she was tossed and wrenched about. She is probably in agony this morning."

She shook her head. "Where did you get this ridiculous idea that women possess such frail constitutions? I didn't teach you that. It must have been your father."

His brow furrowed. Frail constitution? Sara certainly did not have a frail constitution. Was he treating her as such? Deuce it, no. Any woman would be upset by all that had happened in the past few days. Hellfire, in the past month! He wanted to protect her. That was all. He'd failed her before, but this time he would not. He couldn't handle watching her disappear in front of his eyes again.

He turned to his mother. "I understand your point, and I'll tell her. But I think she needs a day or two of peace.

Can you not grant me that? I do not want her bothered today."

"All right, Philip. Your ex-wife has finally released her hold on you, hasn't she?" She reached over and patted his hand. "It couldn't have happened at a better time. Lady Downey is everything you need, son." She smiled at her son as she strolled toward the kitchen. "That was quite a necklace you gave her, by the way. It truly was made for her."

Sara jerked up in bed as soon as she realized the sun was streaming through the windows. The quick movement sent a wave of pain through her. Moving her legs to the side of the bed, she supported her broken fingers and clenched her teeth, determined to stand. Fighting the queasiness in her belly, she washed up quickly and smoothed her hair.

Phoebe's maid entered as she searched for something to wear.

"My lady! Oh my. No. Lady Ardleigh said you mustn't get out of bed. Please! Let me help you back into bed." She wrung her hands, bustling behind Sara.

Sara shook her head. "I'm sorry, but there's something I must do. Please help me get dressed. I must go to my shop."

CHAPTER THIRTY-ONE

SARA STOOD BACK AS FREDERICK opened her shop door. "I don't know, Lady Downey. I still think Lady Ardleigh will be furious with me for taking you out. I don't know why they had to leave so early this morning. We probably ought to have waited for them to return."

They'd apparently gone off to meet the duke, which had left Sara a little miffed. Why hadn't he asked her to come?

"Frederick, I promise not to say a word to the Ardleighs. But now that Stinky has been apprehended and is no longer a threat to me, I must reclaim a few of my possessions."

She tiptoed through the door and stopped, staring at the havoc Miranda Montrose had wreaked on her shop. She couldn't stop herself from running her fingers through the fabric of each ruined gown. Why? What had possessed the woman? She supposed jealousy compelled people to do terrible things, but to threaten someone with a knife? Tear her gowns to shreds?

Pity was the only emotion she could summon for Miranda Montrose. All the damage she'd done hadn't brought the duke back to her.

It felt strange to be back here, ominous, but Stinky's words had motivated her. He'd threatened to burn her shop down, and while he was currently in custody, his threat had reminded her of the one irreplaceable thing hidden in her shop.

Her mother's reticule.

She had hoped Ardleigh or Phoebe would be available

to go along with her, but perhaps it was best that they'd been away. They might have attempted to stop her, and she needed to protect the bag. It was the only memento she had from her mother. Besides, the task would only take a matter of minutes. She would leave as soon as she gathered a few of her things and the reticule.

She made her way up the narrow staircase slowly so as not to jar her arm. She filled a small bag of her personal things along with some night clothes and packed her four favorite day dresses. As she made her way down the stairs, she called for Frederick to help her.

He appeared quickly, red-faced. "Please hurry, my lady. I will not relax until I return you to the carriage."

"I'm almost done. Here, please take this bag out, and I will give you one other sack of dresses to bring." Frederick threw the bag into the carriage and returned quickly. Sara gazed at her dresses. She reached for a pale blue silk gown and a light peach satin trimmed with ribbons and lace around the neckline. "Here, Frederick, if you could arrange these two nicely in the carriage, I will grab my mother's bag and be right behind you. Forget the sack, perhaps we can take them without wrinkling them too much."

She sighed as she found her mother's bag. Miranda had not touched it, thank goodness. She hugged it close to her chest and willed herself not to cry over it. A noise startled her from behind and she turned. Sharp pain erupted in her head before she collapsed into a world of darkness.

Sara opened her eyes and stared at a pile of garbage directly in front of her nose. Peering at her surroundings, she realized she was lying in the alley behind her shop with a cloth stuffed in her mouth. Her sense of smell told her Stinky was not far. The muttering of his voice reached her ears just as she realized he was busy tying her legs together. How could this be happening to her again? Wasn't he supposed to be with the horse patrol? She attempted to yell but found a knife at her throat in an instant.

"Close your mouth, missy, or I'll gut you right here and leave you. You are proving to be almost too much trouble for me. Almost isn't enough to stop ol' Harry, though. No, sir. My boss promised me more money once he got a look at ya. Too bad I haven't the time to sample you meself first." He tugged on the rope securing her legs and dragged her closer to a wagon.

Her head pounded worse than ever, if that were possible. Thinking she heard a voice, she held her breath, hoping help was near. She noticed her back door still slightly ajar, so she stilled in the hopes someone might see her.

An authoritative voice rang out from the front of the shop, unmistakable. It could only be the duchess. She looked about for Stinky, but he had disappeared.

"Please tell me your purpose here, young man."

Frederick hastened to answer. "Oh, Your Grace, Lady Downey wanted to retrieve her mother's bag. She gathered up some things and I settled them in the carriage. She will be right out. I promise to take her straight home."

Sara sighed in relief as she heard the dowager step inside the shop. She would be saved again.

"Sara? Where are you?"

Sara could hear the duchess moving toward her. She tried to yell again, but the gag was too tight. Not a single sound got out. Stinky returned moments later, brandishing his knife. In two quick movements, he hoisted her up over his shoulder and then tossed her in the back of a wagon.

Stinky lowered his face to hers, his stench nearly choking her. "There'll be no more getting away from me this time. Perhaps I'll even have ya before I'm done. Got your nose up in the air and think you're better than me? Well, we'll see." Covering her with a coarse blanket, he climbed up in the box and snapped the reins. Sara kicked but to no avail. The jarring motion inflamed her headache, so she closed her eyes in frustration, thinking of Philip.

The dowager rushed into the dayroom where Philip and the Ardleighs planned their attack against Stinky. Her bones were getting old, but she could still move quickly when necessary.

The butler chased along behind her. "Your Grace, please be careful. Do not hurt yourself."

She marched into the middle of their conversation, dropped Sara's mother's bag onto the tabletop and said, "When will you ever learn to listen to me, Philip? This is all that is left of Sara."

Philip bolted out of his seat and held the reticule up. "What is this? I've never seen it before. And what the bloody hell does that mean?"

Phoebe let out a little scream, reaching for the bag and clutching it to her chest when Philip gave it to her. "This belonged to Sara's mother. She treasured it. She must have returned to the shop to get it. Is that where you found it, Your Grace?"

"I noticed Frederick was there with his carriage, so I stopped to see what he was doing. He said he was waiting for Sara, but when I stepped inside, this was on the floor. Clearly didn't belong there. And something else was amiss…"

Even now, the memory filled her with distaste.

Philip bolted out of his seat. "What, Mother? Please do tell!"

"There was a foul odor throughout the entire place. I called out, but no one answered."

Philip muttered one word before he bounded out of the

room.

"Stinky."

Sara awoke to find her gag had been removed at least, and the softness under her told her she was in a bed and not a wagon. But that was where the good news ended. Both of her feet and her right arm were bound to the bedposts. She heard two voices conversing at the far side of the room.

"What the hell made you bring her here? I don't want her," a woman said.

The man who answered her was obviously Stinky, although she dared not move her head to check. "Your boss man said he would pay me good money for her. She kicks and fights like a cat, that one. She's a mean one."

"Get her out. She's been seen with the Duke of Brentwood. She'll bring trouble down on us, she will. You have to get rid of her."

"Get rid of her? She's a beauty. Once your boss breaks her, she'll make you a lot of money. She's got nice titties, too, even through her clothes. I grabbed a quick feel on the way over."

She heard a resounding slap.

"What was that for?" Stinky asked, his tone an obnoxious whine.

"I told you not to touch the merchandise. You know how the man is. He doesn't want no used goods. Keep your hands off her."

Her eyes teared up as she listened. She knew she had to keep control and not let them know she was awake.

The woman spoke again with a vicious tone as she began to pace in front of the bed, her steps grating on Sara's nerves. "You're not wrong, you fool. She *is* a beauty, and that is exactly why the duke will come looking for her.

You have to get her out of here before it's too late, Stubby."

Stubby? His name was Stubby? Probably for his teeth. She gazed around the room as much as possible without moving her head. Although she could not see much from her vantage point, the walls were covered in gaudy red paper-hangings, bedecked with two paintings of nude figures in obscene positions. She was on a large four-poster bed with a perfumed-soaked coverlet and a mirror above the bed.

Reality slowly made its way through the fog in her brain. Surely, she couldn't be where she thought she was… She stole a quick peek at the woman talking to Stinky. Neither of them glanced her way, thankfully. She was a dark-haired woman with a voluptuous bosom. Her breasts threatened to spill out her clothing, her hair was piled artfully atop her head, and she carried a whip. A whip?

This cannot be. Please, God, don't let this be what I'm thinking.

Her pulse sped up at the mere thought. She was in a house of prostitution. It had to be. The woman must be the madam of the place. Stinky wanted to sell her to the owner so she could whore for him. That word—prostitution—reverberated in her brain. They were going to force her to prostitute? How was that possible?

She forced herself to shut her eyes and picture Philip. He smiled at her, telling her how much he loved her, how he would protect her. He would save her, wouldn't he?

But what if he didn't arrive in time? What if he couldn't find her?

No, she had to figure out a way to save herself.

"And what are we going to do with a strumpet with a broken arm, Stubby? It would tend to get in the way of certain positions."

"It ain't broken, just her fingers. Her mouth still works, don't it? I'll make her earn her keep. She owes me for all the trouble she's caused me, that one."

"If you take that smelly thing out of your pants in front of me, I will cut it off." The whip snapped in the air. "You ought to take a bath on occasion. Your smell is disgusting."

Stinky ran his fingers across the stubble on his chin before spitting into the spittoon in the corner. "Bring me to the boss. I brought him a prime piece of flesh, and I expect to be paid. I want to see him now, before she wakes up."

"Fine, I'll take you. Just so you will believe me and get her out of here." They disappeared out the door and slammed it shut with a clatter.

Sara knew it was her only chance to escape. As soon as they left the room, she tugged at her bindings with all her strength, but to no avail. Her captors were quite adept at tying knots. Glancing at herself in the mirror overhead, she was horrified when she noticed the large bump on the side of her head and the crusted blood matted in her hair. She wanted to cry but was afraid to make a sound.

A soft sound from the corner of the room put her on high alert. Perhaps it was the door opening again. Closing her eyes, she pretended to be asleep, but her heart was thundering in her chest. She had to do something. She had to get out.

"Lady, hey lady, here." She opened her eyes as someone gently jostled her shoulder. A fair-haired young girl glanced down at her, freckles dancing across the bridge of her nose. At her age, she should be attending her first come-out parties.

"Drink this. Who knows how long they will keep you tied up." She offered her a bit of tea. Sara lifted her head to take a sip, alarmed by how much energy it took to do so.

"Please help me. Untie me. I have to get away," she begged the young girl. "I don't belong here. I was kidnapped. I don't even know where I am."

"Shhhh! Not too loud. I don't know when they'll be

back. You are in the House of Candie's Sweet Treats. I
think you can guess what I am and what kind of treats we
are. No, you didn't belong here, but now you do. Once
Stubby brings you here, there is no way out."

"But there has to be. Please help me. I will pay you in
silver if you help me or get a message to the Duke of
Brentwood. Or the Earl of Ardleigh. Please! I cannot stay
here," she pleaded. The girl had to believe her.

"He hurt you pretty bad. What's your name?" the young
girl asked.

"Sara, Lady Sara Downey. I promise to pay you well if
you help me."

"I can't release you," the girl said solemnly. "They will
kill me if I help you. They have done it before. Well, actually, they just broke Anna's leg, and Becky was beaten so
badly she couldn't walk. And poor Marielle, they knocked
all her teeth out."

Sara's mind raced in a thousand directions. Her bindings constricted as she talked. Only now did the reality
of her helplessness dawn on her. "Please help me. I won't
prostitute myself for them. I cannot. That is an impossible thought. Oh my word, how could this happen?" Panic
nauseated her as she tugged and tugged at her bindings.

"That's where a lot of dollymops come from. Candie's
boss has a couple of guys who do the kidnapping for
him. You're stuck here. No one will help you now. I'm
sorry for it. I doubt it will make you feel any better, but I
understand. A month after they kidnapped me, I saw my
pa on the street. I ran to him, I couldn't help myself. Even
though the goon I was with came after me, I still had to
see my father. He turned away, I think because of what I
was wearing. I shamed him. I know that. But it wasn't my
fault. They said my pa bet on the horses and he lost. I was
his payment." The fair-haired girl's head dropped forward
and she stared at her hands. "I know it is hard to accept, but

once you step foot in this house, there isn't no duke that's gonna want you no more."

Sara stared at her in horror. She'd always thought prostitutes sought out their profession. That it was their choice. How could she have been so wrong? This poor girl had been forced into this by her own father? How would she have felt if her own father had done the same to her?

"They cannot do this to young women," she said. "They should be arrested. This is illegal." She tugged at her bindings again, frustrated and powerless.

The girl just shook her head sadly. "Don't fight them, or they will beat you even worse. He beats everyone into submission. Please, don't fight Candie either. She loves to use her whip."

There was no possibility that Sara could accept such a situation, although she didn't see the sense in saying so. Instead, she asked for another sip of tea. She had to keep her strength up. If she was going to fight, she had to be strong. "What's your name?" she asked as she sipped from the cup.

"Well, my real name is Alyssa, but they wouldn't let me keep that name. Here, I am Kitty. I hate it. I am no cat. You can call me Alyssa if you want. Just don't let anybody hear you. I think we could be friends. Most of the other girls here are mean." She smiled at Sara as she brushed the hair off her forehead.

"Alyssa, I am so sorry for what happened to you. But I can help you. I promise to help get you away if you help me. You don't want to stay here, do you?"

The girl shook her head. "I hate being here, but who would take me away? My own father turned his back on me. Some customers aren't so bad. And if you are real nice to the good ones, they come back to you regular and you don't have so many bad ones. Where would I go, anyway? I have no other family. And no man would ever marry me."

"You could work for me. I am a dressmaker. Someday, I will need someone to help me sew. I can teach you to sew if you don't know how. Just get me away from here, and I will help you."

Her eyes pleaded with Alyssa, but the girl jumped up, her eyes full of terror. "They are coming back. I have to go. I will think about it." With that, she turned and ran out the door.

A few minutes later, the door flew open and Stinky strode into the room mumbling.

"Ah, you're awake I see, you stupid bitch! You have caused me nothing but trouble. I will make you pay before this is over." He sneered with his stubby teeth showing as he groped her breast.

She screamed and tried to bite him, but he was too quick for her. He slapped her hard. "Shut up! You just had to talk to the duke in public, didn't ya? Well, if you think your friend is going to save you, yer wrong. Wait and see. I'll still get a prime price for you, even if I have to send you across the ocean. See if I don't. A little more medicine to put you to sleep is what you need. Who knows where you will be when you wake up." Stinky cackled as he grabbed a cup from the chest.

He pinched her nose in an attempt to force her mouth open for the medication. She tossed her head back and forth to prevent him from grabbing her face, but his hold was too strong, and he managed to pour a foul-tasting concoction down her throat. She tried to spit it out, but choked instead and had no choice but to swallow the bitter liquid. Her eyes filled with tears as her world blurred.

Powerless again.

CHAPTER THIRTY-TWO

PHILIP COULD NOT STOP PACING in his library. Gone? How could she be gone? Where the hell was she? He had to find her, he just had to. She was to be his wife, the mother of his children. He wanted her on his arm every day and in his bed every night so he could make slow passionate love to her, or maybe mad passionate love. He'd planned to propose to her, buy her a beautiful emerald ring.

This had turned into a nightmare.

"Brentwood, are you listening?" the Earl of Ardleigh yelled at him. "We've spoken with your mother and Frederick, but they are of no help. We must persist. Pay attention."

"What? Yes, of course I am listening. What was it you said?" He realized his thoughts had been far away. He chastised himself for not paying attention when it was most necessary. He would find her. London was about to be torn apart, brothel by brothel, game hell by game hell, until he found the woman he loved. It was almost dark and they hadn't started yet.

"I said I was outside the shop when she went in, Your Grace. I didn't follow her inside because Frederick was there. I never saw anyone go inside but the lady. When she didn't come out, I went around back in time to see a cart turning at the end of the road. I was on foot, so I could not catch them. But I managed to see where they were headed. I think he took her down near the brothels." The investigator nodded his head to let him know how proud he was of himself.

Philip wished to throttle the man.

"Near the brothels, is that all you have?" He stared at Ridley in disbelief. What, exactly, had he been paying him for? "You were supposed to protect her. I paid you money to watch the place. Did you not see him enter the building? Ridley, I had no idea you were so inept, and I'll see to it that you never get any work again."

The investigator opened his mouth as if to say something, then shut it, his cheeks turning red.

"Brentwood, at least we have something to go on. This is a huge help to us." Ardleigh handed several coins over to the investigator.

"And do you recall, Ardleigh, how many brothels there are in London? It will take us days to search them all. They all have plenty of bully-boys to throw us out as well. I don't imagine too many of them will allow us to search the premises. The day is getting late. We need to make a plan and make haste." He ran a hand through his hair for the tenth time.

"I'll stay and help. I feel responsible," Ridley said, shuffling from one foot to the other with his hands in his pockets. "I...I didn't think anything could happen with Frederick in there with her. How could I have guessed someone would spirit her away like that? I'll go to the brothels with you."

"Fine. We could use everyone's help," Graham said. "We need to divide up. There are six of us now. Philip, they won't dare touch you or the earl. We can split into three groups—some of us can go in the front while the rest sneak in through the back."

"Adam is definitely going with me. You know the area the best. Who ever thought all your rakehelling would prove helpful one day?" Philip drawled.

Adam grinned. "I am happy to help."

Philip rolled his eyes. "We need to get going. Get your pistols."

Stevens, his butler, stuck his head in the door. "Your Grace, Lady Downey is quite a graceful lady. Eli, Charles and I would all like to help find her. We can check the streets while you are inside."

Philip nodded to his butler. Sara had apparently made friends in his household, although that surprised him not at all. How could anyone not like her? She had a heart of gold and her smile lit up any room. "Thank you, Stevens, but I will need you to stay here with the women. Six of us should do it for now. We'll take two vehicles, the phaeton and the carriage. Let's hurry. We have no time to waste."

As his brothers gathered their weapons, Philip turned to Stevens. "Send a messenger to the horse patrol. We could use some extra help in the area."

"Yes, Your Grace. Consider it done." Stevens held the door as the group left.

The dowager duchess stood in the doorway as they exited. "Do be quick about it, Philip. The longer she is out there, the worse her chances are."

Sara awoke in a carriage, gagged, with her feet bound together. Her good hand was bound to her broken one in front. Every jarring bounce sent a jolt of unbearable pain through her. Stinky had to be nearby as the stench was suffocating. After a short ride, they rolled to a stop, and Stinky jumped out without a comment.

"I will be right back, don't let anyone inside. You know I will pay you well for keeping your yap shut," Stinky said to his driver before she heard the sharp click of his heels on the cobblestones.

Philip, where are you? Please find me. I will never put myself at risk again. I thought he was in Newgate. A single tear ran down the side of her face. How could she have known he was free?

Ultimately, it didn't matter. What mattered was that Stinky had her right where he wanted her. The smallest movement caused excruciating pain in her injured fingers and arm. Exhaustion threatened to overtake her. How much more could she endure?

Just like before, she heard her father's voice.

Stay strong, my Sara.

Stinky had given her a strong medicine, and she struggled to stay awake. A strange sound met her ears, a lulling sound, and after a time she realized what she was hearing. Waves slapping against wood. She heard men shouting, too, along with loud banging noises as if they were moving things or stacking large objects. Could she be near the harbor? Were they loading a large ship?

The door jerked open, and two men entered the carriage. Sara lifted her gaze in the hopes of seeing a familiar face. Unfortunately, the only face she recognized was Stinky's. The other man was a stranger.

"She is a beauty, my lord, and she is feisty, too. She will give you a good ride, I think. You won't find many better than this one."

"Shut up, fool, and take yourself outside while I inspect the merchandise. I cannot tolerate your stench." The man's fingers rubbed under his nostrils.

"Fine, but not a sterling under three hundred pounds for her. She is prime flesh. Yes, sir, she is. Check out that skin of hers."

"Get out, I said!" The man practically shoved Stinky out the door, slamming it behind him.

Sara stared up into a pair of cruel eyes. His hair was blond, rather long, but it was immaculately styled, not a single hair astray. He had on a ruffled shirt with a plum velvet jacket. Numerous large jewels adorned his fingers. A dandy? Isn't that what they called men like this?

He ran his finger down her cheek. She pulled back in revulsion. His touch roiled her insides.

"Oh, you are a spirited thing, aren't you?" He tugged her gag off.

"I want to see your teeth, smile for me." He held her face on both sides. His hands were soft and smelled like raw fish.

She attempted to bite him.

He grabbed her broken finger and twisted it, his expression not changing with the act of cruelty. "Here now, we shan't act like that again, shall we?"

She shrieked but stilled instantly as the pain ricocheted to her shoulder and her head at the same time. She closed her eyes so she wouldn't see the pleasure he gained from tormenting her.

"Ah, lovey, you are a pretty one. I might just have to have you, in every way I can think of." He chuckled as he ran his hand up under her skirt to her bottom. "Oh, such long slender legs, too. Imagine what I could do with those."

Sara bucked in revulsion.

He leaned into her with a rabid grin. "You think you are too good for me? We will see about that. You will learn to never look at me like that again."

He reached down and twisted her breast. "Nice tits, too. I will so enjoy breaking you." He tied the gag back on her before he reached down and twisted her nipple. She groaned in pain.

"Don't worry, my dear. It won't be long before you will feel my cock inside you, in so many places." He licked the side of her face before he departed. Her bound hands prevented her from wiping her face, but wiping it would not be enough. She would have to wash a hundred times to feel clean.

"One hundred pounds, my friend. I will have to beat her to get her to do my bidding."

Stinky's agitated voice reached her ears. "She is not going for anything under two hundred pounds. She's prime, she is."

"Where did you find her?"

"She's a widow, a dressmaker. She has no family. Gel was fool enough to live in her shop alone at night. No one will come for her. You won't find one that beautiful inside a brothel and you know it."

Sara's stomach churned as the bartering continued between the two men.

"All right, get her to my cabin before the ship sails, and I will give you one hundred and fifty pounds. Take it or leave it."

A ship! She was going to be put on a ship! Philip could never save her if it set sail. How many countries could he possibly search?

Hot tears burned her eyes. The futility of her situation overwhelmed her, and she couldn't stop thinking about what Stinky had said. He'd been able to do this simply because she'd lived alone. How could that be? A woman could just be kidnapped and sold into slavery? Her dreams of a wonderful life with Philip St. James had just turned to a complete nightmare.

Oh, Philip! Please don't give up. Search for me. I love you.

Philip's nerves were about to totally unravel. How many courtesans had he talked to? Adam had searched dozens of rooms, and they had questioned many, many women, but to no avail. He hoped Ardleigh was having better luck.

This was the last one on this street. He and Adam strode in through the front door. The madam greeted him quickly.

"Why, Your Grace. How pleased we are to have you.

How can I help you? Come see all my lovely girls."

Philip and Adam followed the woman into a bawdy tavern room where several courtesans consorted with a few customers. He searched the room for rich, chestnut locks, but his love was not there. He shook his head.

"None you like here? Follow me and see our specials in the back." The woman leaned toward him to give him an ample view of her bosom, nipples included. "This is where I keep all my new ones, all the young ones, the little touched, the most beautiful. I am sure you will find one that meets your needs in this room."

If he'd had any food in his stomach, he would have lost it. At the same time, he hoped Sara sat in the room of "specials," although the thought of any other man touching her made him see red. If he found her on the lap of another man, he would surely kill the scum, but not before putting his fist in his face.

Adam and Philip stepped into the room. Six women of varying sizes and ages lounged inside. No Sara. His heart fell again. They were running out of options. The madam droned on as he rubbed his hand on his forehead, overcome with despair. Adam quickly sauntered over to a petite blonde. Before Philip could open his mouth, Adam disappeared behind a curtain with her. He turned to give Philip a wink before exiting the room. With any luck, his brother intended to question the girl rather than sample her wares.

"Surely one of these lovelies is to your liking, Your Grace?"

Philip shook his head and turned to leave, but then turned back to the madam. He should at least ask her. "The woman I am looking for is not here. My fiancée was kidnapped. I beg you." He described Sara. "I will pay you a large sum of money if you have any information about her."

"She is a lucky woman, Your Grace. Clearly, you are in love with her. I wish I could help you, but I don't know anything about such a woman."

Philip left the establishment, his shoulders sagging. Adam could catch up with him, he could not bear to be inside for a moment longer. Especially not with the proprietress, Candie, staring at him as if he were the sweet treat.

CHAPTER THIRTY-THREE

PHILIP WAS ABOUT TO CLIMB into the carriage when he saw Ardleigh and Graham headed toward him. He strode over to their phaeton to hear the bad news. The fact that they were alone spoke for itself.

"Any luck, gentlemen?" he kept his voice low so as not to alert anyone within listening range.

"No, sorry," Graham said. "We searched many a room and talked to several of the patrons. We even bribed a couple of footpads in the street. No one has seen anything. She has simply disappeared."

"I take it you haven't had any luck either?" Ardleigh asked.

"Nothing. I can't believe it. There is no sign of her or Stinky anywhere." He dug his boot into the dirt in the ground. What else could they do? Desperation clawed at him, but he would not give up. He would find her. Whatever it took.

"What's next, Brentwood? Any suggestions?" Ardleigh sounded as hopeless as he felt.

"We'll reconvene at my house and decide on our next steps. Perhaps the others have found something." Philip turned around slowly and headed back to his carriage. He opened the door and climbed in.

He found himself staring at Adam and the petite blonde, cuddled up in the back.

"Bloody hell, Adam! Can't you keep it in your pants at all?"

Adam's face broke into a huge grin. "Tell him, Alyssa."

The petite blonde looked up at Philip and said, "I know where your lady is, Your Grace."

Sara's head banged against the inside of the trunk she was in. Every inch of her body would be bruised if she ever escaped her plight. Stinky had helped her out of the carriage, briefly, so that she might relieve herself. Her bladder had been ready to burst after all the bouncing in the carriage. He'd insisted on holding her while she squatted, which had disgusted her, but she'd decided to be agreeable. Thank goodness for pantalets. It was better than lying in her own urine.

The moment she'd stood up, he had stuffed her into this trunk. She was on the move again and in an extremely painful position.

Hurry, Philip. Hurry.

Once Philip changed their plans, he sent a message to Ben and Ridley to meet them at the docks.

"Well, you see, whenever Stubby kidnaps somebody they don't like or a girl who might be too much trouble, they send Stubby down to the docks with 'em. I guess there are some men who pay lots of coin for a sweet-faced girl. They bring them across the seas to be sold in other countries in the Far East." Alyssa's curls bounced as they rode toward the docks. "They always threaten to take us there if we are bad." Her gaze dropped to the floor.

"How did you get her name?" Philip asked. He needed to know if he could trust her.

"She told me. I found her in a room tied to all the bedposts. Stinky and Candie had just left. Sara, Lady Downey, she said she could send me to a duke and an earl, and they would pay me good money to help her. I hate it there, but

I didn't want my legs broken. I didn't want her to be hurt either. So when they took her away, and you showed up... Well, it made me think I might take a chance. Sara said she would hire me to sew for her. I would be happy to work for a lady like her. Or to do anything, really. I've only been there a short time, you know. Ever since my father sold me 'cause he lost on the horses. And he won't take me back. I seen it in his eyes; he won't even look at me now. He's ashamed of me." Tears filled the girl's eyes as she talked. She brushed them away forcefully.

Philip could not believe his ears. He let her babble on because he simply couldn't speak. Such heartless cruelty. He was sick to his stomach at the prospect of getting to the wharf too late or not being able to find Sara in time. How could he possibly find the correct ship quickly enough? They were so close to finding her, but it still might not be enough.

"Don't worry, Miss Alyssa." Adam rubbed her arms to comfort her. "I'm not sure Sara will want her shop open, but either way, we'll help you find another job. What can you do?"

"Adam!" he barked.

"What? Perhaps she can bake or sew or clean. I'm sure Mother could find a place for her. She is always looking for good servants."

"I used to bake a lot of pies and pastries for my church. The reverend, he loved my apple pies and strawberry tarts."

"There you go, Philip. She can bake. We will bring you to see our mother right after we find Lady Downey."

"Do you think she will like me?" Alyssa stared up at Adam with wide eyes.

"Surely she will," he said, tightening his grip around her shoulder.

"Alyssa, I am sure our mother will take care of you," Philip said. "We need you to help us now, though. Can you think of any more details about the carriage Stubby is driving? Or which ship Sara could be in?"

Alyssa stared at the roof for a second, "I have seen the carriage, but I can't remember…"

"Well, think! We need to know now!" he ordered.

Alyssa jumped in her seat and clung to Adam, who glared at him. "I don't think you are helping, Philip."

"Forgive me, Alyssa, I am distraught. Please try to think."

"Yes, Your Grace, I am trying my best." She fingered her skirt as she spoke, her eyes darting from Adam to Philip.

Fortunately, Ardleigh and Graham had followed them in their change of course. When both carriages met at the docks, they had a quick meeting and split into pairs again to attempt to ferret out any information from any locals. After fifteen minutes, they regrouped.

"Nobody is saying anything, Brentwood," Ardleigh said. "They are all tight-lipped. Doesn't matter how much money I show. The area is too large. There are too many ships. We need a better plan." The man's exasperation was clear to everyone.

"We *will* find her. Ridley, you and Ben hit a couple of the local taverns and see what you can find out. Graham, find the shipping office and see which ones are leaving in the next twenty-four hours, and where they're going. Take Ardleigh with you. Adam and I are headed toward the end of the docks. We will work our way in. Meet back here in thirty minutes."

The two of them climbed back into the carriage, which Alyssa had not left, and headed down to the end of the wharf. He couldn't believe the cacophony of voices, peddlers, shipmen. It would be so easy to get lost in this crowd—a thought that sent a shock of fear down his back. After disembarking, they headed toward the last dock. There were two ships loading. The larger one at the end appeared to be a freighter.

"Wait, please, stop for a moment!" Alyssa had her head tipped toward the sky and was slowly turning in a circle, looking around.

Philip's impatience got the best of him. "What? What is it, Alyssa?"

"Something, I don't know for sure." Her gaze roamed the area as she spoke.

"There!" She pointed to an old carriage, hidden by two ramshackle buildings. "Right there, that's it. That's Stubby's carriage!"

Philip took off toward the carriage. He flung the door open and quickly lumbered two steps back, covering his nose. "Bloody hell, that man rots!" He forced himself to search the interior but found nothing.

"That's how I knew he was nearby. I caught his smell in the wind." Alyssa nodded her head proudly.

"Well done, Alyssa, but there's no one inside." Philip turned and searched the docks for anyone resembling Stinky or Sara. "But they can't be far."

Graham came barreling down the street, yelling to them as he went. "Philip, the only two ships leaving"—he stopped to catch his breath—"are those two."

Ardleigh caught up with them, the other three not far behind.

"Great." Philip smiled. He sensed they were close now. "Then we only have two ships to search. Adam, take Alyssa back to our carriage. I don't want Stinky to see her. Graham, you and Ben stay here with Ardleigh. Keep your eye on everything and everyone coming and going from those two ships. Ridley, you're with me."

Philip headed down to the end of the dock. The freighter was the larger of the two ships. The second one looked more like a privately owned pleasure vessel and sat opposite the freighter on the other side of the dock. He decided it was probably for a wealthy individual and so there wouldn't be many places to hide. They headed for the freighter. There had to be many places where someone could stow a prisoner on a freighter.

When they reached the end of the dock, he shouted to the captain of the ship to allow them aboard.

He was waved on, and with his hands fisted at his sides, Philip climbed to the gangway to board the ship. He would find her. He had to.

He loved Sara, he needed her, and his life would be nothing without her.

Sara was locked inside a large trunk, rolling on some kind of cart. She had a small source of light through two holes, but she couldn't see or hear anything. Once she was put on the boat, she probably would have no way out. She might never be free again.

This was her last chance. No matter how much pain it would cause, she tried her best to bounce in the trunk. If she could just rock it enough for someone to see it, maybe they'd free her. Maybe she'd be saved.

Before she could try again, her weight shifted as if she were being steered up a steep incline, probably onto the boat.

Philip shook hands with the captain of the ship and introduced himself. "I am looking for a beautiful young woman who has been kidnapped and brought to the docks to be sold. Have you seen anyone brought on board against their will?"

"Your Grace, I understand your plight and your urgency, but we would never allow anyone to bring someone aboard against their will." The man tugged on the collar around his neck. Sweat broke out on his brow. He was clearly nervous. Did he have something to hide, or did the line of questioning simply discomfit him?

"How many passengers do you have?" Philip asked.

"Less than ten and our accommodations are not comfortable. We deal mostly in trade."

"And do you trade humans, Captain?" His jaw came up a notch as he stared at the captain.

"No, sir, we don't. This is a legal operation. We follow all regulations. There is no young girl on this ship, I guarantee you."

Philip had to admit the man looked incensed at the mere suggestion. Would a guilty man be able to put on such a show?

"Do you mind if we search your cabins, Captain?"

"Yes, I do. You will only slow us down. We have to get moving. You have taken enough of my time already. Please remove yourselves from my ship." As he spoke, two burly men came up behind him.

Philip glanced at Ridley and turned to leave. He headed down the plank in time to see a man pushing a cart with a large trunk on it toward the smaller ship.

In the confines of the small box, Sara willed her body to calm. In order to survive this imprisonment, she needed to be calm, to be in control. Her tongue touched the fabric stuck in her mouth and she choked. *Ignore the sour-tasting gag. You are strong, you have value, you can do this. Your moment will arrive. You must be ready when it does.* The smell of dead fish assaulted the fine hairs in her nostrils. Rough movements jarred her senses again as her new prison bounced over what sounded like old rickety boards. How long could she endure her stifling prison?

Perhaps it was hopeless. She had been sold as if she were a piece of raw meat, and now was about to sail across the ocean. Philip would never find her. Never, ever, ever…

Her eyes closed as she fought for a very shallow breath. The next one was even shallower. Maybe it was time to stop fighting. Maybe this was it, where everything ended.

Her eyes flew open.

Philip! I love you. Don't give up on me. Please find me.

She kicked her legs as hard as she could. How she wished she could get this awful gag out of her mouth so she could shout his name out loud. Twisting and throwing her shoulders inside the small compartment, she rocked and rocked and rocked...

She rocked as hard as she could until the entire trunk swayed under her weight.

Philip!

He spun around to face the smaller boat behind him. Something bothered him about the man and his cargo. It didn't have anything to do with the man's face, which he couldn't see, so perhaps it was the way he was walking? He watched as the man turned and struggled to push the cart up the plank to the ship.

Then it dawned on him. The trunk on the cart was moving. Moving?

Sara?

He yanked his pistol out and bellowed at the man, "Stay where you are!"

Philip charged the man, Ridley following him. The man released the cart at once, turning and racing back up the dock as fast as he could.

"Stop!" Philip yelled. Stinky, it had to be, he was sure of it. The vile man paused for a moment to glance over his shoulder at them. Philip took aim and fired, intent on injuring him so he could not escape. Stinky yelled and grabbed the back of his leg.

He continued running, much slower due to the leg

injury.

Philip shouted out to his brother and Ardleigh, who were approaching the docks. "Stop him! He's the one!"

Stinky made it to the end of the dock and headed up the street, but when he saw the two men charging toward him, he changed direction abruptly, darting directly in the path of two grays pulling a carriage.

One of the grays bucked at the loud sound, but the beast couldn't pull away from the carriage. Philip, Graham, Ardleigh, and Ridley all watched as the horse reared up on its hind legs in fear. The animal's hooves crushed into Stinky and pinned him to the ground. The impact must have snapped his neck.

Philip didn't hesitate. He rushed back to the cart and moved the trunk carefully so he could open it.

All the while, he prayed.

Please, God, let her be in here, let her be alive. I promise to cherish her and love her for the rest of my life. You sent her to me. Please, let us carry out the plan You have for us. I love her!

He opened the trunk, and almost collapsed at what he found. Sara's beautiful green eyes stared up at him. She was contorted, dirty, tangled, clearly in pain, bruised—and the most beautiful sight he had ever been blessed to see. Philip had to restrain himself from shouting out his joy. His eyes searched hers as he yanked her gag off and helped her sit. Rather than cut her bindings immediately, he let her stretch out. She was clearly in pain from the position she had been forced into.

Framing her face with both hands, he kissed her lips softly. "I love you, Sara," he whispered. He held his forehead to hers and sighed, oblivious to everything around him but her, his life. He kissed the tears from her cheeks. "I am so sorry, so sorry. I will never let anything happen to you again." He fought his own tears, finally pulling back to look at her again, wanting to make sure she was truly all right.

Sara gazed up at him. "I knew you would find me, Philip. Thank you. Thank you for not giving up on me. I was so frightened."

"Where were they taking you? Do you know the man in that boat?"

She glanced over her shoulder just as the fair-haired dandy came onto the deck of his ship. His eyes widened at the sight of Philip. "Yes. He paid Stinky money for me. He was going to…"

"Never mind," he said at once. She'd suffered enough and didn't need to recount what the bastards had planned to do. Moving slowly, gently, he lifted her out of her prison and set her on the deck. "Pardon me," he whispered. "I promise to be right back."

Allowing the anger that had been building inside him all day to flare to life, he surged down the dock and jumped onto the dandy's boat. The man had disappeared, but unless he'd dived into the water, there was only one place he could be—in the living area beneath the deck. The small door was locked, but the duke gave it one powerful kick, then another. It burst open and he charged toward the man.

"You can't touch me! I'll destroy you!" the man shrieked.

Philip threw his fist into his face, a satisfying crunch ringing out at the same time as the bastard howled. He dragged him up out of the boat and onto the docks. Ardleigh was already making his way toward him, along with Ben and Graham.

Oddly enough, the boat he was on suddenly left the dock. He couldn't help but smile about that end.

"Escort this fool to the horse patrol," Philip said. "Have him arrested for attempted kidnapping. I'll fill out all the paperwork later."

A small scuffle followed, but the fair-haired man was too

upset about his broken nose to put up much of a fight. Philip's brothers and Ardleigh escorted him down the dock, taking him out of Sara's line of sight.

Philip lifted her gingerly in his arms, kissed the top of her head, and carried her down the dock toward the carriage. When they reached the carriage, Adam and Alyssa bolted out.

"You found her!" Alyssa exclaimed, her eyes bright with excitement.

"See, Alyssa, you did help us," Adam said, giving her a quick hug. "Come, we'll find another way out of here."

"Wait," Sara shouted. "Don't take her back! Philip, please do not let her go back there. It is a horrid place. She can work for me. Alyssa, thank you. Please, Adam, bring her to the Ardleighs. We will take care of her."

Philip kissed her head and said, "Don't worry, love, we will find a place for her."

Ridley helped him get Sara inside the carriage. After they cut her bindings, the investigator climbed up to the driver's seat. They were about to leave, when Graham and Ardleigh jumped in the back.

Philip glared at them both. He'd wanted to be alone with Sara, and they bloody well knew it.

"Sorry, Philip," Graham said with a shrug, "but Adam wanted to take the phaeton with Alyssa. Ben's driving."

"Just close the door. I want to get her home," Philip said.

As soon as Ardleigh got a good look at Sara, he lost all the color in his face. "Oh, my word."

"Damnation, Philip," Graham whispered.

Sara's limbs still looked unnaturally twisted. Her face bore black and blue marks, and she had a huge bump on her head. Philip tried to straighten her legs, but Sara moaned and pleaded with her eyes, "No, please, Philip. It hurts too much."

"Maybe it's best to let them release on their own, Brentwood," Ardleigh said softly.

Philip gently pressed Sara's head down against his shoulder. He didn't have the heart to see the pain in her face. "Sara, I think you need to move them yourself. Start with your toes and wiggle them slowly. Have you been bound for a long time?"

Her head nodded into his shoulder while her good hand clenched his shirt. Her injured arm and fingers had not moved yet. He noticed her fingers had a dusky, pale shade to them he didn't like. He rapped his knuckles on the roof to get Ridley to hurry, then attempted to support her legs without causing her any additional pain.

"When we get her to my place, I will summon the physician to help her," Ardleigh said. "We will take care of you, Sara. You need worry about nothing."

"She is not going with you. She is going to my place," Philip calmly stated.

"Bloody hell, no, Brentwood. That is improper and you know it."

"Ardleigh, you have no say. She is going home with me. We will be getting married soon enough. I have had enough of wondering what is to happen to her next. She stays with me. I will take care of her. You will have to shoot me to do otherwise."

"Sara, do you agree to this? If not, you may certainly return to my home. Sara?" Ardleigh waited for her answer.

She picked her head up just enough to nod her head in agreement. The pain in her eyes was enough to stop their arguing.

CHAPTER THIRTY-FOUR

P HILIP STEPPED INSIDE THE DOOR of Hearthstone Manor with Sara in his arms. His mother and Phoebe ran over to see how she fared.

He headed to the stairway, refusing to stop. He needed to get her to a comfortable bed as soon as possible. "Do not touch her, Mother. She is in a great deal of pain."

"Well, at least you have found her. Bring her up to the guest room, and I will help her get cleaned up." The dowager turned to give orders to the maids.

"No, I will take care of her. I want the bath filled in the duchess's room. She was bound for a long time, and I think the warm water will help her muscles to relax. I will tend her myself."

"Certainly not, Philip." His mother's hands went to her hips as she stared at her son. "No one has been in that room since Caroline left. It is meant for your wife. What you ask is totally improper."

"You are mistaken, Mother, I did not ask." He looked over her head and addressed the maids. "I want steaming hot water brought to the duchess's dressing room along with tea and biscuits, please, and some cheese and fruit."

Before he started up the stairs, he turned to his mother. "My apologies for being short with you, Mother, but Lady Downey is a widow not a young girl. Our staff will watch their tongues or lose their positions, as you know. It would be here or Ardleigh's place, and I would prefer to keep an eye on her myself. Please send a message to the bishop and see that the banns for our marriage are called on Sunday. Contact my solicitor and tell him I need a license. I will not wait long to make Lady Downey my wife."

Sara was still stunned from all the events that had taken place in the last twenty-four hours, but she could hardly tear her gaze from Philip as he gingerly set her in a soft chair in the dressing room. He was so careful and loving. Was this the same man she had yelled at in his townhouse? His eyes were so warm and full of love.

She massaged her legs to relieve the prickling feeling in her skin. Rubbing seemed to help, plus she wiggled and moved as much as she could. She hoped there had been no permanent damage.

Propping her arm, Philip knelt in front of her to plump pillows under her feet. When he finished, he stopped and gazed into her eyes.

"Forgive me for not doing this properly. Sara Downey, I love you with all my heart and I need you by my side forever. Will you do me the honor of becoming my wife?"

She blinked back hot tears. Had he really just proposed to her? She'd heard him mention marriage before, to the others, but she'd decided she must have been delirious. Was this really happening?

Realizing he was awaiting her response, she nodded her head slowly. "Yes, Philip, nothing would make me happier than to be your wife."

Sara reached for him with her one arm, and his lips settled on hers in a possessive kiss.

He pulled back and caressed her cheek. "When you were missing, I was so possessed with purpose. I have never had such a fright."

Eli and Charles arrived with buckets of hot water and dumped them into the large tub. Celia walked in and set down the tea tray she'd prepared.

"I will locate towels, Your Grace." She left briefly and returned with the towels and a robe. The men had already made another two trips with additional buckets of water. "Anything else I can do for you?"

"Thank you, Celia. Make sure that my mother has sent for the physician. Close the door on the way out and don't let anyone else disturb us."

As soon as the door closed behind the maid, Philip began undressing Sara, gently, slowly, careful not to cause further pain.

Her entire body blushed. "Philip, please. I am so dirty. I am sure the maid can help me. You needn't bother with me." She bowed her head in shame. This was not how she'd like him to see her.

"Bother? How can you say such a thing? You have been kidnapped, beaten, abused, and misused. Do you think I care about a little dirt? Please do not insult me, Sara."

He helped her into the steaming water. "Too hot, my love?"

She shook her head. "No, it feels wonderful." She eased her shoulders back to lean against the back of the tub and sighed deeply.

Philip soaped her feet and legs and then massaged her muscles slowly. He worked his way from each calf to her knees, kneading along the way. "Is this helping?"

"Yes, they are loosening up. You have a magic touch, Philip." She smiled at him. Then he touched her injured arm and she cringed. "That still hurts. Please be careful."

He helped wash and rinse her hair and then dried her off. Wrapping the thick white robe around her, he lifted her and set her on his lap.

"Do you want to tell me about everything?" he whispered, holding her close.

Slowly, Sara told him all that had happened. How she

had been struck in the head, tied up in a cart, tied to three bedposts, sold to a dandy, and finally shoved into a trunk. She told him about Alyssa and Candie and about the horrid man who had licked her face. The tears didn't erupt until nearly the end of the story, but when they did, they consumed her. She cried until sobs wracked her body and the only thing left was hiccups. Philip held her through it, running slow strokes across her back or kissing her brow.

When she finished, neither of them spoke for several minutes.

She pulled back and looked up at him. "Philip, where is Stinky now?"

"He's dead, sweet, and he will never bother you again. He ran in front of two horses and startled them. One horse broke his neck."

"Are you sure?" She swiped the remaining tears from her eyes.

"Yes. Graham and Ardleigh both witnessed it up close. If you wish, you can ask them yourself later."

A knock interrupted them. His mother announced the physician and waited for Philip to arrange Sara in bed before granting him entrance. Philip set Sara on her feet and held her to see if she could support her weight.

"Can you walk?" He held her hand as she balanced herself.

She took a step and glanced up at him. "I think so, it feels much better. Thank you." She couldn't stop herself from reaching up and caressing Philip's cheek. His blue eyes caught hers as she smiled.

"I do love you so, Philip."

She awoke in the middle of the night to her own screaming. Sitting up in bed, memories washed back through her, tormenting her, until she recalled that she was in the safety of Philip's manor. As promised, he had held her until she'd fallen asleep. He had then left her to return to his own bed, apparently.

She vaguely remembered something he'd whispered to her in the night. He'd said he didn't think it would be proper to stay with her, given his mother was down the hall, or had he used that as a reason to move to his own bed?

Perhaps he'd only proposed because she was so vulnerable. Now that the tragedy was over, had he realized he did not love her as he'd thought? After all, what could Philip see in her? She didn't have a dowry or any land to offer him. It certainly couldn't be her skills in the bedroom. Miranda Montrose surely knew more than she did. And Duncan had always told her she was timid and boring and lackluster.

Philip appeared in the doorway between their rooms. She hoped he wouldn't notice her tear-stained lashes. It was a wonder the poor man hadn't drowned in all the tears she had shed after her bath. She would not cry again. Men did not care for tears.

But despite all her doubts and self-recrimination, she longed to be in his arms again. She wanted Philip next to her—every night. No better place on earth existed for her than in his arms.

"Is everything all right, Sara? I thought I heard you."

"Just a nightmare. Thank you, I'm fine." She pulled up her blanket. "I'm sorry if I woke you."

Her husband-to-be stood there in his navy blue robe. His hair was tousled and it made him look even more handsome. She couldn't tear her eyes away from the curly dark hair on his chest, remembering how the hairs felt in her fingers and against her nipples. She tried to recall exactly how it thinned around his waist and met up with the darker mat around his…

"Sara?"

"Yes?" She jerked her eyes back up to his face.

"Are you all right?"

"Yes, of course, I am fine."

He said, "You know, I've been thinking. We haven't discussed your business at all."

Her heart leapt into her throat. Surely he would tell her she would have to close the shop. She'd expected as much, but it would hurt to leave it behind. She loved designing.

"I know this will shock many people," he said, looking into her eyes, "but I know your work is important to you. You're talented, and I would like to see you continue your designs. Will you agree to hire a few seamstresses to sew the gowns so that you'll have some time for your husband?"

Her heart leapt into her throat. She'd never thought it possible that she might get to have both Philip and the shop. "I would love to handle it that way. I could use the help, for certain. Thank you, Philip."

He turned to make his way back to bed.

"Philip?" Her hand reached out as if to touch him.

"Yes?" He stuck his head back in the door.

"Are you sure?" Her voice wavered as she spoke, but she didn't look away from him.

"Am I sure about what?"

She cleared her throat as if to gain the courage to speak her thoughts. "Are you sure about us?"

He stepped into the room and leaned his tall, muscular frame against the doorway. His arms crossed in front of him as a slow smile crept across his face.

"You mean, am I sure that I love you?" His arms dropped to his sides as he sauntered her way. "Or am I sure that I want to marry you?"

She watched him, spellbound, as he continued to stroll toward her.

"Or am I sure that I want you more than anything right

now?"

She swallowed as she noticed his arousal beginning to separate his robe. She forced her gaze back to his face.

"Yes." She could feel her blush make its way from her face to her breasts and finally settle as a wash of heat between her thighs.

"Which one are you saying yes to, sweet?" He sat on the side of the bed and set his arms on either side of her before he leaned in to taste her lips.

She stared up at him. "Are you sure you won't change your mind? You know I have no dowry or land. You know I am not as exciting as some of the other women in the *ton*, or as interesting, or as beautiful…" She looked down at her hands.

Philip reached for her chin and lifted it gently until their eyes met. She tried to hide her insecurities but failed miserably. The coverlet fisted even tighter in her hand as she tugged it up to hide herself from him.

"No, sweet, please do not hide from me. You are much too beautiful."

Her eyebrows shot up in surprise. Beautiful? Did he really think she was beautiful?

"Ah, I see you don't believe me. I shall have to convince you then, shan't I?" His eyes sparkled.

Tugging on the coverlet, he removed it before removing her gown.

He kissed her deeply on the mouth. When he pulled back, he said, "I see there are a few things I need to tell you. Will you lie back and listen to me, Sara?"

She nodded as she did as he asked, settling back into the soft mattress.

"I think, perhaps, I need to tell you exactly why I love you. You had a bastard of a first husband who put some very wrong ideas in your mind. I intend to set them straight."

He started at her feet, kissing her ankle and slowly dusting kisses up the outside of her leg as he talked. "The first time I saw you, your beauty almost left me speechless. All I could imagine were these long legs wrapped around me in ecstasy. What beautiful legs you are gifted with." He kissed up the outside of her other leg. "Your green eyes enchanted me. You made clothes for the orphans, you impressed my mother, and mind you, that is not an easy thing to do." His tongue made its way across the middle of her belly, stopping briefly to circle her navel. She closed her eyes in blissful surrender to his sweet torture. She grabbed a handful of his hair.

"Oh, not yet, love, I am far from finished," he said as he pulled her hand away from him. "You are the only woman I know who would turn down a handful of gems because her morality wouldn't allow her to keep them."

He made his way across her belly and up to her nipple. "You have the most perfect breasts I have ever had the pleasure to behold." He suckled her deeply until she cried out.

"You stand in the middle of the *ton* like a goddess with her head held high, no matter what they are saying about you." He stroked his tongue up between the valley of her breasts all the way to her collarbone and nibbled.

"You have the stamina and strength of the strongest man I have ever met." He kissed a trail up her neck. "Had you not rocked that trunk, I may never have found you. You are a fighter to the bitter end." Kissing her tenderly on the mouth, he whispered, "You bear pain as if it is nothing."

Kissing her forehead with both hands cupping her cheeks, he added, "You have the intelligence to run your own business, one profitable enough you were able to pay off most of your husband's debts."

He straightened up on his knees and tossed his robe aside. Sara stared at his naked beauty. His arousal caused her mouth to go dry instantly, but he wasn't finished yet.

Suckling her other breast, he said, "You were in extreme pain after I pulled you out of that trunk, yet the foremost thought in your mind was the slight girl from the brothel who helped you."

He leaned down and started on the inside of her leg, kissing his way up to her damp curls. "But what I love most about you is how you react to my touches, and how I can make you writhe beneath me." His tongue found her nub and he tasted her heat. Her moans of ecstasy brought him back up to her lips to capture her sounds of joy. He pulled himself up to balance his weight on his elbows, then settled between her thighs and teased her slick entrance with his tip.

"Now do you believe that I love you, Sara?"

"Yes, Philip. Please, I need you inside me. I want you now." Spreading her thighs for him, she arched toward him, needing his fullness inside her. She blushed at her wantonness but didn't stop. Reaching for him, she teased herself with his member until she could no longer hang onto him.

"Oh, Philip!" she cried as he entered her.

"And I so love how you call out my name." He smiled at her.

Philip lost complete control. He took one look at the passion in her eyes and grabbed her hips so he could bury himself deeper inside her.

"Am I hurting you, love?" he ground out between thrusts.

"No," she whispered. "I love how you feel inside me."

"Good, because there is no way in hell could I stop. You have no idea how good you feel."

He could tell he was about to explode, so he reached down between them and caressed her nub until he could feel her contractions around him. He swallowed her scream with a kiss and did his best to dull his own roar as they climaxed together.

He held himself on his elbows, cradling Sara's face in his hands. "I love you, Sara Downey, for who you are, and don't ever doubt it. I don't care about land or money. I want my wife to be intelligent, caring, compassionate, and passionate. You are all of those things, and I wish I could erase all the uncertainties caused by your foolish first husband. But you never have reason to doubt my love. I love you, I respect you, and I need you. Please be my wife."

"Oh, Philip! You make me so happy. I cannot think of anywhere I would rather be than in your arms."

He kissed her and rolled onto his side. "How can I help you get comfortable? I am not going back to my bed. I cannot be without you."

Sara squeezed in close to him and put her head on his shoulder. "I want to sleep here…every night."

She was asleep in seconds.

CHAPTER THIRTY-FIVE

Three weeks later

SARA STROLLED INTO PHOEBE'S MORNING room for breakfast. The wedding was not for another two weeks, and the dowager duchess had argued that it would be improper if Philip and Sara were to live together before then. Knowing the power of gossip, Sara had reluctantly agreed. She faced an uphill battle with the *ton* anyway, especially since many of the ladies were jealous of her for having "ensnared" the duke.

But despite their current living situation, they spent as much time together as possible. Philip had settled many of her fears. She knew he treasured her, and the way he looked at her—as if he wanted her nude instantly—made her feel beautiful. The mere thought of that look made her blush.

Her only disappointment was that she had been unable to find the beads to match her mother's bag. She would carry it on her wedding day anyway since it was so special to her, but the pattern was incomplete. The duchess and Phoebe had finally convinced her no one would notice.

"Good morning, Phoebe." Sara smiled at her friend as she filled her plate. She had woken up to find out she had her monthly courses, and it was as good a reason as any to eat heartily. Thankfully, she would not have them on her wedding night.

"Good morning, Sara. You look stunning today, as

always." Phoebe glanced at her as she sat down. "What are your plans for today?"

"I need to go to my shop and see how things are progressing. Alyssa is magical with her needle and thread. I cannot believe how fast she is. With her friend helping as well, I think we will be caught up in no time. Having a man in the shop to take care of the counter makes me feel better about her safety."

"It was very kind of you to hire Alyssa." Phoebe tossed a bit of sugar into her tea.

"She's a lovely girl. If not for her, I could be on a ship bound for some island with a very cruel man." Sara shivered at the thought.

"That's all in the past, thankfully. How does your arm fare?"

"Everything is working well. All the feeling has returned. It does tingle occasionally, but I still don't dare lift with it."

Phoebe's butler walked in and bowed to the ladies. "Pardon me, Lady Downey," he said, handing her a card, "but Her Grace is calling and has brought a friend to visit."

"Of course, show them in." Phoebe waved toward the doorway.

Mary St. James entered the room, followed by a beautiful woman with brown hair and green eyes. She was tall and majestic looking, clad in a quite stylish outfit. Each of the women carried a package. The dowager's was small, but the other woman's package was long and narrow.

Once Phoebe and Sara moved to the settee along with their visitors, the dowager duchess folded her hands in her lap and turned to Sara.

"I am sure you recall I found your reticule in your shop after you were kidnapped. When I examined it, I noticed your mother's initials were sewn inside the lining of the bag. I thought I knew someone with those initials, but I just could not place them at the time."

Sara's heart fluttered as she listened to the dowager. Her palms grew moist and she risked a curious glance at the other woman. Had this woman known her mother?

"After much time, I finally recalled whose initials they were," Mary continued. "It was a love story as I remember it. Your mother, Helen, fell in love with a merchant, your father, but your grandfather would not sanction the marriage as he was a viscount and the businessman had no noble blood. However, as love stories often go, your mother and father ran away and were married anyway. Sadly, your grandfather, the viscount, disowned her."

The brown-haired woman reached for the dowager's hand. "I never stopped loving her, but I was too young to disobey my father. How I have missed her. I was notified of her death, but I never knew she had a daughter." Her eyes teared up as she spoke.

The duchess spoke up. "Sara, I would like you to meet your Aunt Elinor."

Sara's vision blurred from her tears as she stood. "You're my aunt?"

"Yes, my dear." Aunt Elinor smiled. "I would be honored if you would allow me to be a part of your life. You look so much like your mother that I cannot believe it. A part of my beloved sister lives on." She held both hands up to her cheeks and sighed. "You are so beautiful."

Sara and her aunt reached for each other at the same time. "I would like that very much, Aunt Elinor," she said, leaning into the older woman's embrace. Her tears mingled with laughter. She actually had a true aunt. How could she have not known? She could learn so much more about her mother.

"Oh, I have something for you. Your mother loved to sew, just as you do, and she had created her own wedding dress. But because she ran off to marry, she left it behind. I've treasured it all this time, and I wondered if you would like to have it."

Aunt Elinor opened the long package and pulled out a pale blue gown decorated with the same beads as the reticule Sara had treasured for so many years.

"What do you think?" Aunt Elinor's eyebrows rose as she held the dress up for Sara's inspection.

Sara willed her legs to move. The dress was everything she could have dreamed. She stumbled over to it and brushed her hand across the satin skirt, running her fingers across the beaded bodice. "I think it is the most beautiful dress I have ever seen. I would love to wear it on my wedding day."

"I think that would make your mother very happy. Oh, I also brought these if you would like them." She handed Sara the other small sack the dowager held. It was full of a variety of beads, including the very ones she'd been searching for that matched her mother's reticule. She would finally be able to fix it and make it whole again.

Sara choked back her tears enough to thank her aunt and to hug the duchess.

Mary St. James cradled her cheek and said, "It did not matter to me or my son—we love you for who you are. But I always believed you had noble blood in you somewhere."

Sara was speechless.

CHAPTER THIRTY-SIX

S ARA STOOD AT THE BACK of the church and smiled
at Edward Davis, the Earl of Ardleigh, who had agreed
to walk her down the aisle to her husband-to-be.

"You are absolutely lovely in that dress, Sara." He nodded as he perused her gown.

"I cannot believe my good fortune. To have an aunt after all these years, and a man who loves me. Of course, I adore them both. This is definitely the happiest day of my life."

"I couldn't be happier to see you with the duke. You are marrying a good man."

"Yes, I am, and I have you to thank for so much, Lord Ardleigh. You and Phoebe have been so wonderful to me."

The earl beamed at her. "I feared I'd never see Brentwood marry again, but he's a changed man. The fact that he's encouraged you to continue designing your gowns is evidence of that. Someday," he said, dropping his voice to a whisper, "I'll tell him so, but not yet. I don't want his chest puffing out too much."

The earl gave her a kiss on her cheek and tucked her arm in his. They turned toward the front of the church.

She beamed with joy. Her business was doing well. Philip had taken over the financial end of it and hired several seamstresses for her so she could focus on her designs. As she took her first steps down the aisle, she was able to calm her butterflies by focusing on the love of her life, Philip St. James. He was so handsome, as usual. She smiled at her Aunt Elinor and Phoebe as she passed them.

Her gaze locked on Philip's blue eyes as he took her fingers. His eyes were such a warm, beautiful blue.

Finally, the ice had truly melted, not just in his eyes. It had melted in her heart as well.

EPILOGUE

The following spring in London

PHILIP LAUGHED AS HE HELPED his very pregnant wife excitedly pull on her fishing pole. They stood in his favorite place on the dock at his lake.

"Be careful, love. Don't shake our baby up too much. I'll get him for you." He reached over Sara's shoulders to grab the pole and tug.

"Philip, be careful! Don't lose my fish! I can tell this is a special one. I have not caught anything in a long time." Sara bit her lower lip in anticipation.

"I beg to differ with you, wife. You caught something, or your belly wouldn't be sticking out so far," he whispered in her ear.

Sara giggled as she relinquished the pole to her husband. She pinched his arm as she spoke. "I caught this from you and you know it. It was bound to happen, for you cannot keep your hands to yourself."

"Hmph. I still cannot keep my hands off you. You are more beautiful than ever carrying our child." He gave her a quick kiss before gently moving her to the side. Philip was amazed at how much his love had grown for his wife. It was almost a year since Sara Downey had walked into his life and turned it upside down. Soon they would have their first child together. He'd always thought he would want a son first. A strapping boy. But he wanted a little girl who looked just like Sara. They could have sons later.

"Be careful, Philip! Don't lose my fish!" Sara yelled once more with a giggle.

"I am afraid you aren't going to be happy when I reel it in." Philip sighed. He could tell by the tug that it wasn't anything living.

"Yes, I will. I am sure it is bigger than yours. Look at how hard you are pulling. It must be a really big fish." Sara shouted her excitement as her husband fought with the pole.

"It may be bigger than mine, but I don't think it's a fish." He gave one last tug and almost fell on his bottom when it came free.

"What are you talking about?" Sara gasped as she viewed the tangle of seaweed that was on the end of her hook. "Oh, Philip. I thought it was a fish. Oh, poo!"

He gave her his best smile as he held it up for her to see. His laughter echoed across the small valley. He let the large clump of seaweed dangle for his wife's view before he reached for it to throw it back into the lake.

Something caught Sara's eye. "Philip, wait! Don't throw it back yet." She reached for the cluster of weeds and dirt.

"Don't touch it, Sara! You don't know what's in the middle."

"Hold it still, I can see something." She reached into the bundle of weeds and grabbed something hard. Pulling it out, she tugged away pieces of grass and held it up for him to see.

"Look, Philip! It's a toy boat. Where did this come from?" She peered up at her husband as she held out the boat for his inspection.

He dropped the pole and took the boat from his wife, cradling it as if it would shatter. His voice broke as he spoke. "This was my boat."

"Really? Imagine that, finding it now." Sara smiled up at him.

"My father made it for me when I was a child." He set it into the water, holding his hand there for a moment to make sure it floated. Sure enough, it floated on its own to the middle of the lake.

He pulled his wife into a warm embrace and whispered, "I knew you were meant for me."

~ The End ~

DEAR READER,

Thank you for reading! I hope you enjoyed the updated version of The Duke and the Dressmaker. I think Reforming the Duke is a much more appropriate title.

As always, reviews would be greatly appreciated. Sign up for my newsletter on my website at *www.keiramontclair.com*. I send newsletters out with each new release.

Another way to receive notices about my new releases is to follow me on BookBub. Click on the tab in the upper right-hand side of my profile page. You can also write a review on BookBub.

Keira Montclair

www.keiramontclair.com
www.facebook.com/KeiraMontclair
www.pinterest.com/KeiraMontclair

Novels by

Keira Montclair

Jennie and Aedan
#8- HIGHLAND HARMONY-
Avelina and Drew

THE HIGHLAND CLAN
LOKI-Book One
TORRIAN-Book Two
LILY-Book Three
JAKE-Book Four
ASHLYN-Book Five
MOLLY-Book Six
JAMIE AND GRACIE- Book Seven
SORCHA-Book Eight
KYLA-Book Nine
BETHIA-Book Ten
LOKI'S CHRISTMAS STORY-Book Eleven

THE SOULMATE CHRONICLES
#1-TRUSTING A HIGHLANDER

THE SUMMERHILL SERIES-
CONTEMPORARY ROMANCE
#1-ONE SUMMERHILL DAY
#2-A FRESH START FOR TWO
#3-THREE REASONS TO LOVE

STAND-ALONE NOVEL
FALLING FOR THE CHIEFTAIN-Book Three in
Enchanted Falls Trilogy
THE BANISHED HIGHLANDER
REFORMING THE DUKE

ABOUT THE AUTHOR

Keira Montclair is the pen name of an author who lives in Florida with her husband. She loves to write fast-paced, emotional romance, especially with children as secondary characters in her stories.

She has worked as a registered nurse in pediatrics and recovery room nursing. Teaching is another of her loves, and she has taught both high school mathematics and practical nursing.

Now she loves to spend her time writing, but there isn't enough time to write everything she wants! Her Highlander Clan Grant series, comprising of eight standalone novels, is a reader favorite. Her third series, The Highland Clan, set twenty years after the Clan Grant series, focuses on the Grant/Ramsay descendants. She also has a contemporary series set in The Finger Lakes of Western New York.

Her latest series, The Band of Cousins, stems from The Highland Clan but is a stand-alone series.

Contact her through her website, *www.keiramontclair.com*

Printed in Great Britain
by Amazon